SKIRTING THE GORGE

A NOVEL

GERALD R. STANEK

ISBN: 978-0-9747417-5-8

Published by Shiver Hill Books
Printed by Lulu.com

second mother to her. She frequently went to Crestview, the retirement home where Lily now resided, but it wasn't the same as having someone next-door she could rely on, at almost any hour for almost any reason. She couldn't imagine how difficult it must have been for Lily to leave Demerest House, as it was known, after so many years.

The house had been Lily's husband's childhood home. There was a long tradition of a neighborhood Christmas party at Demerest House, dating back to Mr. Demerest's grandfather, who had at one time invited everyone living along Fall Creek Drive, Lakeview Terrace, and Maple Crest Lane. Lily and her husband kept up the tradition for forty-two years, and Lily by herself for another twenty, though over the decades the affair had dwindled in size. Neighbors moved away or passed away, and new neighbors, although invited, did not always warm to the tradition. Lily said she didn't mind too much, because with each year she felt less able to entertain properly.

This year Lily had convinced Michelle, and to Michelle's amazement, Stephen, to hold the fete at their house. Naturally, she let Lily take over the planning and supervision of the food and guest list. It would be a small group, just some old friends, their children if available, and a few students of Stephen's. The Stuarts from across the street had a prior commitment, but sent over a bottle of wine. Mr. Westin, the new occupant of Demerest House had told Lily he would try to stop by.

With so few people expected, a caterer was hardly necessary, but Lily had enlisted the help of Leah Kampnich (a sweet girl she had met when her father updated the kitchen at Demerest House a few years back), to help with the preparations. She had professed an interest in the culinary arts and seemed to have inherited her father's capable hands. She had come on time, but was unsuitably attired,

1

I SAW him coming, the husband, the exemplary professor, encased in his voracious black machine. Its broad beams of light slashed a swath in the darkness, startling the snowflakes, revealing them just as the flux of his passing disrupted their innocent descent, sending them whirling in intricate, invocative convolutions. He paused in the long curving drive to admire his *things*: the glistening snow-laden branches of his stand of pines, the red bow on his wrought iron lamppost, the radiance of his Christmas lights bobbing in perfect scallops along the gables and exposed half-timbers of his impeccably appointed home, dramatically accenting the diagonals of its mock Tudorbethan style.

He did not see me; I did not wish it. I waited in the shadows of the trees, those pines bordering the property, the very ones he thought so effective in blocking prying eyes. What I did that evening and during the subsequent months, I did as a favor to a friend who was anxious for the woman, the wife. It was a final attachment, you see, the last tether, if you will. I did not act with impatience, though in a sense we were all waiting, nor did I act alone, but then to presume such a thing possible would be a misapprehension.

During my time with the Wolcotts, I did not work *for* Michelle, or *against* Stephen, but simply set out to bring certain information to light, in order to aid my friend. I never had anything against the good doctor, except perhaps for his insistence on certain forms, such as being referred to as 'doctor' even though he was not a medical man. Indeed, the doctrinaire Dr. Wolcott could not help but earn my sympathies, coming as he did from a long line of over-thinkers, as trapped as his forebears in marvelous mental architecture.

He became angry when he continued around the drive to the side of the house and nearly bumped into a massive dark green pickup truck parked there, preventing him from pulling his own prestigious vehicle into his well ordered garage. I saw him glare at the side of the truck, where lighter green paint read *Kampnich's Kitchens and Baths*, and watched him storm around the front of the house, checking to see that his directives had been carried out, regarding salt on the walk, wreath on the door, lights hung in precise arcs over the hedge. His mood was evident, but I had no intention of diverting his attention, or redirecting his ire. This was all in Michelle's best interest, in the end. You must break a few eggs; the seed thought must be planted.

Inside, Michelle surveyed the parlor where the party would be taking place. It was a wide space with an open beam ceiling and two broad arched entrances; one coming from the front hall, and the other leading to the dining room. She had draped swags of evergreens around the windows and doorways; partially covering the rich woodwork Stephen prized so much. The tree, a big Scotch pine, she had set up in front of the tall bow window; a few presents were already beneath it, very elegantly wrapped but nevertheless looking a bit lost and forlorn. Stephen's love of wood was again evidenced by the furniture, which was mostly of the Arts and Crafts style, beautiful, hand-rubbed, quarter-sawn, pegged oak. Michelle found most of it uncomfortable. There were two sofas with straight wooden

2

arms and railed backs with rust cushions on the seat only, and two matching chairs. They were arranged carefully on either side of the fireplace. An antique rocker was near the tree, a few stools had been brought in from the kitchen, and there was one worn, beige over-stuffed armchair with ottoman slouching in the far corner. Above the mantle were matching eighteenth century oil portraits of Jacob Worthington Wolcott and his wife Adelaide.

As she scanned the room, Michelle endeavored to see it through Lily's eyes. She had long ago trained herself to see things as Stephen did, to look for the things he felt were important, to make every picture straight, and every pillow upright; all was in order. But what might Lily want that she hadn't had time to ask for, or perhaps thought it too impolite to ask for? Stephen had exclaimed to Lily that the house was 'at your disposal' for the duration of the party, yet they both knew him too well to think he meant it; with Stephen there were always provisos, one of which was you were not necessarily privy to the proviso in question. At any rate, that feeling of Christmas magic had yet to appear. Michelle opened the drapes so the tree would be visible outside, and the snowfall inside. Better, but something was clearly missing, she thought. The doorbell rang.

"I'll get it," she called. The front parlor opened onto what Stephen insisted on referring to as 'the landing', even though there were only three steps down to the small foyer. As one entered the house there was a closet to the left, a door to the right that led to the basement, and those three steps up to the main level. From here, one could walk down a hallway to the right; go straight up the staircase to the second story; or, to the right of the stairs go straight on towards the kitchen. The parlor was to the left, through a broad arch, framed in wide, dark, fluted molding, as were all the doors and windows in the house.

3

"Candles," Michelle muttered to herself as she pushed the pocket doors into their hiding places in the wall, crossed the landing, and stepped down into the foyer. Lily would always have candles. She unhooked the chain, flipped back the deadbolts, and opened the broad paneled front door. A man wearing a formal black overcoat, holding a briefcase and a thermos was standing there.

"Stephen!" she said, surprised that her husband would be standing at the front door rather than come in through the garage. For a split second she had seen him new, as a stranger, as he appeared to others: a tall man with delicate features, wisps of graying blond hair flitting about his aging, yet remarkably taut face. The Christmas lights around the door casing added an extra sheen to his nearly bald head. His wide mouth curled at the corners, his steel-grey eyes were narrowly set; the combination of the two was unnerving, and the familiar look there did not bode well. Was it practiced, she wondered, this habitually ambiguous expression; did he contrive to smile with his mouth but not his eyes, or was it an innate idiosyncrasy?

"Hello dear," he said quietly, carefully wiping his shoes on the outside, then on the inside mats. "What's all this?" he asked, indicating the console by the basement door, on which sat a huge poinsettia and a pile of a dozen or more identically shaped thin packages, wrapped in three or four different combinations of paper and ribbon.

"That's Lily's gift this year, we are not to let anyone leave without one."

"Ah, yes. Perhaps we should have given something out. But free food and drink is quite enough, don't you think? The wreath is very nice this year." He spoke quietly, fully conscious of the presence of others in his home.

"I'm happy with it," she answered with a smile, shutting the door behind him and heading back to the parlor.

4

"Oh Michelle," her husband asked, pausing to methodically click the bolts into place and carefully slide the chain back on, "Might I have a word?" The sound of her name in his mouth grated; he only used it when displeased with her, otherwise it was 'sweetheart' or 'munchkin'. Preempting any hesitation on her part as he joined her on the steps, he took her elbow very firmly in his hand and stated rather than inquired, "You do have a few moments?"

To which she could only mumble "Course," and walk with him down the hallway to his study. While she waited, rubbing her elbow, he very deliberately closed the door, hung up his coat, placed his briefcase on the desk, turned on his computer, and sorted through the day's mail.

"What the hell is that fellow doing here, that *Kampnich*?" he finally said, his voice low in pitch and volume, the name Kampnich uttered with obvious disdain. Michelle began to respond but he cut her off. "You know I don't like these... workmen in the house when I'm not here. Something wrong with the stove?"

"It's not my doing, it's Lily's. And it's not Mr. Kampnich, it's his daughter," she explained patiently, and turning to go added, "Now please come light the fire, people will be here any minute." Michelle returned to the parlor, sighing with relief. Stephen's disapproval was always difficult for her to accept, although he never raised his voice to her. She knew there was nothing he could say to her about it now. Lily was great for getting one off the hook, and he never seemed to bother *her* with any of his little peeves; Lily was impervious to the great professor.

Lily Demerest had lived next door until recently. It had taken a long time for her to admit that the place had become too much for her to contend with, and to move out. It had been hard on Michelle, too, because over the years Lily had become a close confidant, almost a

5

Michelle thought, and wearing far too much perfume. It was cloying.

"Hello Lily, how are you this evening?" Stephen asked, having passed through the parlor to the dining room, where Lily was inspecting some hors d'oeuvres. He stooped and embraced her, kissing the air by the side of her head. She was wearing an evening dress, teal and white, with bits of gold twinkling here and there. An amber silk scarf was wrapped rather tightly about her neck and heavy gold earrings gleamed through her wavy white hair. Though her age was evident, there was a regal elegance about Lily that Michelle envied, if only because Stephen bowed to it.

"Merry Christmas, dear," she said, gripping Stephen's arms tightly so that he might not escape too soon. "Is it too early to say that?" Leah was a head taller than Lily and standing behind her. Michelle saw her unsuccessfully suppressing a smile when Stephen looked at her, as if to say, 'isn't the crazy old lady cute'.

"You must be the Kampnich girl," he said, releasing himself from Lily and holding out his hand.

"Yes, this is Leah," Lily responded, stepping aside, "I believe you know her father."

"Of course, pleased to meet you."

Although his back was to the parlor, Michelle could feel him turning his steely eyes on the girl, half terrorizing, half enchanting. Holding a flame to the wick of a dusty, deformed green pillar that no longer smelled of pine or honeysuckle or whatever scent it had once possessed, her mind was flooded with the memory of the first time that intent, inscrutable gaze had gripped her, as a young grad student. She had felt a sense of privilege, then, just to be in his presence.

7

"Hello," Leah said, giving a nervous little puff of air out of her nose which was not a snort, nor a cough, nor yet a vocalization but possibly a retraction of all three. Michelle could see her blushing from the parlor.

"You're a little young to be driving that monster truck, aren't you?" Stephen asked.

"My dad says it does really well in the snow, and you never can tell with the weather around here."

The girl was quite pretty; button nose, laughing brown eyes, long, thick brown hair that she had tied back with a red ribbon. She was wearing jeans and a red sweater, partly covered by a plain white apron. Michelle thought the jeans were far too tight, and the sweater cut too low.

"Mm, no. Very prudent," Stephen pronounced, "I doubt if we'll get an inch, though. I wonder if I could get you to move the truck so I can put my car in the garage."

"Oh, sure, I'm sorry; I thought I was supposed to…"

"Never mind that, Stephen," Lily interrupted, pulling his arm in an attempt to turn him, which he at first resisted. "You can put it away after everyone's gone. Plenty of parking in the drive. Now go and light the fire, make yourself useful."

"All right then Leah, the truck can wait," he said, smiling with great condescension as he turned around, leaving Leah looking abashed and confused. The baby fat rounding her face *did* give her an appealingly innocent air, Michelle thought. She had a lithe but developed figure, and that wholesome, natural air which seemed to ooze vitality. Suddenly it was obvious why Lily had insisted on hiring her for the evening.

"Is Travis coming?" Stephen asked slyly, for he too had surmised the situation. Lily was always scheming for love.

"Well Bryan's supposed to be picking him up on his way," she answered, ignoring the twinkle in his eye, "but he evidently has some exams coming up next week which he's very worried about, so we'll see."

As Stephen began fiddling with the damper, Michelle abandoned the parlor and followed Lily and Leah into the kitchen.

"Travis is one of my grandsons," Lily was explaining to the girl, "He goes to Cornell."

"Oh."

"He is the last one, the youngest of my youngest."

"Is that why you spoil him so much?" Michelle asked flatly. Lily ignored her.

"His father Bryan is driving up from Pennsylvania just to have cookies and eggnog with his old mother, isn't that nice of him?"

Feeling uncertain how to respond, Leah gave one of her ambiguous little exhalations.

"They're very reliable men, the Demerest boys," Mrs. Demerest averred.

"And terribly handsome," Michelle added playfully, though it was not precisely true for *all* the Demerest boys.

"Now let's get these cookies out to the table," Lily prodded.

2

"FORREST, how are you doing?" asked Richard, stepping across the parlor to greet his old colleague. He had a way of speaking which made every utterance sound like it belonged on stage.

"Oh, 'bout the same as last year, I suppose," Forrest replied, adding, "Can't complain." Whenever he said that, Michelle knew he was about to. Forrest Carlson and Richard Cole had been friends with the Demerests for decades. "My shoulder's been acting up again, but it always does this time of year."

"Sorry to hear that. It's really starting to come down out there," Richard observed. Michelle, lighting some candles on the end tables, saw that the drapes across the bay window had been closed. Stephen must have done that, she thought, when I was in the kitchen. He was noisily crumpling newspaper at the hearth.

"Yeah," Forrest agreed, "I think we're going to get more than they said. Nothing unusual about that though. Guess we'll see the sun again in a few short months, right?"

"Everything well over at McGraw?" Richard asked. McGraw Hall housed the Department of History.

"Oh, fine, fine. Thinking very seriously of retiring, actually," Forrest admitted, "Or I was till my 401k tanked."

"That bad, eh?"

He nodded, seemed hesitant to elaborate. Don't get him started, thought Michelle.

"Richard, how's the play coming along?" she asked while tactically deploying pearlescent green and red coasters in key positions on the coffee and end tables.

"Splendid, just flowing like milk and honey from a bumble cow."

"What play?" Forrest inquired.

"It's just beautiful in here, Michelle," Richard exclaimed, in what she saw as a blatant attempt to change the subject, "You've done a wonderful job with the decorations. When Santa waddles out of that chimney, he won't want to leave."

"Thank you, sir. I just need to get some music going and we'll be all set."

"Where's Lily?" he asked.

"In the kitchen," she replied.

"Of course." Richard immediately headed through the dining room to the kitchen. Forrest chuckled; Michelle smiled at him knowingly. Richard had been in love with Lily for thirty years, and everyone who had seen them together knew it. When Lily's husband Halcomb had died, Richard had still been unhappily married. Now, a widower himself for eight years, he continued to hang on Lily's every word, hoping one day to hear some reciprocation of his attentions. Lily was always kind to him, but it couldn't have escaped his notice that she was kind to everyone. She clearly had no interest in a romance with Richard, or anyone else, yet Richard continued to imagine that they had a special understanding.

"It *is* a magnificent tree, Michelle," noted Forrest, admiring it.

"Thank you, I think it came out well this year. I bought some new red balls, these, with the silver glitter around the top." And she had left off all the green and blue ornaments, on a whim. She was very pleased with it; it gave her an incredible feeling of warmth. Stephen apparently had not noticed the difference.

"Yeah? Well those are nice. I can see how much time you took with it, it's really... comforting."

"I'm so glad you like it," she said, opening the CD player.

"I haven't put a tree up in years. Makes me tired just to think of it," he chuckled.

"Oh, I enjoy it. Maybe you'll do one next year."

"Doubt it. I'm not getting any younger you know. So Richard is in a play?"

"No, he's writing one, according to Lily. But maybe I shouldn't have said anything. You know how long it's been since he's written anything."

"Ah. Well I won't pester him about it then." Richard hadn't been able to write since his wife passed away. Choral Christmas music began to fill the room, *In Dulce Jubilo*. The bell rang again and Stephen went to the door. Michelle quickly crossed the room to open the drapes again.

"For God's sake, Travis hang up the phone," Bryan snapped in a loud whisper as they rose from the foyer. The father was considerably shorter than the son, not as slim as he thought and therefore wearing clothes a tad too tight. He had a ruddy complexion, bushy eyebrows, and eyes that were constantly wide open behind thick rectangular glasses. His fastidiously trimmed short beard bore a hint of grey. Michelle had known Bryan nearly as long as she had known Lily. She liked him, but his was a particularly varied personality. In the morning he tended to be petulant, in the afternoon garrulous, and in the evening, especially when he drank, bawdy. He always seemed to put his foot in his mouth.

"Hey, I really gotta go. Kay, bye," Travis mumbled, snapping his phone shut and shoving it into the pocket of his jeans. He looked nothing like his father, but had not yet begun to look like himself. He was gawky still, and had let his hair grow too long so that it covered his eyes half the time.

"Gretchen couldn't make it?" Michelle asked.

"No, her mother is in the hospital with pneumonia, so she's been there in Harrisburg for the last week."

"Oh dear."

"Well she seems to be over the worst of it, and should be back home in a few days. Gretchen will stay with her there for a while. We'll probably go down for Christmas I guess."

"Well that will be nice for her."

"Hello Travis," said Forrest.

"Hi Mr. Carlson."

"Forrest, got through another year alright, I see," Bryan blustered, taking his hand.

"Can't complain," he grumbled, then surprisingly closed his mouth and turned in the direction of the comfortable armchair. Michelle had wondered how long it would take him to lay a claim. Travis had already taken up a seat by the fire.

Stephen was opening the door for more arrivals; mass introductions followed as Richard and Lily emerged from the kitchen to join the fray. Three of Stephen's graduate students had come, Chieko Yoshida, Ken Lee, and Jeremy Freyberg. With them was Erin — apparently Jeremy's date. The boys were voluble and assertive, dressed smartly, looking and acting the part of Cornellians, each working hard to impress Erin with their witticisms and sophistication. She looked like a model; high cheekbones, long blond hair, sleek black leggings tucked into high-heeled boots, and a clingy dark green

14

velour top. In sharp contrast to both Jeremy and Ken, she held herself aloof and was virtually silent. Michelle didn't care for her.

Chieko was quiet and unassuming, formal yet jovial, beaming at everyone, her eyes mere slits above her broad smile. Her face had a thickness to it; she had a noticeable overbite and a pronounced accent, although her English was good. Ken Lee was just as obviously Californian as he was Asian; his language was idiomatic and current, his manner casual and self-assured.

Last to arrive was Sarah Strickland, one of the graduate students who had been in Richard's program the year before he retired. She was still living in the area, trying very hard to get a position somewhere. For the past year she had been a substitute teacher on call with various school systems, working at Target in the evenings to make ends meet. Michelle and Lily felt quite sorry for her and kept inviting her to any get together available in an effort to advance her professionally, or at the very least, see her married off. As far as they knew, she had never had a long-term relationship and only a handful of dates.

Watching the little group fumbling over their drinks and arranging themselves on the hard backed couches; Michelle noticed all the male eyes following Erin or Leah (who was passing out cups of eggnog), while no one seemed to see Sarah. This irked her more than she could account for. It was true that Sarah's features were fleshed out a bit with a few more years and a few more pounds, but she was still extremely pretty. They had no reason to discount her, yet they did. Why was it so maddening? She was not cold, she was not timid, she was not morose or irritable or vapid; at least Michelle had never thought so. Why did the men ignore her? It was as if she had passed her "best by" date.

"Oh, these are delicious, Mother," Bryan mumbled, his mouth full of green icing and a once holly-shaped cookie. Everyone agreed, with nods and munching smiles, as *Ave Maria* came to their ears from speakers hidden somewhere in the recesses of the ceiling. Michelle, Leah and Lily had brought out the trays of canapés, bruschetta, and sugar cookies. There would be no meal as such, but everyone had plenty to eat.

"Well Leah here iced them," she said, causing the girl to blush and stare at the floor. Michelle could see that Leah would have preferred to remain in the kitchen, but Lily, in a painfully obvious manner, had insisted she sit in the rocker by the fire, near her grandson.

"So tell me Travis, is getting away from the folks all it's cracked up to be?" Richard asked. Travis answered with a shrug and a smirk.

"Thinking of transferring to Penn State? It'll save your father a ton of money," Sarah proposed with a wink. Bryan taught at Penn State.

"No, I don't think so," said Travis.

"Not going back there again, if you can help it, right?" Jeremy laughed.

"Well someone's got to keep an eye on Grandma Demerest, right Grandma?" he suggested, hoping she would back him up.

"That's right, kiddo. You never know when I might start wandering the streets in my nightgown..."

"Nonsense, Lily," Richard protested.

"...and when the authorities stop me I'll say 'fetch my grandson, he's "big man on campus", you can't miss him', and you can come take me home." Everyone laughed.

"I can't imagine you *wandering* anywhere, in any attire, Mother," Bryan argued.

"Well you never know when Alzheimer's might set in dear."

"Or dementia," Travis suggested, still looking alarmed by the suggestion that he return to Pennsylvania.

"Travis," exclaimed Bryan, in an attempt to reprimand his son for disrespect, but he couldn't keep the chuckle out of his voice.

"Senility, stroke, Parkinson's, take your pick," Forrest suggested from the comfy chair in the corner, "live long enough, and it'll happen to all of us."

"I don't think so," Jeremy said thoughtfully. "I don't think it'll happen to me, because by the time I get that old, they'll have figured out what to do about it."

"That's right," Ken agreed confidently, "either gene therapy or nanomedicine, we'll never have to get Alzheimer's, dementia, or any of that stuff."

"So what's it feel like to be the first immortal generation?" Stephen asked, not altogether rhetorically. "Play your cards right, and you'll never die. Clinical immortality, isn't that what they call it? Keep the body going forever, rebuild it if necessary."

"The terror wars have been great for that," Bryan agreed, "Prosthetics has made giant leaps lately."

"It feels great," admitted Jeremy. Cheiko and Ken agreed, laughing. Even Travis and Erin were beginning to liven to the discussion. Leah, too, gave a half-hearted giggle. I don't suppose she knows what they're talking about, thought Michelle, hell, I barely know. But all teens feel immortal, she remembered, trying to recreate that sensation of possibility in her mind.

"We won't need prosthetics," Ken argued, "we'll grow new body parts in the lab. When my brain gets worn out, I'll order a new one."

"What do you mean, we're all going to... to clone ourselves?" Richard sputtered.

"Only as a last resort," Jeremy mused, "Only if the nanotechnology doesn't work well enough to keep your first body working."

"Eventually," said Stephen, "flesh will be abandoned, because synthetic bodies will be so much more durable, and so much stronger. People's minds will be uploaded to an android's hard drive. It's called transhumanism."

"Well don't you think we'd better learn to be decent humans first, before we start transferring our qualities to powerful machines?" Richard posed.

"I'm with you, Richard," Lily said. Richard beamed. "This *transhumanism* should wait until we've had more success with humanism."

"This is all predicated on your survival of the water wars, of course," Forrest submitted for the students' consideration.

"And the food wars, and UFO wars," Sarah added, smirking.

"No, no, I think it's quite likely at least one of these young people will live for hundreds of years, if not forever," Stephen asserted seriously.

"Really?" Lily responded, eyeing him carefully.

"Yes. At the pace these technologies are developing, it's entirely possible."

"Well they're fools if they want to live forever," Forrest argued.

"Didn't Patton say that?" asked Bryan. Stephen ignored them and addressed the young people.

"Of course, play your cards wrong, a way to end your life can always be found," he reminded them portentously, with his knowing, unsmiling smile.

"He did in the movie," Forrest answered Bryan, "which is a far greater measure of truth than anything which might have actually happened."

"What kind of a thing is that to say?" Lily demanded, glaring at Stephen. He did not respond, but Michelle watched his smug smile fade.

"Well I agree with him," Richard continued dramatically, "living a long life is not as important as living a fulfilling life, as doing something worthwhile with the time you *do* have."

The doorbell rang. Michelle rose gracefully before Lily could spring from her stool. She couldn't think who was missing.

"Like dying for your country, so that someone else can live a long life," remarked Forrest, as she went down into the foyer, cursing Stephen's paranoia under her breath. She loosed the chain and turned the deadbolts yet again, and opened the door.

The man standing on the Wolcott's doorstep was a complete stranger to Michelle. He was shorter and younger than Stephen, broad shouldered, his short brown curly hair was uncombed, there was a week's worth of beard on his rugged face, he had no coat, no hat, just a thick white sweater and jeans. His shoes looked like work boots, spattered with paint. He was holding a bottle of wine.

"Hi. Uh… Lily invited me, I just moved in next door? Well not just, a couple months ago."

"Six months actually," Michelle corrected, "You must be Mr. Westin."

"Kyle," he said, stepping in, holding out the bottle of wine clumsily. She noticed he didn't bother to wipe his feet. She took the bottle; their fingers touched accidentally. She shivered and closed the door. An effusion of warmth accompanied his cologne as he passed by her, which struck her as odd, since it was so cold out and he was

19

underdressed. Was it cologne, or turpentine? She remembered the rumor that he was an artist, had Lily told her that?

Once in the summer when she had been changing the sheets in the guest bedroom, she had glanced out the window to enjoy the dappled look of the sun sifting through the dancing maple leaves, and as a branch was lifted by the breeze, she saw, or thought she saw through an open window of Demerest House, a flash of nudity — not an arm or shoulder but a torso, or hip, or thigh, hairless, probably feminine, passing voluptuously into and out of the golden rhomboid of light described by the window frame. The branch moved down and up again, the leaves fluttered and waved, but the flesh was gone. Later that day she had looked out of a room downstairs, tried to see across the yard into the same window, and thought she could make out the shape of an easel with a canvas on it, its back to her.

"Michelle Wolcott, so glad to meet you at last. I trust you got our little house warming gift, I rang the bell several days in a row, but you never answered," she noted. He had a blank look on his face. "The brownies?" she suggested, "I left them in the garage? On top of your car, actually."

"Oh, that was you? I thought it was Lily, I…"

"No, it was from Stephen and myself, just like the card said." Kyle's mouth opened in the shape of the word 'card', but was saved from uttering it by Lily who was standing at the top of the steps, waiting.

"Mr. Westin, how good of you to come," she said enthusiastically. Michelle stepped aside, closing the door behind him.

"Kyle, please," he said, rising to Lily and taking her hand.

Amidst the introduction of the newcomer the group shuffled about, some hoping to gain a more comfortable seat, some getting another glass of wine. Erin asked for the bathroom, Jeremy made a quiet call on his phone. Leah, in her red sweater and hair ribbon, brought Kyle some eggnog and cookies.

"You're very Christmassy," he said to her, taking her offerings. She smiled.

"Where are you from Mr. Westin?" Richard inquired.

"Most recently Soho."

"And how are you finding the weather up here?"

"Love it. Love the fresh air."

"Oh, me too," Cheiko professed, "I just love it here, the fall was so beautiful, and the snow is so pretty."

Forrest chuckled in the corner. Sarah and Bryan turned towards him expectantly, wondering what was so funny.

"Everyone says that the first year or two," he observed dryly.

"Oh look!" Leah exclaimed, pointing out the window.

3

I HAD seen Michelle through the open door, very nearly as Mr. Westin had seen her, for I was at that time standing behind him, peering through the juniper. He didn't know I was there, he was too engrossed by the sight of her, by the aura of light suffusing that copious crown of hair, which softly embraced her kind face; by the obliging grace expressed in the set of her shoulders, the angle of her wrist, the tilt of her head; by the evocative, compact hands emerging from the long sleeves of that form-fitting blush-colored cashmere dress.

Once the fellow was admitted to the house, I proceeded. The power of the visual prompt for the subject (as I had just been reminded so eloquently) must never be underestimated. I strode casually in front of the bay window. The girl, Leah, saw me first, as she was crossing the room with a tray in her hands. She exclaimed and pointed, nearly dropping the tray; the others looked in turn: Travis, Sarah, Bryan, Ken, Kyle, Michelle, Erin, Richard, Stephen, Jeremy, Cheiko, Forrest, and Lily. They all saw me, but I gave my gaze to Michelle only, holding prettily still with one paw up in the air until I felt her knowing with certainty that I was for her. Then I scampered away into the tall pines.

"Magnificent," Richard boomed.

"Wow, I've never seen one before, that was totally awesome," added Ken. Everyone stood staring through the glass at the tracks in the snow, or at the spot in the darkness where it had vanished with a flick of its tail, as if they had witnessed a supernatural event.

"So beautiful," Cheiko breathed. Kyle, who happened to be standing between Cheiko and Michelle, quietly pronounced it "portentous."

Michelle was speechless. She looked at Kyle from the corner of her eye but did not move her head.

"Doesn't that mean something, when you see a fox?" Lily asked.

Stephen, as he stepped away from the window, said, "Means there'll be one less squirrel in the yard tomorrow." Lily ignored him and turned to Richard expectantly.

"Mythologically? Well, the fox is universally known as a trickster, a thief, not to be trusted," he began in his most pedantic tones, assuming a grand confidence from the fact that Lily looked to *him* for answers, "There's the French *Reynard*, of course, most famous for cuckolding..."

"But what does it mean if you see one?" she persisted, "Is it seven years bad luck, does it mean you're going to meet your own true love..."

"If you see a fox in Tompkins County it means six more months of winter," put in Forrest, resuming his post in the corner.

"Yes, no matter what time of year you see it," Bryan added. Everyone laughed and began moving away from the window. Michelle was left there alone, inhaling the lingering odor of the artist, noticing again the turpentine beneath the musky cologne.

"What about in China, Ken," queried Richard, trying to shift the onus, "are there any fox superstitions?"

"I have no idea, I'm from Palo Alto."

"Oh."

"I believe in China, fox spirits are usually portrayed as inhabiting young women," Cheiko said with a laugh, "and are... how would you say... unsatisfiable?"

"You mean insatiable?" Sarah suggested. Travis and Bryan laughed excitedly.

"Ah, yes," Cheiko giggled, "Insatiable. But in Japan," she continued, her soft voice taking on a mysterious quality, "the foxes are messengers of *Inari*. They are called *Kitsune* and they appear in human form, standing up and walking on their hind legs, so one does not know it is a *Kitsune* at all, until it is too late and they have completed their task. And you can never be certain if a *Kitsune* is going to trick you, or guide you, because all *kami* have two aspects or souls, the *nigi-mitama*, — gentle soul, and the *ara-mitama*, — assertive soul."

"So the fox is the messenger god in Shinto, like Mercury in Greek mythology," Jeremy surmised.

"Oh, no," she said, shaking her head, "*Kitsune* are very important to the Japanese mythology," Cheiko agreed, "but *kami* are not like gods, and most are not anthropomorphized as the *Kitsune* sometimes are. In the traditional understanding, *all things* have *kami*. Each tree, each river, each forest, even each rock, everything has spirit." This kind of notion had never made sense to Michelle; trees maybe, they were alive, but rocks?

"So they would be more like the Greek *daimon*, or the Roman *genius?*" Kyle wondered.

25

"Perhaps," Cheiko agreed cheerfully, "It is not really my area of expertise." Apparently satisfied with this, Kyle did not reply. Michelle, focused on the windowpane, watched the reflection of his white sweater move fluidly into the dining room.

"Drawing parallels across cultures is problematic," Richard warned, "some things simply don't correlate.

"Correct me if I'm wrong," Bryan prefaced, being under the impression that there were no areas outside of *his* expertise, "But the difference would be that *kami* are not divine, they are very much of the earth."

"I really don't know," Cheiko chuckled, "I just wanted to offer my little knowledge because of the fox."

Michelle felt sorry for her; she had no idea she would be sparking such stupid debate. It was dangerous to open your mouth around so many professors. Kyle had taken the hint, and let the subject drop. Still facing the window, she watched his reflection help itself to bruschetta and wine from trays left on the long red-cloaked table. His head and hands were dim in the window - barely there above the strong gleam of the white sweater, like an apparition of some kind, a headless visitor from another dimension.

"I think a better analogy would be that of the Buddhist *deva*," Richard argued.

"No, no," objected Bryan, "the *deva* is a being in its own right. The *kami* is the essence of the place or thing, not a supernatural being, but the *idea* of the most excellent maple or oak. The finest Fall Creek Gorge existing of any possible Fall Creek Gorge."

"You're comparing Shinto *kami* to Plato's Form of the Good?"

"Well... yes, I suppose so. What do you think, Cheiko?"

"Maybe. I'm not really familiar with Plato. I think perhaps *kami* is not very translatable."

"Well who teaches this sort of thing on campus," Lily asked, "We must know someone."

"I'm afraid I'll forget about it by tomorrow, Mother," Bryan confessed.

"So was our little *Kitsune* trying to trick us, or guide us?" Stephen inquired coolly.

Michelle turned away from the windowpane and strode elegantly toward the dining room to check on her guest.

"Perhaps this one was just a fox," responded Cheiko. "Perhaps as you say, he was only after a squirrel."

"My grandpa always says," put in Leah, "if a fox is crossing your path and it stops and turns back, it's bad luck, but if it keeps going, it's good luck, and if it looks at you, it's a blessing."

"There you have it," Bryan said in the living room, "from the salt of the earth. Your grandfather is a hunter, I suppose?"

"Yeah. He and my dad go every year."

"Are you finding enough to eat?" Michelle inquired quietly.

"Oh yes," replied Kyle, munching.

"Did you try the salmon canapés?" she asked, noticing there were none on the table. Kyle looked around too, as if to say 'what canapés'.

"Oh, I think there are more, let me go check." Michelle passed through to the kitchen; Kyle remained, sipping his wine and examining the grouping of floral watercolors on the dining room wall.

"Rumor has it *you're* an artist," commented Stephen, who had joined him abruptly. Kyle, pausing to swallow, said, "I neither confirm nor deny."

"What do you think of these?" his host asked, nodding toward the paintings, which Kyle had not ceased to scan. One was of bearded blue irises, another of variegated tulips in various stages of bud, a third of deep magenta peonies, and the fourth was of daffodils. They were in matching gold frames but they did not quite go together somehow.

"Static. Too tight. Not enough contrast."

"You don't say?" Stephen pushed, that half smile creeping over his face as Michelle reappeared with the hors d'oeuvres.

"Mmm. Art shouldn't be so strict. You've got to abandon the obvious at some point and delve into the soul of the subject."

"Interesting."

"Can I get you anything else Mr. Westin? Some more eggnog perhaps?" Michelle asked.

"No thank you, I've got the wine here. The food is all delicious, by the way."

"Thank you, but that's all Lily's doing you know. And Leah helped her," she pointed out, taking a tray into the living room, wondering if they had been talking about art in general, or about the florals in particular. Had he noticed her signature on them? Stephen was probably informing him now, relishing Kyle's embarrassment. She circled about, plying her guests with more food, keeping her ear trained on the two men's voices but unable to pick out any words. Presently they passed through the room.

"A little hobby of mine," Stephen was saying, and she knew he was going to show Kyle the prints lining the hallway; this was a requisite for aesthetically inclined guests. He was fiercely proud of them. They were handsomely mounted in gunmetal grey frames, each perfectly illuminated by recessed fixtures in the ceiling, their titles inscribed on the concrete colored matting with elegant black calligraphy: *Chateau d'If, Santo Stefano, Devil's Island, Goli Otok, Robben Island, Alcatraz*. He would watch his guests read them, and wait for the little flinch of recognition to cross their faces. Then he would feed them a tidbit, a charming anecdote of inhumane conditions or failed escape attempts. Michelle went down the hall after them, under pretext of needing something from the linen closet.

"They're very well done," the artist declared, "Interesting subject matter." Each was delineated with sharp black outlines and intricate hatching.

"They're more history than art, really. Most of these are now museums," Stephen explained. "There are more upstairs, some of the civil war sites, Johnson's Island, Rock Island, but these are my favorites. I've been to each of them actually."

"Never thought of them as vacation destinations," Kyle quipped.

"No, not exactly. Fascinating places though. For instance, did you know at Chateau d'If you could *buy* a better cell in the tower, one with a fireplace and a window? Provided you were of noble birth of course. The common folk were locked in the lightless lower levels, even underground, with sewage falling from above, and water seeping up from below."

"And I thought justice was blind," Kyle commented.

"Did you really? An idealist, then."

"Perhaps. Ideals are important. Speaking as an artist, I've found that a poor vision is a poor place to start."

"Yes," Stephen laughed, "I suppose that's true. Have *you* ever done any etching, Mr. Westin?"

"No, I haven't. Not really my palette, black," he said.

"It can be a… stark reality I suppose, if you look at it that way. You know one must etch the plate in reverse in order for them to print properly."

29

"I am familiar with the process," Kyle said, a little testily. Having retrieved some napkins from the closet, Michelle noisily closed it and started back down the hall.

"Is this the restroom?" the artist asked as she passed, pointing to a door which was ajar. Brass fixtures gleamed from it's darkened interior.

"Yes of course," she answered, gesturing for him to enter, which he did, flipping on the light as he closed the door.

"The man knows nothing about art," Stephen haughtily informed her as they rejoined the party.

4

"TRAVIS seems to be adjusting well to college," noted Forrest. The young people were all outside, rolling and patting and throwing snow. Lily had insisted that Travis make her a snowman. He was reluctant until she ordered Leah to help him. Ken and Jeremy, seeming eager to impress Erin with their mastery of the natural world, soon joined them. Michelle had found some extra boots and gloves in the foyer closet. Forrest, watching them laugh and romp about from his comfy throne in the corner, looked as if he were trying to summon lost memories.

"Yes, he's doing fine," Bryan agreed, "I wonder about his room-mate, though."

"Oh, I thought you were going to bring him along," Lily remembered.

"We invited him, but he declined."

"You should have insisted," she scolded.

"I was quite insistent, Mother, I assure you, but the boy would not be swayed."

"Is that the German boy you told me about? What's his name, Andreas?" inquired Richard. Lily nodded.

"Well he probably thought you didn't mean it. You must learn to be less intimidating," she said.

"For goodness sakes, Mother, I did not *intimidate* him, I was quite warm and encouraging. He's just not the social sort. Ask Travis,

31

he'll tell you. Just stays in their room most of the time, studying. No friends to speak of. Doesn't seem to be doing too well in his classes either."

"What's he studying?" Michelle asked.

"Engineering of some kind. Robotics I think."

"He's probably just a little homesick, still getting used to America," Richard suggested.

"I think it's more than culture shock," Bryan said, "He's... one of the quiet ones. Can't connect."

"Some of them just don't *get* it," Stephen agreed, "I wouldn't wonder if he ends up at the bottom of a gorge."

"Stephen!" Lily exclaimed.

"Now Lily, it's no one's fault, it's in his genes, obviously. It's evident he's a loner, which more than ever is anathema on campus. And in the wide world."

"It's a wonder they don't all take the leap, faced with this interminable gray," Forrest put in.

"I'd have to agree," Bryan averred, "about Andreas. He certainly won't last academically. No confidence, no *esprit de corps*. It's not about personal achievement anymore, it's about teamwork, communication, social networking."

"Nonsense," Richard boomed, smiling broadly, "Why, you know nothing of him, how can you make such a generalization? For all you know he is a genius, he may be the next Einstein."

"Well if he is, no one will ever know, will they? He has no fighting instinct, he's afraid of engagement. He'll wind up fodder for his betters, pushed aside like any dolt willing to work at Walmart."

"But how can you call those who would push aside someone just because of where they work 'better'?" Michelle asked crossly.

"Come on, Michelle, you know what I mean."

"All great ideas arise from the individual, not the team," Richard's resonant voice asserted persuasively, "the herd cannot think out of the box."

"That's the kind of unsubstantiated misconception a properly developed collaboration would never propound," Stephen countered.

"I agree," Bryan said, "Ontogeny follows phylogeny. It may appear that the spark comes from a single individual, but the group exists first, supporting and directing that individual. Without the team, an idea is never fully developed, never properly explored."

"You mean exploited," submitted Kyle. He had been quietly consuming cookies and wine. Michelle glanced at him, caught his eye, and somehow felt he was defending her. The others ignored him.

"Working alone can be likened to existing in a semi-conscious or minimally conscious state. A well connected psyche is more aware, has more information available to it, and in the end is making a far greater contribution to the whole," Stephen explained, "And as a student of robotics and artificial intelligence, that boy should be well aware of this. Part of the presumed advantage of mind uploading will be the ability to easily connect multiple minds in a hardwired matrix of consciousness."

"But linking minds can only dilute the spirit," Richard boomed, his great cheeks waggling, "The entire cosmos is in here," he declared, slapping his flabby chest with one hand, "It must be brought out pure, unadulterated, uncensored by mob mentality. Kyle, you're an artist, back me up on this."

"Well, if by cosmos you mean the voices in my head, then, no, we deny our secret existences," Kyle quipped.

"I contain multitudes?" Sarah quoted irrelevantly.

33

"Yes," Richard confirmed, winking at her. She loved her old professor; you could see it in her face. And why not, Michelle too loved the thrum of his TV announcer voice, his easy laughter, his courage and loyalty.

"But isn't that solipsistic, Richard?" Michelle suggested. Kyle turned his head slightly, as if looking at the professor, but Michelle felt his eyes lingering on her, on the cashmere, on her hair and face. Just as his eyes were about to meet hers, she looked away, and met Stephen's eyes instead. Had he seen her, watching Kyle watching her?

"No, it's romantic," Richard replied. "It takes a hero, someone with tremendous courage to bring forth the eternal flame and hold it high so that others may see."

"You mean a human superorganism, like a bee hive?" Bryan directed this question to Stephen, both of who had so discounted their opposition as to drop them from the conversation entirely.

"These two are hopeless," Richard mumbled under his breath so Sarah and Michelle could hear.

"Exactly. But more than mere stigmergy;" Stephen added, "distributed cognition. You could think of it as an extension of what we have now with the internet, cell phones, and all the associated social networking tools. Only communications will go directly into the brain, or the mind in the case of nonorganic existence."

"But we already *are* linked," Lily said. She had been listening intently. The others looked at her blankly.

"In Christ," she said. Then her face took on a sheepish look, as if she hadn't intended to say that out loud. Michelle felt for her. It was definitely the wrong crowd for a religious remark, not that Lily considered herself deeply religious, although she did go to church frequently. In fact she had often attempted to persuade Michelle to accompany her, but Michelle had been raised by atheists. Rather than go to Lily's church, she had acquiesced to periodic 'philosophical' discussions aimed at imparting *some* sort of belief, which, due to her great respect and affection for Lily, had in part succeeded. She did now believe in something, but remained unsure what it was.

Since her husband had passed, Lily considered herself head of the family, yet she also professed that her family increased every day, with each person she met. She felt a great responsibility to advise where advice was needed, to guide quietly where advice would not be heeded, to set an example if nothing else could be done, and suggested this was an obligation everyone should take on. She took this task very seriously, but it did not weigh on her, because the activity itself sustained her faith that her advice was apt and her guidance guided. To her, it could not be otherwise. Sometimes Michelle acknowledged her wisdom and aid, sometimes she tolerated it, and only occasionally did she think of her elderly friend as a meddling pain in the ass.

Through their discussions, Michelle had found that while Lily considered herself a Christian (and when asked, certainly replied that she did believe in one God), her faith did not descend on her from any specific dogma; it arose organically from the fertile soil of her existence. She possessed a great deal of common sense, compassion, and experience, and these married to form a practical unconscious conception of God as amalgam, as the sum of interpersonal relationships and chance encounters. It followed inherently that *keeping* faith required activity, engagement, and involvement. This was Lily's true creed. She felt linked to all the people around her on a deeper, or higher level, and she could sense that they were linked to others around them whom she did not even know in a normal way, but *through* them she did, and those people knew others, and they in turn knew others, and so she knew we are all linked — *In Christ*, that was how these feelings were named in her mind. But she shouldn't have said it that way. After a moment, she tried to rephrase her thought.

"I mean, don't you feel that there is a, a... collective unconscious?"

"Of course, Mother," Bryan said, "But that's just it, it's *unconscious*. What Stephen is talking about is a conscious connection, which theoretically might be possible in the future. If people's minds are contained in computers, you see, they could be linked much the same way different hard drives are linked now."

"So the team *becomes* an individual consciousness," Stephen clarified.

"Oh, I see," Lily said, rising, signifying that she was done with the conversation. She stepped away and situated herself in front of the window, beside Forrest.

"What do you think, Forrest?" It was a rhetorical question. Everyone knew he didn't offer opinions on anything but his own malaise. They looked out the big bay window together, at the young people enjoying themselves.

"I think Frosty's just about done," he said.

"Yes, they're doing a fine job," she agreed.

"My God, talk about Big Brother," Richard blustered in Lily's defense, "as if we aren't being programmed enough by the corporate media machine. Where's your soul, man, how can you talk so blithely of existing inside silicon chips and... and... *circuitry* and being *run* from on high like some *app* on your precious dingleberry phone. The very idea is intolerable." Lily didn't seem to hear him.

"Oh look, there goes Travis," she exclaimed gleefully, pointing. The bay window shook with a loud whump. Michelle jumped. A round white spot had appeared just above the sill; a snowball fight had broken out. Travis had run by the window in an evasive maneuver; someone, perhaps Jeremy, perhaps Erin, had just missed him and struck the glass instead. Lily was completely changed, the hurt look had evaporated from her face; she had become absorbed in the action outside. It wasn't as if the consciousness conversation had stopped, it continued without her.

"It's simple mathematics, Richard," Stephen coolly continued, after turning momentarily to scowl at the snow stuck to his window, "the unit is one thing, the set another. As long as cognizance is confined to the unit, the full capacities of the set are not being utilized."

I must have had too much eggnog, Michelle thought, because they're not making sense anymore. Kyle made a comment about bluetooth brainwashing; Michelle chuckled too loudly. Stephen looked at her askance. She rose, turned her back to him and stepped into the red glow of the tree, leaning over the back of Lily's chair.

Stephen had a habit of turning parties into lectures or debates. He enjoyed pitting one camp against another, then sanctimoniously pronouncing judgment on all. Bryan continued spewing bits and pieces of the latest studies he had read on brain imaging during meditation and how that applied to quantum mechanics in the emergent noosphere, or the effect of the principles of decision downloading and the laws of fluid dynamics on the distribution and use of cultural memes in the War on Thought, or some such pretentious theorizing. Richard ineffectually defended himself by quoting antiquated literature.

Sleepily, Michelle watched Lily watching the students, feeling vaguely jealous of both. Outside, Leah was standing behind Erin, feeding her snowballs. Lily waved, motioned, was on the edge of her seat, grinning. "Come on," Michelle heard her say under her breath, "go get him!"

Is that what it's like to live *in Christ*, Michelle wondered; she's out there *with* them. Whereas I can only witness, she can *experience* their play. How does that work? What the hell's wrong with me, that I can't share their joy?

5

THE NIGHT was incredibly silent; the wet snow fell thickly, muffling all sound. Travis watched his breath floating away. There was no wind, no traffic noise. The yard was dim, compared to the front with all its Christmas lights. A dark pinkish radiance dwindled as it rose from the horizon; the ground, slightly lighter than the surrounding woods, glowed a ghostly blue.

A single porch light winked through the trees, their bare limbs reaching up like crooked fingers, welcoming the barrage of flakes. That's Grandma's house, he thought, that light. Except not anymore. It reminded him of all the summer nights he had spent there, sleeping on the terrace or in the gazebo, watching the fireflies magically hovering through the garden, appearing here, then there as if blinking in and out of existence. It seemed incredibly sad that she had had to move away from it, sadder still that he would never spend another summer there, in that garden, in his childhood.

It turned out that Jeremy had a good aim, now Travis found himself at the back of the house alone, a snowball in each hand, trying to calm his breathing and listen for pursuers. No one came. Chickens. After a minute or two he continued around the house, and saw a big green truck parked up by the garage. Green letters on the side read: *Kampnich's Kitchens and Baths,* and below that, *347-5979.* He took out his phone and started punching the number in.

A snowball hit him in the middle of the back.

"Uh," He grunted as he whirled and ducked, looking for a target to fire at. The phone fell from his hand. Leah hit him again with another one, down low, in the leg.

"Wait, I dropped my phone," he protested, but she rushed him, and pushed him over onto the ground, rubbing snow into the back of his head and laughing.

"Jeez, you got snow all down my shirt!" Travis yelled, scrambling to his feet. Damn, she smells good, he thought. She had picked up the phone and glanced at the almost finished entry on the screen.

"Need work done on your kitchen?" she asked, "or your bath?"

"I, uh… was just…"

"Twenty percent discount if you mention this snowball fight," she quipped, tossing the phone back to him. He wiped the snow off and put it back into his pocket. They stood looking at each other a moment, tense, alert, awaiting the next move. Then he jerked down to scoop up some snow. She took off running and squealing, looking back frequently. He didn't run, but patiently formed a good firm snowball, then threw it at the moving target. She turned, saw it coming, and deftly avoided it.

"Seventy-six!" she yelled at him, then disappeared around the corner of the house.

"What?" He trudged back to the front door, thinking. Then it hit him, and he pulled out his phone, altering the final two digits of the entry to seven, six.

"Oh, it's cold out there," Ken exclaimed, coming back into the parlor and heading for the fire. Soon the rest of the snowman crew were shaking off their hats and stomping up from the foyer, their faces glowing with the chill.

"Look," Jeremy said to Erin, holding up his phone, "my sister just sent me these pictures of her new baby girl."

"Ooh, how cute!"

"Can I see?" Sarah asked, and so Jeremy made his way around the room, clicking through a half dozen pictures of a wrinkled pink bundle.

"Wow, so you're an Uncle," Ken said.

"I know, isn't it crazy?"

"What's her name?"

"Doesn't that make you feel old?" Leah asked.

"Alice Ann."

"How adorable," Richard proclaimed.

"No, well yeah, but she's like seven years older than me, so she's really happy about it."

"She is so tiny," Cheiko said, "So sweet, the little fingers."

"That makes her all of what, 30?" Bryan asked.

"Yeah, she didn't want to wait too long, cause she didn't want any, you know, problems."

Michelle took her turn looking, her envy growing with each picture.

"Oh gosh, look at that face," she cooed. "Do you know Connie Ward is going to be a grandmother?" she said, turning, realizing too late that of course Jeremy didn't know who Connie Ward was.

"Who?"

"Mm, never mind," Michelle mumbled, flipping her hand to excuse her mistake, and looking about for Lily, who did know whom Connie Ward was. Connie taught in Stephen's department, she was younger than Stephen, barely older than Michelle. Her daughter had been born while she was still in college, now the daughter was expecting.

"Thank you for sharing those, she's so beautiful," Michelle said, a tear in her eye. She felt heaviness in her chest, she sighed and sank down beside Sarah on the couch. One forlorn Santa was left on the tray, its blue iced eyes had been smudged by a reindeer's hoof; she picked it up and bit off its head.

* * *

"You just need a little more confidence," said Bryan, "It's all about attitude, Sarah. Attitude and image."

They were standing near some shelving in a corner of the parlor, where Sarah had been looking at the books. He had a glass of wine in one hand, the other was pressed against the wall, to steady himself. Most of the young people had left, gone to find more interesting parties or home to cram for finals. Sarah could hear someone talking in the dining room, and she knew the women were in the kitchen because she had purposefully avoided the vicinity, having no desire to help with the cleaning up. Mr. Carlson looked like he was asleep in the chair across the room.

Professor Demerest was a head taller than Sarah; his winy breath filled the corner where she stood, his comb-over dangled down at her, bouncing on his bushy eyebrows and those thick glasses. She was repulsed, yet somehow flattered by his attention. She assumed his mother had put him up to 'advising' her.

"It's about that first impression, you know?"

"Uh-huh," she said, nodding, trying not to look at him.

"You see, right there," he continued sagely, "You're too shy. You must learn to look at people when they talk to you, Sarah. Show people you deserve to be here."

"I'll take that into consideration, Professor Demerest, thank you."

"Please, call me Bryan. You'll find I'm not as formal as old King Cole," he said, meaning Professor Cole, who *could* be pretty formal at times, Sarah thought. She smiled.

"There, you see? That's a better impression already. You can't overestimate the value of a well-crafted smile. Now let me ask you something Sarah. Do you write down your goals?"

"Yes," she lied. Someone had suggested that to her before, but it seemed so stupid. It wasn't as though she was going to forget what she wanted. Standing this close to him, Bryan looked younger to her, except for the grey in his beard.

"Do you visualize? You need to *see* yourself in the job. When you go for an interview, you need to walk into the room like you own it. You *do,* you know." Now she looked up at him, trying to figure out what he meant or if he were too drunk to mean anything. He smiled broadly; she smiled back. She tried to look him in the eyes, but the tilt of his head and the thickness of his glasses made the position of his gaze ambiguous. Was he looking over her head? At her mouth? She wasn't certain that they were making eye contact. She felt nauseous, shaky in her stomach.

"And let me tell you something, *confidentially*," Bryan went on, grinning at the alliteration he had just conceived, "You have every reason to be *confident*, you are still a very attractive woman." Sarah couldn't help but blush at this, even though it was a backhanded compliment, even though she didn't believe it. He's definitely drunk, she thought, grinning, pulling her hair back from her ears.

"Especially when you smile," he assured her, "Don't you understand? *You* have all the power. Don't be afraid to use it."

43

"Well thank you," she said. He took another sip of wine. His eyes seemed to be focused on her lips. Was he trying to lean toward her, or was he just unsteady?

"Because you could have any job you want, you know, if you smile."

"Now I know you've had too much to drink," she chuckled, leaning back against the bookshelf.

"No I haven't, I'm serious. Any job in your field. You just need an interview coach. I want you to call me the next time you have an interview, and I'll walk you through it. Can you do that for me?"

"Alright. Sure."

"You might want to do something with your hair, though," he decided.

"What?"

"And wear a black skirt, and you know, buy a decent bra, something with a little more... lift."

The anxious shaky energy in Sarah's stomach shot up through her arm, in a completely involuntary and supremely satisfying explosive jolt; she found herself looking deeply, penetratingly into his stunned eyes, recognizing that those annoying, obfuscating, thick lenses were no longer in the way, knowing at last that he *saw* her. Then came the realization that she had knocked the glasses off his face, that she had slapped him that hard, that her hand stung from the force of it, that something or someone had taken her over, if only for a moment.

Michelle heard the sound, a crack, like a book hitting the floor, followed immediately by the unmistakable sound of glass crashing and shattering. She rushed out of the kitchen the back way, by the stairs, and saw Sarah down in the foyer pulling her coat out of the front closet.

"You're leaving?" she asked, stepping down after her. Sarah nodded. She seemed upset.

"Are you okay? What happened?"

"Nothing. Professor Demerest dropped his wine glass. I've got to get going."

"Can you drive alright?"

"I'm fine. Better check on him, though," she added, nodding in the direction of the parlor and rolling her eyes, "he's really wasted." Michelle glanced up and saw Bryan standing in the archway, wiping his glasses on his shirt, squinting down at them. Sarah was opening the door.

"Well I think he was planning to spend the night anyway, but thanks for looking out for him. You think the roads are okay?"

"Yeah, it stopped a long time ago, I'm sure the plow's been through already. Well, good night."

"Oh, don't forget your gift from Lily," Michelle said, snatching one of the packages from the console and handing it to her.

"Please thank her for me. Thank you for inviting me."

"You're welcome. Merry Christmas."

6

WHILE she was mopping up the wine and sweeping the glass off the floor and mopping again, Michelle saw Kyle Westin catch Leah as she was passing through to the dining room. He spoke softly to her and handed her what looked like a business card. She smiled and nodded her head, the red ribbon in her hair bouncing jauntily. He made another quiet comment and the girl laughed, putting the card in her pocket.

"Well it's been a pleasure to meet you," Michelle heard him say, taking Leah's hand in his. She had seen him earlier extracting a laugh from the more reserved Erin, whispering in *her* ear, handing her a card in a similar manner. What was he up to?

"You're not leaving," Lily exclaimed, crossing from the fireplace, where she had been talking quietly with Bryan.

"Oh, I think I'd better," the artist confirmed, "Gotta get my beauty sleep, you know."

"Well thank you for coming, Mr. Westin," Michelle said. In this light his dark eyes looked greenish. There were dimples beneath the whiskers.

"Please, call me Kyle. I'm sorry I didn't stop by sooner, and… sorry about the brownies. They were delicious, by the way."

"Oh, good. Glad you enjoyed them." She passed the broom and dustpan to Leah, who returned to the kitchen.

47

"I get rather involved in my work, I'm afraid, and…"

"No need to apologize," Michelle assured him, extending her hand. He took it firmly, did not shake it, just held it, looking at her. She looked away. His hand was very warm.

"I really like these watercolors, by the way," he said, nodding at the dining room wall.

"Oh? You don't think they're too… static?" she probed.

"No, no. They're exacting. Very precise."

"Michelle painted them," Lily divulged. Kyle released Michelle's hand. She covered it with her other hand, crossing them in front of her.

"Really? I didn't know you paint."

"Yes, when I have time. Mostly in the summer," she said, glancing again at his eyes. He was still looking right at her, or… at her hair maybe. She looked away again, felt the blood rushing to her face.

"Well they're very nice. And I like the way they're framed."

"Sometimes I wish I could paint with a little more, I don't know… abandon."

"Perhaps Kyle can give you a few pointers some time," Lily suggested.

"Sure, anytime."

"Well, abandon can be overrated," said Stephen, appearing at Michelle's side, putting his arm around her waist and pulling her tightly to him, "I think you've made an excellent study, sweetheart. Looks like a spring garden."

"Yes, I really like them," Kyle repeated, "Thank you for inviting me Lily," he added, extending his hand towards her. She grasped it, pulled it down, forcing him to bend over and accept a brief embrace.

"Not at all, welcome to the neighborhood. How are you enjoying the house?"

"Oh, It's fantastic. I'm sure you miss it."

"I'm afraid I do, I'm afraid I do miss it."

"Well stop by anytime. Although apparently I can't be trusted to answer the door." Michelle and Lily chuckled.

"And feel free to stop by here," Stephen countered, "Just call first."

"It is a big house," said Lily, ignoring Stephen.

"Well I always have music on when I paint, sometimes I have it cranked pretty loud."

"You'll have to get the doorbell wired directly into your studio, then," Stephen suggested, "I know a handyman who can do that for you."

"Yeah, maybe. That might be a good idea I guess. Well…" He took a step towards the door. Lily went with him. Michelle moved to follow, and Stephen walked with her, still holding her around the waist, releasing her only after he saw that the chain was hanging loose. He glared at her with a look of disgust as he took up position at the door so that it could be properly secured.

"Good night, Kyle. Merry Christmas if I don't see you," Lily said, handing him one of the remaining gifts.

"Oh, thank you. Merry Christmas to you."

"He's such a charming man," Lily remarked as she and Michelle sat down by the fire.

"Who's charming?" Richard asked, returning from the bathroom.

"Mr. Westin, don't you think so?"

"If you say so, Lily dear. Seems nice enough I suppose."

49

"Disappointed she didn't say you?" Forrest teased, waking from his nap, "The great Richard Cole is the most charming of all, right Lily?"

Michelle chuckled.

"Did I hear that you've changed your mind about retiring, Forrest?" she asked, "I thought you'd already put your house on the market."

"What happened here?" Stephen demanded, seeing the wet spot on his polished oak floor.

"That's entirely my fault, Stephen," confessed Bryan, "I'm so sorry. The glass just slipped out of my hand."

"Glass? Michelle, did you sweep this properly?" he asked. "We don't want anyone stepping on any shards." Without waiting for an answer, he went off toward the kitchen, presumably to retrieve the broom and sweep it again. As if he ever walks through the parlor without shoes on, she thought.

"I have listed it," Forrest answered, "It's just I'm not sure I can afford to stop working, what with the alimony, and..."

"Of course you can," Richard rumbled, "Don't put it off, that's my advice. Life's too short. Best thing I ever did, retire. Should have done it sooner." Forrest shrugged and looked unconvinced.

"Good luck selling your house in this market," Bryan warned.

"Actually, I've already had an offer. Bit low, but I'm thinking about it."

"Take it," Richard advised, "You can live off the proceeds for years. There's an apartment available in my building, utilities included, you can walk to everything, sell your car if you have to. You won't regret it."

Stephen reappeared with the vacuum and began unwinding its cord.

"No, if I retire, it's Florida for me. Been going down there for January break the last couple years, looked at a few condos. I'm just not sure I can afford one now."

"That should be no problem, the bottom has dropped out of that market," Stephen remarked, "You could pick up a condo for a song, now. If that's the sort of environment which appeals to you. Try Orlando." He stood with his foot over the power button of the vacuum, as if daring them to continue the conversation. Michelle wanted to slap him.

"I was thinking Ft. Lauderdale," Forrest revealed. He didn't look offended in the least, as if he didn't realize Stephen was belittling him. Was he oblivious, or had he risen above it, Michelle wondered. Perhaps Stephen only seems snide to me because I'm with him every day. He flicked the length of vacuum cord with his left hand in what Michelle saw as a threatening gesture.

"Well I'd better be going," Forrest sighed, heaving himself out of his nest.

"Are you sure?"

"Me too. If Forrest is leaving, the party *must* be over," quipped Richard sarcastically. "Can I give you a ride home, Lily?"

"No," she answered. "Michelle and Stephen have been kind enough to put Bryan up for the night, and I'm going to stay too. There are few things we need to discuss." Bryan looked at his mother quizzically.

"In the morning, dear," she assured him, patting him on the knee. He gave a grunt as if to suggest he was not so drunk that he could not discuss whatever it was she wished to discuss.

"Good night, Stephen," Richard boomed, "It's been a lovely affair."

"Oh, let me get the door for you."

51

"I'm coming too," Forrest informed him, hugging Lily and Michelle briefly before Richard took his more demonstrative turn.

"Do it now," Richard reiterated as they donned their coats, "you could be dead tomorrow."

"Richard, don't be morbid," Lily admonished. "I'm sure it'll all work out," she assured Forrest, "You never know what's around the corner. I think good things are in your future."

After the pair left, Stephen carefully locked and chained the front door. Then he began turning off lights, snuffing candles, and drawing the drapes while Michelle ran the vacuum. Leah appeared in the dining room arch. She had been cleaning in the kitchen. Lily paid her and she left through the garage. Michelle put the coasters away, wiped down the coffee table, and switched off the music and the tree lights. Then she double checked the kitchen, put coffee in the coffee maker and turned on the dishwasher. Stephen did not like to rise to a house in disarray. He helped Bryan up to his room while Michelle got Lily settled in hers.

I lingered in the vicinity, listening, observing, inhaling the smell of the pines. I had forgotten the chilling joy of snow.

7

SARAH Strickland sat on her couch eating French fries, with the canned laughter of the late show in her ears, rereading that which she had scanned earlier in the day, now finding new meanings:

> This is a time for all signs to move forward and work toward accepting new patterns. Start making those choices that you have struggled with in the past. New relationships are possible now; maintain open lines of communication with others. Information is coming in the following weeks that you may not know what to do with, but illumination is at hand, and a new understanding will help you to step through that door and allow you to regain control over your life.

Perhaps I overreacted, she thought, perhaps he was right about it all; perhaps I do need a new hairstyle and a new bra. But why did he have to be so creepy about it? She squirted some more ketchup onto her plate and shoved another fry into her mouth in an effort to expunge Bryan's leer from her mind. 'You have all the power. Don't be afraid to use it,' he had said.

"I have power," she said aloud, "since when?" That *would* be a new understanding, she thought, tossing the paper aside and picking up the little square package from Lily. She was going to save it, wait till Christmas to open it, but decided that was pointless, since she already knew from the size and weight it was a small wall calendar. Everyone had received one as they left the party. Hers was wrapped in gold foil with a red bow, which she now removed and carefully set aside. After peeling off the foil she verified that it was indeed a calendar; the artwork was soft looking, undefined, not so much fuzzy as rough, like chalk on the sidewalk. There were figures for some of the months, elegant women holding round children, or faces of solemn looking men; the clothing and complexions had a sort of third world feeling, but whether they were meant to be Arabic, African or Indian, she could not tell. Most of the images were more vague, perhaps representing the moon over a lake, or a mountain range or a body supine. The cover showed a starry sky over a dark teal field; in the center, levitating magically, was a window frame with billowy curtains and through the window one could see the same scene portrayed in daylight, the radiant sun on green rolling hills. Written in elongated letters in the night sky was a single word: Rumi. It was a fourteen-month calendar; she opened it to the first month, December. There was an image of a woman, her face turned aside, she looked like she were in pain or had been crying. Below the image, printed in flowing script intended to look like handwriting was the following quote:

The wound is the place where the Light enters you.

* * *

Lily put on her nightgown and tried to put away her irritation with her son. He wouldn't tell her what had passed between him and Sarah, but it was clear he had had too much to drink. And he had dismissed her in front of the others when she spoke of Christ, as if faith were foolish. She could forgive him of course, he was under considerable stress, what with Gretchen's mother in the hospital, and he *had* been kind enough to drive up and spend the weekend helping her with some legal matters, yet it irked her to be treated as if she could not understand the conversation, or had nothing of value to contribute. It had seemed to her they were going to a lot of trouble to theorize about constructing a system that already exists. Halcomb knew what she meant.

She and Halcomb had been married for sixty-three years, during forty-two of which Halcomb had been alive; they were no less married now. She often spoke to him, in her mind, many times a day in fact. He seemed to speak back; of course one could not say for certain that he was perceiving her presence as much as she was perceiving his, but she never doubted it, just as she never doubted that Christ, or the Father, or the collective unconscious if you pre-ferred, was responding to her thoughts. People and things reacted to her needs, desires, and intentions. Someone was listening. Perhaps everyone was listening. Sometimes it felt like everyone were linked *in Halcomb Demerest.* This thought seemed blasphemous, but if that was the way God made her feel, how could it be? If she were driv-ing somewhere, and lost her way, she knew that Hal knew which way she should turn, and she inquired of him, and he answered. If she forgot someone's name they had both known for many years, he would inform her. For larger questions, she sent her inquiries or notices of need or prayers to Christ, but it was all done without thinking, it was all one and the same to her, there were innumerable divine presences available, spirits or angels or Hal, or her mother or father or the Father. Innumerable but one.

The window of the guest room Lily slept in that night faced Demerest House. She could not resist peeking through the blinds at the home in which she had spent the majority of her years, raised her children, truly come to know and love her husband, and coddled her grandchildren. It was odd to see the space between the two houses from this opposite point of view, to see a completely different face of the features she knew so well: the low stone wall, the curve of the flower beds she had tended year after year, the branches of every beech, maple, and fir (some of which she had helped Halcomb to plant), the stumps and knolls in the yard, the slope of the land itself; all looked different from this side. It was a disturbing feeling - in the best sense - expansive, as if she had found a new chapter in a beloved book. The connection she felt to the place suddenly felt more intimate and complete than it had before.

How strange, she thought, to see the old house on a wintry night and be outside of it, bittersweet. Her home spoke to her across the ghost-grey yard in a voice just as forlorn as it had been the past twenty years. It wanted children, parties, laughter and light to fill its rooms. Someone must provide these, eventually, or the walls would close in on themselves. She still harbored hopes that one of her grandchildren would keep the place in the family, but none of them seemed to have any desire to live in little old Ithaca, except perhaps Travis, and it was far too early to know where he would want to settle.

There was a light on, high in the master bedroom. Did he sleep in it, she wondered, the sleigh bed, all alone as she had done, or did he use a different room? The bedroom of Lily's apartment at Crestview was rather tight; she had been unable to take the magnificent king-sized antique with her to her new home, it remained at Demerest House where it belonged, along with a number of other key furnishings. She slept just as well on the unassuming twin that suited the dimensions of her new life, but she did miss the dark cherry curves of the great bed. She shut the blinds tightly and turned inward.

The interval between donning her nightgown and turning out the light was the one time of the day Lily allowed herself a pang of self-pity, a twinge of sorrow. Through the lonely years she had been able to imagine Halcomb waiting there propped on pillows against the warm wood of that big bed, a book in his hand, his bushy eyebrows raised in an effort to stay awake and focus on the page, peering through his bifocals at her as she slipped under the covers, smiling his welcome; so many long winter nights they had traveled together in that sleigh. As long as she had the bed she had been able to sense him beside her in the night. There seemed to be no room for him at Crestview, his shoes and ties, his desk and files, his favorite chair all finally out of her world. During the day it was fine, he still seemed to be with her as she went about her business, but sometimes now at night...

Lily had always prayed, in church on Sunday, at table before her meals, and just about anytime she saw someone in need or was in need herself, she sent out a prayer. But since leaving Demerest House she had begun to pray every night at her bedside again, like she had as a child, on her knees with hands clasped and eyes closed. Besides being a good way to keep the spirit humble, it kept her from dwelling on the change of furniture, and kneeling was good for the posture. If she were honest with herself, she would have to admit that she no longer prayed as she had when she was a girl or a young woman, and that she probably didn't pray as Reverend Thomas might advise her to. She had long ago taken charge of her own prayer and no longer thought about what exactly she was doing; she was simply praying. She might have a particular person in mind, or a specific question to ask, or a simple wish to feel God's presence;

but there were many nights when feelings or ideas were given to her during prayer. Did they come direct from God? From Jesus, Mary, an angel, or Halcomb? She did not know, she no longer questioned the source, she had absolute faith that what she was given in prayer was for someone's benefit, and if at all possible she should act on these thoughts. It might take her months or years to understand exactly what she should do, if anything, or exactly how to proceed, but *not* embracing these gifts was unthinkable.

Here, this close to the old house, she felt her husband's presence strongly, and her mind was full of people and problems as she knelt beside the bed to pray. She knew Halcomb or Christ would help her to help those in her life. There was Sarah of course; Lily had hoped Bryan would be able to help her, but now his drunkenness seemed to have made things worse. Yet immediately upon closing her eyes, she received the distinct impression that whatever had passed between them was a step forward, for both of them.

Then there was Leah; she was sure she had done the right thing there; she sensed a spark between them. Travis would open her eyes to the world's possibilities, and Leah would bolster his confidence. She would have to keep an eye on them, though. They were both too young to form a permanent attachment. But what about this boy, Andreas, Travis's roommate? Lily was very worried about him, after what Stephen had said about ending up at the bottom of the gorge. He must be looked after, so far away from home. She would suggest that Travis should take him to church. She would ask Stephen to warn his advisors to watch out for him. Perhaps he should be on some medication. She prayed very hard on this young man she had not yet met.

It was Michelle that worried her most of all, she could not think why. She had had a bout with depression several years ago, but seemed to have come completely out of it. Now Lily thought it might be returning. It wasn't anything she had said or done. There was something... *grey* about her. Halcomb knew. In actuality, Lily had been praying for her all day (since she had arrived to help with the decorations), holding her in her mind, requesting assistance on her behalf. Now, kneeling there in her nightgown, she made the choice again, to give. She opened her mind and her heart for them — this was how she prayed — she drew in the love, from God, from Christ, from Halcomb, she did not seek to qualify it or discover its origin, she simply felt it, drew it in, and directed it back out to those who seemed in need, to Michelle and Andreas and Sarah and Travis and Leah and Bryan and Gretchen and her mother and Richard and Forrest and Stephen and Kyle and Ken and Cheiko and Jeremy and... and... what was that girl's name? Erin and Reverend Thomas and Doctor Pankow and Catherine Spivak and...

* * *

Michelle lay awake in bed, feeling slightly dizzy, staring at the curtains as though she could see through them and the foggy glass, watching the snow falling in her mind's eye, remembering the fox; its red coat, shimmering white vest, and little black boots, the way it looked her in the eye like a promise, the sense of expectancy it had imparted. What had Mr. Westin said... *portentous*. Maybe it was that word which struck her more than the fox itself.

Kyle was an odd man. Interesting, funny, but odd. Why had she been rude to him about the brownies, she wondered, after all they were only brownies, and what did he mean by 'static', exactly? What was *wrong* with her paintings, could he show her? She felt her face flush with shame for them. Was she a mere dilettante, was that

59

what he thought? Lily had said he showed in New York, but did he *sell* any? She had sold two watercolors the previous spring, $500 each — nothing to sneer at. Who was he to come into her house and criticize? Of course he hadn't *known*. He was only answering a question honestly, and he was sorry when he realized, she heard it in his voice as he was leaving, when he lied and said he liked them. He somehow apologized with the tone, the timbre of his lie. His voice *touched* me, she thought; there had been a physicality about it, he had reached out. The sound was not commanding like Stephen's, nor deep and rich like Richard's, but there had been a kindness, a pledge of goodwill, which she had felt when he spoke, regardless of the words spoken. Was she... attracted to him, she wondered, then felt a pang of recognition that, yes, she was. Had Stephen noticed it, when she herself had just now become aware of it? Had she fawned over him at the party, glanced his way too often or perked up at his conversation? She turned her head and looked at Stephen, sound asleep beside her. No, there was nothing he could have noticed, she had done none of those things. But there was a part of her which had glommed on to a part of him, or an idea that was a part of him, or something in her had recognized that something in him was contiguous on some other plane or in some other world, as if they already knew each other, yet only that small part. Had she known him in another life, did she even believe in all that, was this warm feeling proof of it, or was she just horny? It was not the feeling of family, the comfortable assurance of shared experiences, but... an acknowledgement of spirit, the commonality of the great beyond — *Namaste*. What was there about him that gave this impression? He did not remind her of anyone she could think of, rather, in a confusing way, he reminded her of himself.

Michelle and Stephen had been married for fifteen years, yet in many ways he remained a stranger to her, so very *other*. She and Stephen had shared so much, yet there were parts of him he refused to reveal, and parts of her he refused to acknowledge. As her understanding of this had grown, the assurance she had once felt with him had eroded. She still took great comfort in his presence. She still wanted him, still wanted to be there beside him, still wanted to share his life. Lily had tried to tell her once what her own marriage was like, how they had been so much a unit, how when Halcomb died it felt like half of her had been ripped away. Michelle couldn't really understand, though in a way she had been envious of their connection. She thought of Lily across the hall in the guestroom, so completely alone, she thought of Sarah, never really having had anyone in her life, and she turned her body towards Stephen and lay her arm across his chest, feeling incredibly grateful that he was there.

8

FALL Creek winds its way through Tompkins County slowly, coming in at the village of McLean and meandering through Freeville, tiny Etna, and sedate Forest Home before pausing at Beebe Lake. After escaping Beebe dam it courses through campus and cascades dramatically down to Stewart Park and Cayuga Lake, leaving the deep shale-walled Fall Creek Gorge behind. Skirting the gorge is a trail, enchanting in summer, often treacherous in winter, always beautiful. Between the bridges at Thurston and Stewart Avenues, there is a bridge for pedestrians, which connects to the gorge trail. Apart from these bridges, the gorge is visible from a handful of campus buildings, frat houses, and private residences. The home of Stephen and Michelle Wolcott is one such address.

The Wolcott's master bathroom has one window, high on the wall beside the commode. Though small, it offers what is, to Michelle, the best view of any window in the house, because it is the only second story window that faces the gorge. The view from the bedroom windows is that of neighboring houses or the backyard and sparse woods beyond. From the bathroom, Michelle can see a little section of the gorge, at least for seven or eight months a year, when the branches are bare. Taking in this view has become a ritual, part of her morning ablutions; she wraps her hair in a towel, spreads paste on her toothbrush, and stands on tiptoe to check the mood of the world.

The pattern of this certain stretch of the gorge wall Michelle knows as well as that of the quilt on her bed or the Oriental rug on the living room floor. She cannot see the creek from her vantage point, but each day she looks out at her personal expanse of the landscape and notes the changes: snowfall, leaf fall, rock fall, leaf bud, bird nests, streaming rain. She recognizes the array of trees lining the opposite side of the gorge, some leaning over the edge where the shale continually gives way, as if in the act of falling, as if a vast forest were marching relentlessly forward, forcing their vanguard into the chasm. Several times she has noticed that large clumps of shale had slipped away, their absence suddenly more conspicuous than their presence ever was.

The gorge trail is easily accessible by crossing Fall Creek Drive, but during the winter its use is restricted. She sometimes attempts it anyway, using ski poles to assist her in keeping her balance, but only when Stephen is out of the house. He considers it foolhardy and irresponsible.

The morning after the Christmas party, Michelle looked out of the window at the foggy smear of snow and barren trees and wet rock, and for some reason thought of the fox. A mental image of him trotting the trail flitted across her mind, as if they had an appointment she was late for. She hadn't been for a good hike since before Thanksgiving, but it was quite cold, a high of ten degrees was expected. Besides, Stephen would be home all day. He had been up for a while, and undoubtedly Lily had preceded him. She dressed hurriedly and went down; the smell of coffee met her on the stairs. She heard voices as she approached the kitchen.

"...I suppose you'll have to spend Christmas with Robert," Bryan was saying.

"Certainly not. You know I can't abide Los Angeles. Not for Christmas," said Lily.

"Why don't you come to Madrid with us, Lily?" Stephen offered. What the hell is he doing, thought Michelle, as she entered the room. Of course he knew she would never say yes.

"No, no. You two need some time alone. Perhaps I'll spend Christmas with my new friends at Crestview."

"We're alone all the time," Stephen countered.

"I mean alone *together*," said Lily significantly.

"Good morning, Michelle," Bryan said. The other two had their backs to her.

"Good morning. I'm surprised to see you so... alert this morning, Bryan."

"Awake, yes, alert could be contested. I would have slept in, but I need to get home."

"Right. So what happened with Sarah last night?" she asked. Bryan blushed above his beard.

"I don't remember exactly *what* I said, but I do know she took offense. Slapped my glasses off."

"You don't remember," Stephen chuckled incredulously. Bryan cleared his throat.

"I'll call her and apologize. I'm sure she realizes, whatever it was, that I didn't really mean it. I may have had too much to drink."

"May have?" Stephen leered.

"Can I get anyone anything?" Michelle asked. She noticed they had gotten into the last of the Christmas cookies.

"Don't call her," Lily suggested, "I'll call her. You send her a note."

"I will call her, Mother," he said firmly, "It was my mistake, I will make the apology. Besides, I think I may know of an opening for her. Dr. Rasmussen owes me a favor."

"Oh, well that would be terrific," Lily exclaimed. As if it were *her* career on the line, Michelle thought, I'd bet Sarah doesn't get that excited. Yet it's not affected, she really feels it. How does she manage that, where does it come from?

"I can't promise anything, Mother."

"Does anyone want any breakfast? I can whip up some pancakes," Michelle offered. Thankfully, everyone politely declined. The very idea made her nauseous.

"Now what about Travis's roommate, what can we do for him?"

"Mother, you can't force a student to get help, the resources are there for anyone who wants them, but..."

"I mean it, now, we can't sit idly by if we know someone's in trouble," she persisted, "Can't you get the boy some counseling?" Bryan sighed and shook his head.

"Travis said he's already spoken to the RA about it, but Andreas is adept at putting up a passable front. You can't commit someone who's functioning and no danger to others."

"In this case, Lily, I think the most effective measure would be to encourage Travis to make more of an effort to befriend the boy," Stephen suggested, that superior smile on his face. Lily turned to Bryan and opened her mouth, but Bryan preempted her.

"I'll speak to him, Mother, but what more can you expect of him? He's got his studies to worry about. It's not as though he has shunned him, you know. His concern is the reason we're discussing it at all."

"You're right. I just hope you have made it clear to him that we have a duty to help those around us."

"Of course I have."

"I'm sure it'll all work out," said Stephen, but Michelle had the distinct impression he didn't mean it. "Now if you'll excuse me, I have some things to attend to. Good to see you Bryan." The two men shook hands and Stephen went off in the direction of his study, with the clear intention of remaining there until lunchtime or beyond.

Michelle had long ago given up on trying to understand what it was that kept her husband so occupied. There was always one more call to be made, one more student group to advise, one more grant to be written, one more TA to reprimand, one more committee to meet with, one more symposium to attend. She could not pinpoint precisely when she had slipped down the list of priorities, but it seemed her name was now so far from the top that it was on another page altogether.

She had suspected an affair at one time, in the third year of their marriage. Out of the blue he was coming home late, staying up all hours in his study on the phone or the computer, and traveling more than previously. He had received a promotion of sorts he had said, but as he was already the head of the department she had found that unconvincing. She had searched his pockets for weeks but found nothing, she had checked his shirts for lipstick and sniffed them for perfume and examined his jackets for stray hairs. She had listened at his study door but had heard no laughter, no terms of endearment, nothing personal at all.

One night she had surprised him by bringing supper to his office on campus and interrupting him in a meeting with three men she had never met before. He had made no attempt to introduce them, and not one of them had smiled at her as he hustled her out of the room, saying later only that she was very thoughtful, the meal was delicious, but he would prefer if she never came to the campus unannounced again. She had demanded to know if he were involved in something illegal. He calmly sat with her and apologized, saying he could see now that he had neglected her, and that he was very sorry, but he could not tell her anything more about his work, except that he was doing an increasing amount of consulting, some of which may well have national security ramifications, and he was not at liberty to discuss it. He had been credible; she had wanted nothing more than to be placated, to have her confidence in him restored. She had not understood what an important person he was.

"Are you alright, dear?" asked Lily. Michelle realized she had been semi-present, silently brooding. There was something uncomfortable about the conversation they'd been having which had caused her to withdraw — diagnosing the roommate when he wasn't there to defend himself, as though he were insane to be a little down so far from home.

"Yes, sorry. You're sure you don't want some eggs or something," Michelle offered. She was vaguely aware that Bryan had excused himself to shower and pack his bag while she had been absently stirring her coffee.

"No, thank you, I had a cookie," said Lily, smiling like a naughty child. It was wonderful to have Lily back in the kitchen. They had spent so many hours through the years chatting over coffee. There was a time Michelle had relied on her, but now that Lily was at Crestview the closeness Michelle had once felt for her was dissipating. She was starting to feel the difference in their ages.

"Oh. So how are you doing? How are things going at the new place?"

"Just wonderful. Everyone's so friendly. And the food! I never expected it to be so good. I'm sure I've gained ten pounds." This was something Lily had said the last three times Michelle had seen her. She gave the same reply.

"Nonsense, you look as skinny as ever."

"And how's Linda?" asked Lily. Before she had married Michelle had had a few close friends, who had for the most part drifted out of her life. Linda was one.

"I presume she's fine. I see her posts on Facebook now and then." Linda was still in town, but long ago she got pregnant and never escaped the house again. Going to see her had only made Michelle sad and envious. Lily knew this, which made her question mildly irritating. Have I changed, wondered Michelle, feeling impatient with her old friend, or is she not as lucid as she used to be?

"You two should get together more often."

"Yes, maybe I'll call her," sighed Michelle, rubbing the back of her neck. She didn't forget at all, Michelle realized, she's *hinting* again.

"Do, and let me know how she's doing. And her little boy, what's his name, Brandon, how old is he now?"

"Yes, Brandon. He must be ten. No, eleven."

"Eleven! Oh my goodness, how can that be?" asked Lily, shaking her head in disbelief. Michelle tried to smile.

"And her daughter Mia is eight." The memory of holding little Mia made her heart ache. No, it was the memory of the way it had made her feel — jealous. Excluded from one of life's great joys. Stephen had told her up front he didn't want children. She had thought she was fine with it. She sighed again, heavily, and drank from her cup, avoiding Lily's eyes. "Well you must go visit them, and tell them I said hi."

"I will." Can she not see how hard that would be for me, Michelle wondered. Maybe not, she had four, and all those grandchildren, she has no concept.

"How are things with you and Stephen?"

"Fine. You know how they are; Stephen is Stephen. Nothing unusual if that's what you're asking." She stood, turned toward the sink, but sat on the stool again, holding her head.

"You haven't been having the migraines again?"

"No. Just a little dizzy. My neck's pretty tight."

"You'd better have that seen to."

"Yes. I'll make an appointment with Sam. Right after we get back from Madrid."

"I'm so glad you're going, that's just the thing, get him away from work for a few days. You'll both feel so much better. But you know if you ever need to talk about anything..."

"I've got your number," responded Michelle briskly. She didn't want to talk about these things with Lily anymore. She knew all of Lily's responses, all of her advice. Lily was very concerned, but she was not always sympathetic. There was something about her that made Michelle feel lazy or inadequate, like a weak-willed whiner. A *wallower*. Well maybe she was, but she didn't want to be reminded of it. That's what was so great about Sam. There were no judgments, no arguments, just occasionally a suggestion, or the possibility of a palliative. You could just lie there and say nothing if you wanted to, or you could jabber on and Sam would just listen. Stephen did not care for the tall hippie cum shaman, from the moment he set eyes on the tie-dyed poncho, the frizzy ponytail, the amulet; he had made his disapproval known. He did not care for that smell of incense and cinnamon, and particularly he had not cared for the suggestion that he and Michelle try couples Tantric yoga. So it had been a few years since she had had a good massage. She missed Sam.

70

9

ON NEW Year's Eve at the Eurostars Madrid Tower, Michelle slipped into her sexiest teddy, a sheer red nothing of ruffled lace. They had been at a gathering, she had had three glasses of champagne; Stephen had had one as far as she knew. He was so annoyingly disciplined; so diligently moderate. He was in the bathroom. They had been at opposite ends of the room at midnight and had not kissed, so she didn't know if he were in the mood. She heard his voice in conversation, on his cell phone again. Just let him come out without his damned pajamas, she thought, situating herself on the bed in what she hoped was an alluring pose.

Michelle had been eagerly anticipating this Madrid trip for months; her mind related it directly to their honeymoon fifteen years earlier, one week of which had been spent in Barcelona, the other in Paris. In Barcelona they had had a fire in their room. Perhaps that was why thoughts of the honeymoon were forever related to their first excursion together, that weekend in Quebec. Why did her mind continually revisit that, why had that been a seminal moment in their relationship, what had occurred? A few shared hours during which they found they had the same taste in movies (romantic costume dramas), the same favorite novel (*Wings of the Dove*), the same penchant for crème brulée. They had stayed at the Auberge Saint-Antoine, walked the streets of the old city arm in arm, and lain in front of the fireplace drinking champagne, giggling like children and tearily admitting to each other how lonely they had been. They had converged; inhabiting the same space in a way neither had ever done before, or sadly, since. At least that is what *she* had felt, that is the love she had experienced and had expected to relive on the honeymoon. It is what she continued to wish for them whenever they got away from the routine, continued to hope for there in the bed of the extravagant, modern, clean, cold Madrid Tower.

He was still on the phone. It was chilly; the teddy gave no warmth whatsoever. She suddenly felt embarrassed, ashamed somehow for even having brought it on the trip. It had been a gift from Marcia, received at the bridal shower, occasionally brought out on their anniversary or Valentine's Day. Now that she had it on, it seemed vulgar somehow, too blunt an instrument. What if he did come out wearing pajamas, and she was sprawled there on display like a drunken slut? All she wanted was to somehow recreate that feeling, that Quebec-related feeling of real togetherness, the joy of knowing one another, the unity Lily and Halcomb apparently shared for so many years. She didn't want Stephen to think he had not been attentive enough, or that he wasn't good in bed, she didn't want to insult him in any way or to imply anything other than that she loved him, and she wanted him. And she knew he still loved her, despite his detachment. He was simply focused on other things. She slipped under the covers and clasped her knees to her chest.

Stephen and Michelle had not lived together before they were married, and she had had no idea that he owned pajamas. They had been lovers. Well isn't that the way with most couples, things slack off after the honeymoon, and she was glad at the time, she reminded herself. Stephen was a very focused man. When he turned his mind to something, it *would* be accomplished. It was one of the things she respected most about him, one of the qualities that made him exceptional, one of the reasons she had fallen in love with him. He had turned that focus on her, she had felt its irresistible power and been swept away by the Wolcott charm, the sly smile, the fulgurating steel eyes. The honeymoon had been nearly overwhelming, he was too intent; she began to feel he looked on her as an opponent. Parts of her felt beaten.

When they got back to Ithaca Stephen started wearing a sweatshirt to bed, saying he was cold. The fall term commenced and his focus shifted. She had been relieved. When winter arrived the sweatshirt was replaced with the full pajamas she had never seen before. He did keep the house cold, and it was *his* house, she felt that still; his family's money, his tenured position, his well-established life she had entered. She began wearing a big T-shirt to bed. So their contact had become gradually less intimate, their conversations more formal, their lovemaking had become sex, then the sex had become brief, then infrequent. She hadn't minded really, it hadn't been the sex that drew her to him, but she often missed the feel of his skin on hers.

Warmer now, her eyes closed, Michelle stretched out. She felt a pivoting sensation, not unpleasant, as if her feet, legs and torso were turning at an angle from the bed, as if she were slipping out of herself, as if she were being pushed gently into something else. *Taking a turn*, she thought, smiling, going with it. If she relaxed a little bit more, she thought, let go one more degree, she would pop out and float free.

For me, it was a first attempt at opening the door, a trial run if you will, to test the current of resistance. I approached in the prescribed manner, from the left, not to inhabit, not to control, but to instigate the contemplative process. Witnessing one's thoughts is the first step; a modicum of disjunction is frequently effective. I was well satisfied.

Stephen emerged from the bathroom bathed and bare and smiling at her. But seeing she was already asleep, he donned his pajamas before getting into bed. Their night of lovemaking was only her dream.

* * *

"Sarah?"

"Yes." Sarah Strickland had just returned home, she had been called in that day to Monrovia high school to baby sit through six long periods of aggravation and tedium. She stood in her canary colored parka over the kitchen sink of her little apartment, looking out the frosty window at the snow falling onto the yellow plastic slide of the neighbor's swing set.

"It's Bryan Demerest."

To the west, the sky looked almost clear there; the low sun was pouring a lemon cast through the thin layer of clouds.

"Sarah, I'm calling to apologize. For the things I said at the Christmas party, I'm afraid I was pretty drunk; I didn't mean what I said. I mean I'm not sure I even remember everything I said, but I'm pretty sure I said some things I didn't mean. I hope you can forgive me."

She set the spoon down on the counter, but still did not respond

"And I want to apologize for taking so long to apologize. My mother-in-law has been in the hospital and Gretchen's been with her constantly so I've been having to... well I won't bother you with the details, but I had wanted to get back to you sooner, that is to apologize, and assure you I meant no offense. Even though what I may have said should probably be considered offensive. I'm really sorry and I want to do something to make it up to you. Can you forgive me? Sarah?"

"Do what?"

"Sorry?"

"Do what to make it up to me?" she elucidated. Her nose was filled with the memory of his horrible breath, she blinked at his thick contorted lenses; she could see his comb-over dangling above her.

"Well anything I can. I feel just horrible about it. Can you forgive me?"

"I guess so. You were pretty smashed."

"Well I hope we can still be friends Sarah, and I really mean that."

"Sure."

"So listen, I think I may be able to get you an interview down here at Penn State. Do you think that's something you'd be interested in?"

"What's the position?" Her stomach gurgled loudly; she felt a tightening at her solar plexus.

"Well it's just a TA, but I think if you play your cards right…"

"Play my cards right with who? With you?"

"Jesus Christ, Sarah, that's not what I mean at all! I'm trying to help you for God's sake, that's all I meant in the first place. You know people *can* help you if you let them. You needn't see me at all; I won't even be there. It's just an interview anyway; I make no guarantees of any kind. No one is out to *get* you, you know."

"Sorry."

"As I understand it there is an assistant professorship coming open next year. The idea is to get you in there now, and let them get to know you..."

"Alright. Yes, thank you very much Bryan. I'm sorry to be so touchy."

"I completely understand. You have every right to be suspicious of me, and as I say I can't guarantee anything, but there are a couple of people who owe me favors."

"Thank you. Apology accepted."

"Wonderful. I'll email the particulars."

"Fine."

"And Sarah, I did mean what I said about... that you have every reason to be confident about... I do mean that."

Still looking out the window, Sarah set the phone down and picked up the spoon. While they had spoken, the horizon had turned from yellowish to pink. The play slide was no longer yellow, but dull beige because of the waning light. Her reflection was now visible in the window, her focus shifted; she saw the straggly brown hair, the lumpish face. All this while her hand had been working the spoon in the carton of butter pecan, scraping up another mouthful, and it brought it up to the face reflected in the window, and Sarah saw what she was doing. Guiltily she tossed the spoon in the sink, clapped the lid on the ice cream container and stuffed it back in the freezer. Stuck on the freezer door (with a Christmas tree magnet she had appropriated from her mother's fridge the week before), was a sheet from a small spiral notebook with bits of torn paper still hanging from the margin. At the top she had scrawled *Goals 2010*. Below that was a list of three items:

1)get job   2)lose weight   3)find love

10

MICHELLE opened the drapes wide to let in some light, and sneezed at the sun. She was back from Europe; Stephen had remained to attend a conference in Bern. Stephen liked to keep the drapes closed tightly over all the windows in the winter, to keep heating costs down, but... he wasn't there to object. She was finally going to change the sheets in the guest bedroom where Lily had slept the night of the Christmas party. This was the last task remaining from the season, except removing the outside lights. She would put off having that done until Stephen became angry. If it were up to her, they would continue to brighten the evenings until spring, but for Stephen there were rules to be followed, conventions to be observed, order from chaos, always. She had already taken down all the decorations and ornaments and packed the tree away in its box.

It was a clear, crisp winter day; the sun had melted the frost on the window, forming little puddles on the sill. Snow was falling in clumps from the gray branches where it had been clinging since the night before. Pulling the comforter onto the floor and yanking on the sheets, she remembered the last time she had done this, in the summer after Stephen's sister had been with them, when the trees had been at their greenest, when the dancing leaves had revealed the corner of an easel, and a form moving by a window of Demerest

House. She stood, the bundle of linen in her arms, and looked out across the yard to that same window. Its blinds were down.

After putting the sheets in the washer, Michelle went to check her email. Her 'office', if you could call it that, was a small room between the pantry and the laundry room, directly below the guest room she had just taken the sheets from. It had a daybed (placed there in the off chance their house were ever full with visitors), and an antique writing desk, some nice teak bookshelves, a small TV and DVD player, and a short chest of drawers. This room was her little sanctuary, it was the only room Stephen left completely to her. He took the décor of the rest of the house quite seriously and while he might tell her to 'handle' this or that, he always had his input and expected it to be followed. This room he left to her to do what she wanted. At first she had wanted to make it *just so*, she had chosen colors and purchased paint, but then for some reason she decided to leave it basically as it was, bland — beige walls, brown carpet, peach trim. She had tired of fussing over the house. The room's contents were mostly things left over from the apartment she had had before they were married; not sentimental things, but furnishings she had found too useful to discard, even when Stephen had found fault with their quality or condition. It was here she deposited her laptop, here she retired to read when alone in the house, here she made her novice attempts at meditation, here she practiced yoga, and here she sometimes spent the night when Stephen was out of town and their bedroom seemed too lonely.

She plopped down on the flowery spread of the daybed and opened the computer. There was a brief email from Stephen:

Munchkin,

Hope you are well, I'm exhausted. Another dinner
tonight. Hope the speaker is better than last night's or
I may fall face first into my soup. Will call from the
airport, should be around 2pm your time, day after
tomorrow. Kisses

She replied thus:

Sorry it's so tedious. Don't get too worn out. Maybe
you can sleep at the dinner, when no one's looking
;) Cold here, but sunny today. Wish you were here
to warm me up. Bring some of that famous Swiss
chocolate? Luv u

She checked the weather to see what was expected for his
return flight, though she hardly needed to. Every night between Hal-
loween and Memorial Day there was a good chance of lake effect
snow. On Facebook there were some pictures of Connie Ward's new
granddaughter, one showing the hospital band still on her tiny wrist,
another of her scrunched newborn face, the little cap on her head;
one of excruciatingly sweet little feet, which made Michelle grin
and coo. She scrolled down and saw Sophie Dobazni, a student of
Stephen's from several years ago. She had been tagged in a picture
taken at Cornell and resurrected by one of the other students in the
group. Michelle clicked the picture and moused over the faces, revealing their names. Some looked familiar, a girl she remembered
for her annoyingly pointed smile, the name, she had forgotten — Rebecca Burnbaum. Soon she found herself navigating through albums
of photos of unknown happy people posing at black tie parties, in
sports bars, in backyards, on waterfronts, at Tenochtitlan, eventually
arriving at an album titled 'Ian', which showed a little boy riding a

tricycle, his face exploded in a monstrous grin, as though about to run over the picture taker. There were more pictures of Ian; sitting in a kiddie pool with a confused golden retriever, blowing out six candles on an Incredible Hulk cake, his little cheeks puffed out like a balloon, and one of baby Ian sleeping on his father's stomach, his diapered butt stuck up in the air. He has Rebecca's smile, Michelle noticed, pointy, and definite.

She loved Facebook; she had a lot of friends in her list, many of which were not really in her life anymore, except there on the computer. Most of her friends from her early years in Ithaca, like Linda and Marcia, had been absorbed into the disciplined, scheduled world of homework, sporting events, rehearsals, and family vacations. Of course there were many students and visiting academics she and Stephen had entertained over the years that had moved away, some of these she had found online. No one refused her friend requests, but she only read their posts and looked at their photos, she rarely commented, they had little in common, they weren't really her friends. That was okay. The best part of the network was anonymously peering into the lives of friends of friends, seeing the joy on their faces, in their pictures, in that record of those rare moments in their lives which they deemed worthy of attempting to preserve with a photograph and maybe a caption: Ian learns to ride. It didn't matter that she would never meet Ian; it might well be that the best of him was in those photos.

Michelle returned to her homepage and typed Linda Morse into the search box. Linda's familiar face popped up; she sent her a message: How're the kids? Lily says hi.

Rubbing the back of her neck, she sighed and suddenly felt very weepy. She still had not gotten past it, seeing them move from being a couple to being a family. True, almost every baby picture filled her with longing, but there was so much more tied up with Linda and Dennis because she had seen at first hand what she was missing out on. Envy was only the beginning; there was frustration, anger, grief. Then there was the guilt; she felt guilty for being envious, for being sad whenever she saw Linda, for being angry with Stephen, for her completely indefensible sense of injustice, and for wallowing in self-pity.

Michelle and Stephen had agreed when they married, no children. Seeing Brandon nursing had changed her mind, but Stephen was adamant. Linda was outraged that any man would try to limit his wife in that way; her advice was to leave him, or at the least to adopt, but Michelle defended Stephen. It was one of the few times she had seen him make his point without vehemence, without sarcasm or condescension. He simply could not consent to bring any living thing into being, he said, it was too cruel, the world was too harsh a place. It was sad, she admitted, but he had been upfront about it. Linda could not understand her passivity. Privately, deep down, Michelle had come to believe that she didn't deserve a child.

Why was she rehashing all this today, Michelle wondered, why was she feeling so emotional? These were exactly the sorts of thought patterns she should refrain from. She went to the kitchen and poured herself a glass of wine, then returned to the computer.

She liked to check the collectible section of craigslist every week because her father still collected clocks. Of course she had only ever seen *one* worthy of being considered and it was gone before she could get hold of the seller, but it was worth a try. Once she found some quality dollhouse furniture for herself, the best of which was there on the shelf beside her where she could see it every day. The dollhouse, which her father had made for her fourth birthday, was somewhere in the attic, probably being eaten by mold or

81

mice. She had purchased a tiny Spanish style sideboard in Madrid, it was here now with her other favorite pieces on the bookshelf. Stephen didn't think much of this little hobby, and while he tried not to interfere, he could not help but reveal, on occasion, his disdain for childish things. Therefore she made every effort to purchase only the finest quality miniatures. Today there was nothing to find under collectibles.

The 'artists' link was another she always checked; in case any shows were coming up she hadn't heard about. There was a call for artists of comic book art for a show in Elmira, a notice for the upcoming Spring Bouquet show which she had already received an email about, and a listing which read: Model Wanted (Cayuga Heights). She took another sip of wine and clicked it.

> Females wanted to model, relaxed atmosphere, various body types considered, clothing optional. Submit photo. Good heat in studio. $10—$20/hr. depending on experience.

The only contact information was the anonymous craigslist email address. Michelle chuckled. Oh my God, she thought, looking again across the yard to Demerest House, it's got to be him. She typed 'Kyle Westin' into the Google search box and hit return. His website came up and she clicked it. The browser window went black, a thin silver line slid across near the top, and menu items faded up from the black background.

about | gallery | events | contact

Michelle clicked *about*. A photo of Kyle appeared, palette in hand, paint smeared on his forehead, his face displaying apparent absorption in his work; this dissolved and a second picture emerged, in which he was gesturing with his brush, mouth open as if in conversation; this gave way to a third image which showed him laughing, as if the photographer had told a dirty joke, then a fourth photo of him turning off the lights in his studio, which dissolved into the first one again. They looked professional, but posed, she thought, his wavy hair somehow looked purposefully disarrayed. The text on the page read:

> Kyle Westin was born in Portland, Maine, and received early artistic training from his uncle, Gordon Westin, an established illustrator. He continued his education in painting at MassArt in Boston. He now lives in Soho. His work can be seen at the Carlton Gallery in Manhattan, and the Fleischmann Gallery in Boston.

> "I have to work in oil, because the vibrancy of the colors cannot be matched in any other medium, and I love the way it feels when I put my brush to the canvas. The flow, the depth, you can't get that with anything else. It calls to me. The work should be a sensual experience for the painter as well as the viewer; otherwise, why bother? You might just as well take a photo."

> "My subject is the female form for the same reason the Greeks sculpted Venus, for the same reason the ancient Egyptians painted Isis, for the same reason the Hindus worship Shakti. To quote the *Saundaryalahari*:

'If Shiva is united with Shakti, he is able to create.
If he is not, he is incapable even of stirring.'

If one fails to acknowledge the goddess, there can
be only the abyss, sorrow, and tedium. Once one
concedes the primacy of Venus, there is at least the
possibility of joy.

"Oh my God," Michelle laughed, "He's insane." And out of
date, she thought, or is he ashamed to admit to living in Ithaca?
Bad for his image I suppose. Then she clicked on *gallery*, which
opened a slideshow of a few dozen images. "Jesus, what a pervert,"
she said aloud, but she didn't mean it; there was nothing *perverted*
about them at all, nothing one would consider obscene, no crotch
shots, no violence, nothing even dark in mood. It was just the idea
that her neighbor, a man she had met and made brownies for, and
invited into her home and shared eggnog with, spent all his time
painting nude women. It was unsettling somehow, but not really because of the paintings, they were basically harmless. She took them
all in as they came and went, then stopped the slideshow and flipped
through them one by one, studying them, *reading* them the best she
could, trying to look beyond the first glance which registered 'naked
woman' and exploitation.

He seemed to have been through several stages over the years.
There were many paintings of idealized, perfectly formed women
or parts of women portrayed in 'glamorous' fashion: a close up of
lustrous red lips, polished fingernails stretching the waistband of
sheer lingerie, a leggy blond leaning over the hood of a curvaceous
convertible. Then there was a group that seemed less glossy in style
but full of reflected light. The subjects, while still quite beautiful,
did not seem idealized or imaginary, and appeared posed in perfectly

natural positions, except they were naked: seated at a dining room table set with two place settings, lying on a blanket in the grass with a book in hand, sitting on her heels before a fireplace petting a cat.

A third grouping seemed to be the most recent, and the most unusual stylistically; the lines were more exaggerated, the settings surrealistic, and the models, while in a way very ordinary speci-mens, seemed somehow *more* sexual, supernaturally feminine: a bulbous woman sitting cross-legged under a tree, her chestnut hair braided and twined with its convoluted trunks and branches, with a little Buddha baby seated in her lap; a smiling, spindly girl standing in a carousel whose ponies were all satyrs and centaurs and uni-corns, smearing and blurring their hooves and horns round the edge of the canvas in the haste of their revolutionary motion; a pendulous matron with an immense bouquet of flowers in her hand, squatting before a Celtic cross in a misty graveyard.

The work was good, as far as Michelle could tell, they weren't really to her taste of course, but as she looked she began to see what he meant when he said her paintings were static. His, particularly the last group, were the opposite — fluid, dynamic, emotive. There was nothing misogynistic about them; voyeuristic perhaps, a few might be called disturbing, yet they did all seem to be reverential toward women, they did 'worship the goddess' in some sense. And the colors were unbelievable; they weren't garish, but the intensity, the luminosity was exciting. They were beautiful.

She clicked *events* and glanced at the list of shows, all but one were past. The next was almost a year away. Then she clicked *con-tact*, just because she had clicked all the other options. A form came up, requesting name, email, and comment. She finished her wine and started to fill it out, typed in 'incredible, gorgeous colors', then backspaced and typed in 'static... tight, too much contrast', then she closed the window without clicking 'submit'.

11

TRAVIS thumbed the number 347-5976 and held the phone to his ear. One, two, three rings. Shit, do I want to leave a message, he wondered.

"Took you long enough," a female voice said.

"Leah?"

"Who'd you think was going to answer my phone?"

"I don't know if you remember me, this is Travis, we met at a Christmas party, at Demerest House. Sorry, I mean at the Wolcott's house."

"Oh, are you the guy with the butterfly tattoo on your neck?"

"Wha..."

"Did you ever get your chopper running again?" Holy crap, I can't believe I said that, thought Leah, trying to keep a straight face.

"No, I'm sorry, this is Travis Demerest. We made a snowman, my grandmother Lily Demerest had you there helping in the kitchen, remember?"

"How did you get this number?"

"You gave it... are you screwing with me?" he laughed nervously.

"Not yet. Well maybe just a little," she giggled.

"Shit, I didn't know you were such a freak, Leah."

"Me neither. I guess you bring it out."

"God. Then you normally hang with bikers."

"You know it."

"Right. So you wouldn't want to go to a movie or something with me, since I don't have a chopper."

"I suppose I could make an exception."

"Cool. Only thing is… I don't have a car either."

"Loser."

"Jesus, are you always this mean?" Travis chuckled.

"No. Only with losers."

"So do *you* have a car?"

"No. My dad lets me use his truck sometimes, but only for work or school."

"Loser."

"Dork."

"Freak."

"Douche."

"Well… what should we do?"

"I guess we'll have to walk."

"Where, Cinemapolis?"

"What's playing?"

"Dunno. You wanna just come up to my dorm?"

"Yeah right. Why don't we meet at the Shortstop? I'm hungry."

"Where's that again?"

"I thought you used to spend summers here."

"Yeah but my grandmother doesn't exactly hang with the students. I know I've seen it driving by."

"It's on Seneca. Meet me there in half an hour."

"What's the cross street?"

"I don't know."

"How am I supposed to know if I can get there in half an hour if I don't know where it is?"

"Figure it out, Mr. Ivy League."

"Let's make it 45 minutes."

"Kay."

An hour later they were sitting in a booth, Travis eating a Dinosaur BBQ pork sandwich, and Leah having a cheese steak.

"How did you know it was me? On the phone?" he asked, running his fingers through his hat hair, hoping he looked presentable. Still cold, Leah kept her hat on, it was red and fuzzy with a floppy little brim and it cupped her luxurious brown hair to her round face. She looked vibrant against the faded brick colored vinyl. Her cheeks were flushed with the cold, her puffy winter coat made her seem incredibly soft and squeezable.

"I don't get a lot of calls from Pennsylvania," she said, noting that his eyes were brown, and his brows girlishly thin. Not his best feature. She liked his chin; it was kind of narrow and pronounced. His beard had not yet fully come in; he looked like he was trying to grow a moustache without much success. He was thinner than she remembered, wiry. Nice full lips, straight white teeth. He'd had a haircut since she saw him last, it looked much better.

"How did you know it was a Pennsylvania number then?"

"One of my grandmothers lives in Altoona."

"Oh. Well you freaked me out, I was about to hang up."

"Ha, that was fun. You're like, 'we made a snowman, remember?'"

"Yeah, yeah. I'll get you back. When you least expect it. You've asked for it now. And I still owe you for that snow down my back."

She's so cute when she smiles, he thought, and she smells incredible. God I want to kiss her.

"Ooo, I'm shakin' in my boots."

"So where do you live?" he asked.

"Couple blocks that way," answered Leah, pointing out the window.

"Great, so I had to walk for miles and freeze my ass off and you come all of two blocks."

"Poor baby. But you were ready to make me walk all the way to your dorm."

"Well I would have warmed you up when you got there."

"Pig." They both chewed for a while, enjoying the food.

"So... your dad makes kitchen cabinets and stuff?"

"Yeah. And my uncle. And my brother."

"Cool. My dad teaches at Penn State."

"I heard. What's he teach?"

"Economics. Business."

"Is that what you're studying?"

"No way. Maybe. I haven't declared a major yet. Maybe psychology. Prelaw. I don't know. My mom and dad expect me to get a doctorate and everything but it's just so hard to face like another six years of school. I mean some classes are interesting, but there's just so much hypocrisy you know? So much fuss over stuff no body really cares about."

"Yeah. I know what you mean," Leah said, although she wasn't sure she did.

"I mean, you read three books on the same topic and they all disagree with each other, and everyone spends all their time arguing you know, the fine points and they never get around to *doing* anything about anything. I just don't know if I can get in step with

90

the whole system. I mean in a way it would be easy to just go along. I can see myself ending up just like my dad, you know. And it would be okay I guess. I mean he's got a pretty cushy job in a lot of ways, but he's not really happy, you know? You think you're dad's happy, being a contractor? Does he like it?"

"I don't know. Never really thought about it. He's pretty grumpy most of the time actually. I don't think it's so much what they do. They're old, you know? Old people are never happy, are they? I don't know any that are."

"I guess not."

"And why are we talking about them anyway? Old people are depressing."

"Sorry," he chuckled.

"Except for your grandma. *She's* happy."

"Yeah, she's totally got it figured out. I've never seen her in a bad mood. You know I think she wanted me to ask you out."

"What? Did she say that?"

"No, but... I'm pretty sure she was hoping we would hit it off."

"Why do you think so?" Leah asked, remembering how she felt so out of place and useless at the Christmas party.

"I don't know, she's just always asking me if I have a girlfriend, and I've never really had a steady one so I can never say anything. Every summer she would find some excuse to invite some neighborhood girl to her house so I could meet them."

"Oh shit, you're kidding! Gross!"

"Yeah, it was pretty stupid. I think she worries that I'm gay."

"And are you?" Leah asked, smirking.

"No," he laughed, "I've just never really... you're the first one I've liked," he claimed. Leah didn't know what to think, was she supposed to believe he was a virgin?

91

"So she's like your pimp?"

"No, she'd be like *your* pimp. She'd be my *procuress*," he laughed.

"Jesus, does she know you're such a perv? I think you're making this whole thing up," Leah protested, but remembered that Lily had told her about her grandson before they met, mentioned him by name and said what a great guy he was.

"No, really, I think if you called her now she would say you should come back to the dorm with me."

"Yeah, right," she laughed, taking out her phone, "so what's her number?" Travis laughed that she called his bluff, but did not give it to her.

"Come on, what's her number, gutless?"

"So what are you going to study?" he asked, changing the subject.

"Me? I don't know. I'm not sure I'm going to college."

"No? Why not? Are your grades really awful or something?"

"No. Jerk. My grades are fine. I guess. We can't all get into the hot shit schools. I'm just not sure I want to go. I mean, my uncle went and he's just installing cabinets same as my dad, and my cousin went and got a degree in English and couldn't do anything with it and now she works in shoe store at the mall for next to nothing, so I don't know why I should pay all this money for some degree I'll probably never use."

"But you're smarter than them. I think you should definitely go."

"You *just* told me how it's full of hypocrisy and you can't find anything you want to study, but you expect me to want to go."

"See? I'm learning how to be a good hypocrite already. There's no end to the useful skills you can learn at a fine educational institution. Have you applied anywhere?"

"Yeah. Syracuse, Colgate, IC. I could always go to SUNY. I just don't know what I would major in."

"Well what's your favorite subject?"

"Home Ec."

"You're kidding," Travis laughed.

"Screw you, I like to cook."

"Sorry. That's cool." They ate quietly for a while, watched the snow falling.

"God, you're pretty," Travis said when he had finished chewing. Leah exhaled in that adorable way she had, not quite a laugh, not quite a snort, not quite a cough.

"Dork," she said, smiling. Guys were such idiots, she thought. She had yet to learn how to accept a compliment gracefully. She did not want to be romanced so much as she wanted a friend. Not that she didn't want to mess around. Just... how can you take someone seriously who says something like that?

"So. You wanna come back to my dorm?" Travis asked when he finished chewing. Leah smiled and shook her head.

"You don't give up, do you?"

"How would a loser ever get to be a winner if he gave up?"

"It's pretty late."

"It is not, it's nine-thirty."

"I'd better go home. My dad'll be waiting."

"He doesn't expect you home at nine thirty. Come on."

"No, I'm not walking all the way up there, how will I get home?"

"I'll walk you home. Just for a few minutes. I want to show you something."

"Yeah, right," she laughed. "I think I know what you want to show me."

"Come on, just walk with me. You can leave whenever you want."

"Good to know I have your permission."

"I just mean I'm not a creep or anything. For God's sake, you know my grandmother. If I get pushy you can tell on me, right? Just come back with me. It's not like I'm going to slip you a rufie or anything."

"Woa!" she laughed, "Just the fact you brought it up shows you've thought about it, though."

"No, no. I just mean you can trust me."

"How many girls have you date raped, Travis?"

"Come on, don't be stupid."

"Now I'm stupid, oh, you're really smooth."

"Ahgh. Come on, you know you want to."

"What makes you so sure? How do you know what I want?"

"You wouldn't have given me your number if you didn't. You know you like me or you wouldn't be here. And I think you're incredibly hot."

"Shut up. What are we gonna do, make out while your roommate watches?"

"He won't be there. Trust me, he's never around anymore. When I do see him he doesn't say much. I think he might have a girlfriend."

"Good for him. Guess he's not as much of a loser as you." That one hurt a little, she could see on his face. Well it had to be done. Did he really think she was going to fuck him after one sandwich?

"I gotta go," she said.

"Can I walk you home?"

"Sure."

In bed that night, lying curled on her side, one hand between her legs, listening to Beyonce sing *if you liked it then you shoulda put a ring on it,* Leah thought about Travis's face; his jaw, his lips, his pathetic moustache. She did like him. She liked the little kiss on the cheek she had allowed him on the porch steps. Did he really like her, or was he just saying that to get her undressed; it was easy to see he *could* be really nice, but she wondered if he *would* ever be as nice as he could be, or would he turn out to be a jerk like his father, coming on to girls half his age. Did she care if he were nice, reliable, or loyal? Did she want a ring on it? That's what I'm supposed to want, she thought, I'm supposed to want the ring and the promises, but I don't really see why. Could I really become a part of that family, that wealth? It's not like they're billionaires, but still, will I ever see Europe otherwise, have a house by the lake? Do those things matter to me, she wondered. Would it be so awful if I just let him fuck me? He looked like he might be good at it, she thought, I should have gone to his dorm, there might not be another chance. When was it okay to sleep with someone just because they asked you and you felt like it? She was eighteen, did that make it okay? If that made her a slut, did she care? It's my life, she thought, I won't get another, probably. And if you really like someone, love them, why do you want him to make promises? Why wouldn't you want them just to be happy and do what makes them happy? She pulled the quilt tighter around herself, turned off her ipod, and dreamt about Travis's lips.

12

AFTER having removed them from the box, Michelle folded the cardboard carefully, print side in, and stuffed it along with the receipt, warrantee, etc. into the kitchen trash, not the recycle bin. Then she gathered trash from the bathroom and some old food from the fridge and dumped it on top of the empty box, carefully tied the bag, took it out to the garage, and put it in the garbage can. The new little binoculars she took to her office. Stephen had a fine pair of wide angle field glasses of course, but he kept them in the study; they were quite large and heavy, and she didn't much enjoy using them, and if she borrowed them and for some reason forgot to return them, he would miss them, and then he would quiz her about what kinds of birds she had seen, when he knew she wasn't really very good at identifying them. She had often thought of getting herself her own, more delicate pair. That day when she saw them at the store, she told herself, now maybe I can learn some of the birds and next time we see something unusual I'll surprise him. She stepped to the window, to try them out. I'll have to get my own Peterson's guide to study, she thought.

Her office faced east, towards Demerest House. There were many trees between their houses, several maples, a couple of beech, a large oak and some conifers. High in the grey branches one could see large nests. Stephen had told her those belonged to the crows.

She fiddled with the dial on the binoculars; they were quite good, she thought. The windows of Demerest House came into focus. The blinds were closed. She could zoom in enough to see individual slats. She moved her view up to the third story where there were two similar windows. One had its blinds open, but all she could see from this angle was that the overhead ceiling light was on. What am I doing, she wondered, and returned the focus of the glasses back to the trees. Scanning with her new eyes, she identified several smaller nests here and there, but no obvious occupants or activity. A bird jumped from branch to branch of one of the beeches; she followed it briefly, decided it was a finch and turned away from the window.

In the corner of the room beside the daybed was a teak bookcase. This was where she kept all the things she didn't want Stephen to see, it wasn't as though she were keeping them from him really, she just didn't want to aggravate him. Her Tibetan bowl she kept here, and the meditation CD's, and the incense, and the books she knew he didn't like. It wasn't that he *disapproved* of these things exactly, but he had a habit of belittling them, which she found disheartening. 'Magical thinking' he would say, and smirk that way with his mouth but not his steely eyes. She tried not to give him the opportunity, by keeping these things in her office and using them only when he was out of the house. They were 'hidden' in plain sight. It was a system she felt worked pretty well for both of them, but part of her knew it was not quite right. It was weak of her not to address it. With other people Michelle was self-possessed, even assertive; with Stephen she had always been deferential. She saw now it was her own fault, she had allowed the relationship to begin that way, she had wanted him, wanted him precisely because he commanded respect, from nearly everyone. He had a way of implying authority without needing to assert it. He deflected dissent with the slightest facial expression, the most minimal vocalization, an exhalation through the nose. People were afraid of him, not physically necessarily, but afraid of his disapproval, and if he sensed that fear, he would reward you with a nugget of praise for your cleverness, as if to say, 'Good for you, you're right, I am powerful.' She had to admit to herself that she had found that attractive once. Did she still?

Above the bookcase she had hung the Rumi calendar that Lily had given her for Christmas. She read again this month's quote:

Gratitude is the sovereign antidote that transforms Wrath into Grace

She pulled a handful of titles off the second shelf: *The Power of Intention, 10 Questions for the Dalai Lama, Ask and It Is Given, You Can Heal Your Life*, and tucked the binoculars up against the back, returning the books in front of them. On the bottom shelf, in between *The Spontaneous Fulfillment of Desire* and *The Answer is You*, was a slim leather bound journal, deep emerald, with marbled green endpapers and ivory parchment leaves. Fixed in the binding was a pink marking ribbon with a pewter ankh tied to the end. Marcia had given it to her, she had left it untouched for many years and had only recently begun using it, not so much as a diary but as a gratitude book. She couldn't remember where she first read about the technique, but it was recommended frequently as a daily exercise to both reinforce the positive aspects of what is good about your life, and to attract what you desire to you by writing about what you *intend* as if it already *is*, by bringing a concrete immediacy to your feelings about what you want to see in your life, and from what she had read, it was the power of the feelings which set this universal law of attraction in motion. This process made for odd journal entries, but it did seem to make her more grateful for what she had, and so she intended to continue. She turned a fresh page, picked up a pen and spent some minutes writing, considering, and writing again, composing at length the following:

> *I am so thankful it was sunny today. I am grateful for this beautiful home, and for my health. I am so fortunate to have an attentive husband, and that our marriage is strong. I am grateful for all Stephen does for me, and that he is so steady, honest, and kind. I am thankful that he finds me attractive, that he wants me and is there for me. I am happy to be losing weight, and that I am taking care of my body. I am grateful that Stephen has taken an interest in Mr. Westin, and that we are making new friends. I am thankful it's going to be sunny tomorrow.*

After returning the book to its place, she put a yoga DVD into the player and began breathing deeply in preparation. She used to go with Marcia to the Wellness Center at the Corners for yoga, but that was many years ago when Sam was still the instructor. She had thought about making an appointment for a massage, for the knot in her neck, but decided she could stretch it out herself. Besides, it was a New Year's resolution to get back into shape. She told herself she didn't need to take a class to workout, but the truth was she hadn't played the yoga tape in a year; it had quickly become a bore, and if Stephen were home she was too self-conscious to use it. Sun salutation was a good beginning. She faced the window rather than the screen, and did as the yoga master bid: breathe.

* * *

Wearing heels, flab-squeezing, body-shaping power hose, a beige pencil skirt, a magic bra which made cleavage miraculously appear at the neck of her yellow silk blouse, several subtle, professionally applied hair extensions, false eyelashes and quiet but extensive makeup, Sarah Strickland walked purposefully into the conference room for her interview, envisioning the paycheck already in her hands. Butterflies filled her stomach, her solar plexus was vibrating intensely, and the corners of her mouth twitched slightly, because they were receiving mixed signals and were attempting to be prepared to both smile and pout. She refused to give in to the dismay that arose on seeing that there were three women on the panel, and only one man; Bryan had promised at least two.

"Ms. Strickland?" the man inquired. He was mid forties, trim, clean-shaven, and wearing a toupee. His slate colored suit was immaculate, his shirt completely wrinkle free, the Windsor knot of his red tie structurally perfect. He had a pleasant yet detached smile.

"Yes," she said, "How are you today?"

"Very well," he replied, "please have a seat." She did so, confidently looking him in the eyes, doing her best to make her smile natural and unaffected. He met her eyes and returned to the papers before him; she had the distinct impression from his inflection and the tilt of his head that he was gay. Bravely maintaining her smile, she next met the gaze of the young woman to his right, probably a student representative, and said "Hello." She looked anorexic, was casually dressed, slumped in her seat, and with a grave nod gave Sarah the feeling she had already dismissed her. She then greeted the other two women in turn, doing her best to send them warmth and give them the impression of strength, competence, and professionalism. The third person at the table was older, matronly, open, reminded Sarah of a chubby Lily. This was encouraging, but it was the fourth panelist whom she finally felt a connection with.

She appeared to be in her early thirties, was fair skinned, and had short black hair, which was beautifully cut and accentuated her angular features. Her lipstick and nails were chianti red, she wore a black business suit and her fingers slowly massaged the sleek black pen she held in her right hand. Her large dark eyes seemed to be assessing Sarah's outfit, makeup, and hair. Shit, I've overdone it, she thought, she knows it's not my real hair, fuck. Finally the woman met Sarah's gaze, for a long while with no reaction at all, then a very slight curve turned the side of her mouth. Sarah relaxed. There was something about that hint of a smile. It reminded her somehow of Bryan. Was this the person who owed him a favor?

"Can you tell us why you wish to be considered for this post?" the man asked. Sarah inhaled deeply and bloomed.

* * *

The darkness welcomed her, gave her room to expand. The wind bit her face and the cold air snapped her mind alert. There was a light, dry snow falling. Her boots made a crunching noise as she walked. The porch light revealed tracks crisscrossing the yard, squirrel's mostly, but after looking for a while she found the ones made by the little black boots, and she began to follow them. Drifts veiled the banks of the path, occasionally swallowing her knees. She had a miner's light on her head, and its light scuttled before her, just seconds behind its quarry. A moment was spent wondering where the miner's light had come from.

I supplied an answer: Uncle Peter, not mining, spelunking. Minimal, specific continuity is preferred when seeking oneiric contact.

She raced ahead, the leather fringe of her buckskin slapping on her thighs, but there was no time to question that, her mind was occupied with the task of negotiating the roots and rocks and mud, pushing herself through the roll and swell of the waist deep snow. For a brief eternity she kept on, revisiting familiar twists and turns through the winding wood, following the dancing light and the fox prints in the snow. The clouds were low, and the breath of the earth rose all around. Her bow was drawn, and I led her on.

The steel and concrete deck of the pedestrian bridge hangs from cables draped between the towers anchored on either side of Fall Creek Gorge. Mounted on each tower is a bright light, but the circles of illumination emitted from these bulbs do not quite meet; there is a shadowy area, a darkness over the center of the gorge. A thin fog rose from the water to welcome the snow streaking down through the lamplight. As Michelle approached and looked through the trees at the bridge, she thought she saw someone there in the shadow, not walking but looking over the rail down into the gorge, as though watching the sound of the cascade rise out of the black. She made her way into the glow of light below the tower, and it seemed to her the hooded figure put a foot on the lower cross bar and raised itself, leaning over the rail, pulling with its arms as if it were about to heave itself up and over and Michelle had an instinctive protective reaction.

"Wait!" she shouted, feeling her throat trying to make the sound, running, grasping at the cloak, at the white-tipped tail that thrust out at her from the cloth, but it was too late, the black booted feet flipped over the railing, the hood swooped back as he fell from her, his bearded face dropping into the abysmal fog, his hand pulling her down after him.

"No!" she screamed. This time Michelle succeeded in making a sound, a muffled plaintive grunt which woke her, yet those eyes — pleading, inviting, knowing — were slow to release her. She took a deep breath, tried to slow the pounding in her chest, fought not to plummet into those eyes. She was in the daybed, in her office; Stephen was out of town again. Rolling over, away from the wall, she found it was still quite dark out. She did not want to wake, nor did she want to return to that dream. Through the slats of the blinds she could see a light, upstairs at Demerest House. It comforted her. She stared at it until she fell asleep again.

In the morning, Michelle put on her neoprene pants, got her ski poles out of the closet, and crossed over to the trail. She knew it was foolish, or at the very least, morbid, but she felt compelled to go and look in the gorge. She had never had a premonitory dream that she knew of, but she did believe in them. And though the details of the dream had faded, it had left a strong impression. Someone had fallen from the bridge, she could not recall it clearly, but the feeling remained, a bond to something otherworldly, both past and future.

It was early, cold, and sleeting, yet she was glad to be out in the clean air. The trail usually had a calming effect on Michelle, no matter the time of year. The smell of the moist leaves under the snow, the hushed sound of the creek coursing through the gorge, the occasional squirrel or rabbit scuffling away; that immediate connection to nature was reviving, more so than meditation or yoga or painting.

Sam had recommended the trail as a place of refuge and recovery, calling it the walking cure. Michelle suffered from migraines, she couldn't say exactly when they had started. They had become more frequent after Marcia moved to Colorado. This was after Linda got pregnant for the second time, just after Stephen got his 'promotion'. When she had gone to the office with dinner that night, disturbed his meeting, accused him of infidelity and/or nebulous criminal activity, she had been forced to her knees with the pain behind her eyes. Stephen didn't understand the difference between a migraine and a headache; he had seen it as a breakdown, insisting that she see a specialist, by which he meant a psychiatrist. The word paranoia had been mentioned, and then she had seen her own obsession, seen the irrationality of her feelings. He had made her ashamed; she had let emotion conquer reason like a child. Dr. Wilson had prescribed antidepressants, Linda had suggested light therapy; the long, grey Ithaca winter invariably exacted its due and she was no exception.

Once she had the pills, Stephen became very supportive, suggesting she take some time for herself, treat herself at a spa, spend more time with friends. Taking his recommendations to heart, she finished the semester, and then gave up her office position. She went to the cinema in the middle of the day, attended concerts at Ithaca College with Lily, volunteered at Loaves and Fishes, took watercolor classes, joined a book club and found herself reading Deepak Chopra and Wayne Dwyer and Michael Beckwith. Michelle learned that it wasn't about Stephen at all; it was about herself. She had been looking to him for personal fulfillment; she had been comparing her marriage to that of Linda and Dennis, or Lily and Halcomb, when everyone knew that they had been abnormally codependent. Michelle was fortunate to be her own person, she was independent and whole and strong.

She went to tai chi and yoga classes, where she met mystical Sam, who was never pushy but seemed to know about everything alternative, from Reike to ayurvedic medicine, and had enthusiastically encouraged her to walk the trail every day. It wasn't just about the exercise, it was about *space*. It was about being in the moment, and absorbing energy from nature. Gradually, over the course of months, with each tracing of the trail, with every deer sighting or squirrel conversation, she had become more a part of the world again. Her sense of self expanded; that is the way Sam put it. That is what she had to do to climb out of the dark abyss she had fallen into, grow beyond it. The migraines had all but disappeared. She had just been a little down since Lily moved out.

Unfortunately, today the hike was not making her clearer. The blanket of overcast sky felt oppressive and ominous, rather than comforting. Normally the snowy weather made her want to stay snuggled up, watching movies, making chili. Today she wanted to run, she wanted to howl. She began to move faster, leaning on the ski poles to maintain her footing, feeling the sleet stinging her face. She had a sense of running through decades of time, her cerebral process shifting away from systematic analysis toward an equally lucid instinctive perception, as if moving past the time when Cornell came to dominate the landscape, which was neither before nor after, only different, the way Colorado is different from Kansas, and which comes before or after depends entirely on the direction you're traveling. The impression of buckskin, its smell, its texture, flashed across her body, with a veracity both compelling and surprising. That interval of the dream reconstituted itself in her mind, and she seemed to know the world in a different Age, before industry divorced mankind from the earth.

The dream had made Michelle anxious, but she didn't realize just how keyed up she was until she got to the bridge and recognized the unusual intensity with which she inspected the area, because she could not believe there was no one there. She stood in the center of the span, breathing hard, feeling out of shape, leaning on the railing suspended over the chasm, searching the monochromatic landscape for a speck of color or the shape of a body; some sign of the fallen figure the dream world had shown her, which she dreaded finding but could not fail to look for. Nothing caught her eye except the movement of the water trickling over the icy rocks, the wind bending the forlorn cedars, the sleet bouncing off the grubby slate and sleeping oaks. At one point she thought she heard a cry, that heart wrenching sound only a baby can make, but there was no one there. It must have been the wind, or some animal. She listened, but it did not come again.

Something in Michelle was profoundly disappointed, as if an augury of change had been rescinded. The back of her neck tightened in a horrible knot. Her mouth was dry, her nose wet, and her chest hurt from sucking in the frigid air, but she would not leave. Surely there was *something,* some reason for the dream, some justification for the way she felt, some presence there in the gorge; there *must* be. *Everything has spirit,* she remembered that girl saying, Cheiko, the Japanese student with the bad teeth. *Kami* she had said. *Each tree, each forest, each river, each rock.* But there was nothing there. She felt the migraine coming on. Shivering, she took out her cellphone, found Sam's number and called to set up an appointment.

13

SAM KEPT a little office at the house on Linn Street, in what used to be the back porch. Clients affectionately referred to it as the Healing Room. Not much had changed, Michelle noted as she disrobed and climbed between the sheets on the massage table. The three large brass singing bowls still sat on their cushions on the floor. The folding screen with its Japanese style painting of mountains and birds and fluffy white clouds still stood in the corner. Several large candles were glowing like they had not been extinguished or replaced since she had last seen them three years ago. The air was thick with the smell of incense and essential oils. The same anatomical posters hung on the walls; the black and white ones depicting acupressure points and meridians, the creepy flayed-man muscle chart, and the one that read *The Chakras* on top. It was Michelle's favorite, because of the color, and because it helped her visualize her chakras coming into balance.

The only thing Michelle did not recognize was a sculpture, about two feet high, of a couple coupling. It was primitive in style, probably Indian, she thought, ebony colored, depicting an ugly man or monster or ferocious god of some sort, seated in a cross-legged pose, and a beautiful, small and incredibly flexible woman mounted in his lap, facing him in ecstasy.

"That's new," she said when Sam returned.

"Oh? Has it been that long since I've seen you? I've had that a while."

"I was thinking it's been about three years."

"Wow. So how have you been?"

"Good. Pretty good, but I've been having trouble with my neck the last several weeks, and the other day it triggered a horrible migraine."

"Okay, let's see what we can do. My hands might be a little cold at first," Sam advised, gently pulling Michelle's head to the left with one hand, massaging the right *levator scapulae* with the other.

"Well that sculpture is called *Turning the Shakti*."

"Oh. Where have I heard that recently? Shakti. Or was it Shiva."

"Shakti is the female and Shiva is the male. The Shakti energy has been turned to face Shiva. It represents the importance of turning inward in the pursuit of selflessness."

"Isn't that backwards?"

"Sounds like it, but the idea is to turn away from judging others, and begin judging yourself instead. In this way you begin to focus on making others happy, rather than expecting the outside world to focus on you."

"Oh. It looks like they know how to make each other happy."

"Yes," Sam agreed, tilting Michelle's head to work on the left side of her neck. "Have you done any yoga lately? You're very tight."

"Yes. Not enough I guess."

"How often do you go?"

"I've been doing it at home. Haven't been to class in a while."

"Oh? Why's that?"

"Haven't felt like it. I don't really know anyone there anymore. Maybe I'll go next week."

"It might help. How are things going at home?"

"Same. Fine."

"Good."

It was obvious to Sam that Michelle was not ready to talk about it. That was okay. All in its proper time. Sam had always endeavored to cultivate in clients an understanding of the mind body connection, without (wisely) addressing the specific electromagnetic fields or arrays, otherwise known as the *subtle bodies,* or the mechanics of their interaction with the physical body. It had always seemed sufficient to suggest that certain chronic pains may be linked to particular habitual thoughts or emotions, and how it may also be beneficial to deal with the cause of the emotion rather than to address the body only; that one could think of the body as a closet, and one should be careful what one keeps. Life events or emotions one can't let go of have to be stored somewhere; memories, including memories of pain, are not only retained in the brain, but in the muscles, in the organs, even in the bones. Sam hoped to impart awareness, not just of a body/spirit connection, but of the body as *metaphor* of the spirit.

Michelle had taken to these concepts readily on a mental level, however Sam had noticed that she had not taken them to heart; she was not always forthcoming with herself regarding the origins of her troubles. It was good that she had returned at last; she was still in process.

"Have you been meditating at all?"

"Some. I never seem to get anywhere."

"That's because there's nowhere to go, Michelle. You're trying too hard. It's not about trying or going, it's about being."

"Right. I know. I just think too much."

"Close your eyes," Sam ordered, pushing both hands as far as possible under Michelle's back, then pulling them out, ever so

111

slowly, keeping the pressure up, feeling the energy flow. Sam used to try to push it into people, to wield it like a tool, but that was many years ago. Back then it had seemed as if one *had* to pull it up from the earth, or out of the air, to *exert*.

"I want you to take a deep breath and let all the tension go." Eventually one learns to wait, simply wait with open heart and it flows. Calm the mind, awaken the spirit, breathe, and the shudder will come, due to the change of vibration; Sam used to follow it, almost in awe, attend it moving up the legs and spine, along the arms, or more often from the crown chakra down. For a long time now it had come automatically, there was no waiting or watching, the base frequency had modulated upward; just open the hands and it flowed, as if running to ground, seeking out the cold spots, the holes.

Tenderly Sam stroked her temples, brow, and jaw. She was breathing better, balance was returning. The ears now, gently stroking, then down both sides of the neck to her shoulders, just pressure, flow. Now down the arms, together, then individually, working the muscles, pulling from the wrist, rubbing the palms, then each finger. Michelle sighed. She was relaxing, the resistance was subsiding, Sam could sense it. Her sorrow and fear were washing away, yet longing and confusion remained. She might progress now, though — divulge the source of the knot.

"Oh God, that feels good," Michelle professed tearfully.

Sam smiled, and felt her gratitude, and let it go. This was the key; not only the pain and the hurt and the bad things must be released, but the good things as well, and above all, the love. This was the hardest thing to understand, Sam realized, that it should be necessary to detach from the love itself, but it was true. All attachments,

112

all emotions, good or bad, cause wave interference, obstructing the current of the vibration.

Sam quietly continued soothing Michelle's muscles, working down the obliques, then the hip flexors, helping them to let go of their burdens, waiting patiently for her to open up, as she used to do.

"Funny thing happened to me the other day," she began, "on the trail across from my house."

"Oh?"

"On the bridge actually. It was weird. I thought I heard something. I felt like... I wasn't alone, but I knew there was no one there, you know?"

"We are never totally alone," Sam reminded her.

"But I felt like... a presence. I mean, not just Mother Nature, or God, but... a *personality*. If that makes any sense."

"I think I know what you mean. What happened?"

"Well nothing. But I expected something to. Have you ever felt a spirit in the gorge?" she asked.

"Like a ghost? I've never seen one," Sam replied, "but I wouldn't be surprised. A lot of people have died there over the years."

"No, I mean... do you think the gorge has a spirit, a soul?"

"Oh. Well everything has its spiritual side."

"Even rocks?" asked Michelle. Sam took a breath, slowed the rhythm of the hands. A delicate balance was necessary. Too much information would be counter-productive, only adding to the confusion, the tension.

"Even rocks. The world is not as it seems. It's all about patterns, Michelle. Waves within waves. Solid matter is not really solid; it's made up of vibrating patterns of energy. Even rocks are mostly space."

"Right, I know, but that's not the same as having a spirit."

"Well, I think Science will eventually conclude that spiritual energy is just as real and just as measurable as electromagnetism and gravity, and that the laws which govern it are just as precise and beautiful as all the ones they already know."

"So you're saying rocks have souls."

"It's not that they *have* souls, it's that they *are* soul." How do I explain, Sam wondered, oiling and massaging her calves, that there is actually nothing of her which is *not* spirit. "In the ocean, there are currents and whirlpools and swells and crests and breakers and surf, but these are just names for different patterns of the same force." Sam paused between the movement and the breath to let this sink in. "There are aspects of every thing which we cannot see, whether we have named that specific pattern of energy Michelle, or Sam, or Rover, or juniper, or shale, or Fall Creek."

"Mm hmm. I guess what I'm really asking, is do they *know* it. I mean do you think the gorge is aware that it is the gorge?"

Sam did not answer right away, wondering what she was getting at, debating the best way to approach understanding, yet set the mind at rest and allow concerns to fall away.

"Yes. But words are not the only way to communicate. Sequentially is not the only way to think. Reason is not the only way to hold awareness. Do you think the gorge knew *you* were there?"

"I don't know," Michelle sighed, "I don't know what I think. It was just weird. Like it was angry. Or sad. And I had déjà vu, but from a dream. Anyway that's when the migraine started to kick in."

"I see," Sam said, pulling on her ankles, stretching her out, elongating the vessel. "Sounds like something is trying to surface. You remember what we talked about before, don't you?"

"That migraines come from resisting? Yes. I try not to, I really do. Just go with the flow." She sighed heavily.

"I know it's not as easy as it sounds, Michelle. The important thing is not to worry. Try to see what you've been resisting. Acknowledge that you've been hesitant, or stubborn, or frightened. Let it come up, become conscious of it, don't turn away. Many times if we look at the issue head on, understand what it's really about; it will cease to be an issue. You may find that you are the only obstruction on the path you desire to take."

Michelle said little else during the remainder of their time, allowing them both to focus on the flow, the balance, the healing.

"If your neck tightens up again, you know where to find me," Sam said afterward, helping her on with her coat, giving her a quick hug.

"And who's this?" Michelle inquired as she opened the door to leave and a lanky, light gray tabby came trotting in. The bold, scruffy looking cat jumped on the massage table, sniffing and twitching its tail.

"That's Scaramouche the Swashbuckler," Sam revealed in a singsong voice, "and he knows he's not allowed in the Healing Room, don't you Mouchey? He likes to sit at the captain's table in the galley and watch the birds feeding on deck." Michelle played along.

"Oh my goodness! You sound like a fancy kitty, Mr. Swashbuckler." Once spoken to, he turned away with quintessential feline disdain, blinked his green eyes slowly, and affected ennui at the presence of a guest in his domain.

"He showed up out back one morning last fall, looking like death warmed over, eyeing the juncos. I opened the door and he didn't have the strength or sense to run off, so I brought him in."

"You're a good Samaritan. Strays make me nervous. Stephen hates cats anyway."

"He keeps me company on long winter nights. We have tea and crumpets together. Well, actually he doesn't care for tea, and he thinks we're having salmon pâté together, but mine is usually a piece of toast."

"If he's such a swashbuckler, shouldn't you be sharing grog and hardtack?" Michelle pointed out as she crossed the threshold.

"That's it," laughed Sam, "see you soon."

"I'll call."

Samantha Reyes waved as Michelle drove away, past the banks of cruddy, crusted, melting snow. The air had the wet, slightly fetid smell of the first thaw, when dead things warmed enough to release their odors. It was beginning to get dark. The grey sky was merging with the grey ground, separated only by the thin fingers of the trees. Heaven and Earth, as above, so below. Sam went back inside, into the Healing Room and lit some incense. She put Mouchey into the kitchen and closed the door. Taking a moment to get comfortable on a gold silk zafu, easing her legs into *Sukhasana* pose, she glanced again at the calendar on the wall, its image of a woman in a burka, and the words for that month:

> *This is love, to fly toward a secret sky,*
> *To cause a hundred veils to fall each moment,*
> *First to let go of life,*
> *Finally, to take a step without feet.*

Bearing this in mind, breathing deeply, she pulled a large singing bowl to her and began to ring it by rubbing the mallet around

116

its rim, massaging it to summon its deep vibration. She did this for a minute or two, until she could feel the oscillation coming up strongly through the root chakra, then she set the mallet down and let it sing. She felt the quiver running up her spine, up her neck and out the top of her head, she made the choice to *let go*, get out of its way, relinquish control, let it overtake the frequency of her own chi. She allowed the acceleration, the rise in pitch, the escalation of energy, until her entire body began to feel tingly, then numb. This was followed by the heaviness, the largeness, as though her head were a water balloon; big, weighty, resonant, just breathing, just vibrating, until she did not feel a *body* at all, only lift, rising up and out until she was there with them, beyond, seeing her self, her person, as merely a tiny part of the being she truly was, which was just as physical, just as real, just as cohesive as the small entity known as Sam, yet expansive, inclusive, permeative, fluid.

Most of her life Sam had felt other entities in her, around her, through her, beings of light. She had never feared them, as children often do, they were never monsters to her, foes, though she felt them pushing and pulling. She saw them as guardians, or guiding spirits, shielding, circling, centering, or sometimes as peers, doubles inhabiting parallel worlds. They seemed to exist in a different dimension, a lesser *density,* the 'higher plane' people spoke of. Her body was comprised of them, theirs were composed within and without hers, pervading yet discrete, as if assembled with the very same particles but according to a disparate, preternatural mathematics, coexisting at a higher velocity, wavelength, or amplitude, ever-present but at the edge of cognizance.

For many years they were quiet in their resonance, now, with her renewed focus on meditation — two or three times a day, sometimes for hours — she felt closer to them than ever, closer to *there*

117

than ever, wherever it was they thrived. She had recently been experiencing a pervasive low humming, accompanied by uncontainable tingling in the limbs, and the appearance, during wakeful periods, of certain crystalline shapes, luminous octahedrons, hovering at eye level. They seemed anxious, as if waiting for her, as if she was the final one, and with her collusion or submission their goal was at hand. She shared their insistence, felt under their auspices, allowed herself to build... a presentiment of ascension, of phase transition, of the sublime sublimation of body from here to there, or perhaps more accurately, from here to *here*, for she knew *there* was only a construct, an illusion. Still, it was nothing she could hurry, nothing she could force; one cannot push the river. Time was not a deceit she had mastery of. She was required only to keep the vortexes open, even to those entities, ideals, and forms of opposing polarity. Ascension to successive echelons in the pyramid of awareness is an act of inclusion requiring unconditional acceptance of all that lies below.

14

"OH, I haven't been here in ages," Lily said, as Richard helped remove her coat. Beneath she wore a beige jacket with outrageously large flowers embroidered on it in gold thread, and a white silk scarf with gold fringe.

"I'm so glad you could come Lily, it's always such a treat to see you. You look ravishing," Richard's deep baritone rumbled.

"Stop it now, you see me all the time."

"It always seems like ages, like you ration yourself out, only so many visits per year. We should see each other every week." He held her chair and helped her scoot up to the small table. They were in a little café in the Dewitt Mall, which had once been Ithaca's public high school, but had long since been converted to shops and apartments.

"But then you would tire of me."

"Never," he boomed.

"They've changed the menu, looks like."

"Yes, it's much better now. There's a young couple running it now, Shayna and Ivan. They're adorable. Scary, but adorable. Both of them tattooed up and down, well you'll see."

"What? I don't know if I'm up for this."

"You should try the turkey panini, it's fantastic," Richard suggested, settling his girth on the small seat. He wore a pale blue V-neck sweater over a pinkish shirt and looked like an Easter egg.

"How was Los Angeles?" He asked.

"Warm," Lily answered, smiling, "wonderfully warm."

"And the grandchildren still growing like weeds I presume?"

"No actually, I think they finished with that some time ago. Jen is twenty-eight you know, and Mark just turned twenty-five."

"My God, I can't believe it! We are ancient."

"Nonsense. We're in our prime, Richard, as Halcomb used to say."

"Yes, but that was *twenty* years ago. Ah, here she is, speak of the devil." A young woman came to take their order. Tattoos covered her arms and neck as Richard had promised. She also had a stud in her nose and one in her lip. Her hair was an unnaturally blue shade of black. Twenty years, Lily wondered, can it really be that long?

"Hi Professor Cole, how are you doing?" Shayla asked.

"It's just Richard now, I'm retired you know."

"Well what would you like just Richard, or do you need a few minutes?"

"No no, this is my good friend Lily, I was just telling her about you and Ivan."

"You promised to keep quiet about that," Shayla teased. Richard laughed his booming laugh.

"You see what I mean," he said, turning to Lily, "I just love this place. Now, I'll have the California Club, and if you could leave off the avocado and the sprouts and slip a couple extra pieces of bacon on that I would be so pleased. And the lady will have the turkey panini."

"No," Lily interjected, "I believe I'll have the Santa Fe Chicken Salad."

"Alrighty, we'll get those right out to you," the young woman promised, heading back to the kitchen.

"I'm sorry, Richard, I just don't think I can stomach such a hefty sandwich at the moment," Lily explained.

"Oh, have whatever you like, the salad is delicious too."

"You've had it?"

"I've had everything," Richard laughed, his blue eyes twinkling with gustatorial delight.

"You come here often then, do you?"

"Well someone has to. It's important to support the local businesses, don't you think?"

"Of course, but…"

"I hate to see a restaurant go under. It's such a labor of love to begin with."

"Yes."

"I feel it's my duty to bestow my patronage on them," Richard laughed, "I really do!"

"Oh, for Pete's sake Richard, don't be so arrogant."

"It's not arrogance," he protested, but lowered his voice a bit. "I'm absolutely sincere. Those of us who can must support the hard working masses, nobless oblige and all that. They don't support each other you know, they're the ones supporting the corporations."

"Nobless Oblige? I had no idea you were such a blue blood."

"Well I can pretend, can't I? Makes me feel important I guess. I always make it a point to tip well, and spread the word. If someone does good work, you have to spread the word. Which reminds me…" He reached into his pocket and produced a business card. Lily took it and read:

StainsAway Carpet Cleaning — Commercial —
Residential — Dave Northrup.

"Carpet Cleaning?"

"He's amazing. Got a horrible odor out of one of my rentals."

"I haven't got any rentals, Richard."

"What about Demerest House, that artist fellow must have rubbed paint in the carpet by now."

"But you know Halcomb could not abide wall to wall carpeting. It hides the beauty of the wood."

"Oh, I forgot. Well give it to Michelle; give it to anyone with carpet. You know people. The man's a genius, and he's got kids to support. Here, take another," he insisted, handing her another of Dave Northrup's business cards, "If we can't muster him up some business I may have to have carpet installed in my dining room just so I can have it cleaned."

"Oh honestly. Alright. I think you're carrying this patronage a bit too far."

"Well I've lately come to realize it's the only thing I do well. Perhaps the only thing I've ever done in this world that has ever really amounted to anything." The beaming smile had slowly faded, and Lily saw, for a moment, a little boy inside that big ogre face.

"Self-pity? From *you,* Richard? You surprise me."

"Not self-pity, just self-knowledge. A little late in life, but welcome, all the same."

"There isn't any chance we're talking about your play, now, is there? How's that coming along?"

"I gave that up months ago, Lily, I told you that at Christmas."

"You most certainly did not. And why, may I ask have you given it up?"

"It was terrible. Horrid piece of trash."

"I don't believe you. Richard, you're so dramatic. How could you possibly fail to write great drama?"

"Hmm, it was *too* dramatic. I lose my sense of humor when I write Lily. No, the world will benefit from my decision to let it drop."

"Come on, don't give up so easily. How can I read it if you don't finish it? I've really been looking forward to it. Where's your ambition?"

"The death of my ambition has thankfully preceded my own, and honestly Lily, I don't think I've ever been happier."

"Well then I'm happy for you."

"I think I just needed the play as a crutch to lean on when I retired from teaching. I had to have that to focus on. Thank you," he said to Shayna who had brought them water.

"Thank you. Could I have some lemon for my water please?" Lily asked.

"Sure," she said, retreating.

"I feel quite different, really," Richard revealed, his voice dropping to a soft rumble, "for the first time in my life I am… at peace I guess, with myself. Sometimes I still feel guilty. Lazy maybe. But it's as if a great weight has been lifted. A burden I've carried all my life. Ambition might be one word for it. Ego might be another."

"Richard, you're the least egotistical person I know."

"I wasn't implying that. Maybe justification is the word I'm looking for. I don't know how to describe it, but I see now that my entire life of work was for nothing."

"Oh, Richard, that's nonsense! What about all your students?"

"Well I don't mean futile, that's not it. I mean as though... as though I didn't have to live it that way at all. I mean this burden that I've lately set down... I never had to carry it at all. I mean it defines you, your work, doesn't it? You *have* to do it because without it you don't exist, or there's no justification for your existence. And then it's done and you still exist, and it turns out no one is asking you to justify anything, and they never really were, it was just in your mind all along. Do you know what I mean?"

"I think you're still getting used to retirement, Richard."

"I don't know how to explain it, Lily, what's been going through my mind lately, but there has been a... *shift* as it were. And now it seems to me..." he said, pausing to drink and formulate his words, "that there is no better way for me to be of service to humanity than to bestow — on those burdened with the heavy weight of ambition — the gift of... well," he laughed, "of servicing me."

"Richard, really!"

"I know how it sounds," he laughed, "but when you think about it, there's nothing of more value I can give. Don't you see, I am now giving others what all my students gave me; a *raison d'être*, a sense of accomplishment, an *identity,* however unwanted it might be. They need me to need them, all these workers. What would my doctors do without me, for instance? And my accountant, and my barber, and the dry cleaner, and Shayna and Ivan. I am proud to say I have the good grace to use others well, in the antique sense of the word. I finally see how all those aristocrats in all those novels I taught for all those years were able to sleep at night; they *believed* in the importance of their position. Their existence needed no justification; their belief that their position came from God made it so. And what strikes me as marvelously ironic, is that I think I see now that I might have lived my entire life in this way, doing nothing more than being someone else's employment. All that was needed was my own permission, my own willingness to see it as a useful contribution to society. It *is* enough you see; someone has to be the mirror that reflects the light everyone is trying to bring out from under their bushel basket, it might as well be me. There is no higher ambition. I was really the only one saying it could not be so."

"But what about all your students? Surely what you taught them was more important than just paying for a haircut," Lily argued.

"Was it? I imagine they've forgotten what I tried to teach them, as well they might, it was of little enough importance. And I daresay they've all forgotten *me*. Except Sarah." There was the pity again, Lily thought, and the little boy expression. She could see him embedded in that Easter egg bulk, just begging for a hug. But she knew if she gave him one, the little boy would disappear and a ridiculous Don Juan would emerge. They had been through it before, a few times since Halcomb's death. Why is it men have such trouble releasing their romantic notions, she wondered. If he needs a hug and a little reassurance, why can't he accept exactly that, why must it be couched in amorous terms?

"Oh that reminds me," she said, "I think Bryan may have gotten her in at Penn State."

"Really? That's wonderful!"

"Yes, she went down there last week for an interview, so keep your fingers crossed."

"Oh, I will, poor girl. She could use a break."

"Here you are," Shayla announced, setting the food before them.

"Mmm, looks delicious," Richard declared.

"Yes, thank you, dear," said Lily.

"Here you are," Shayla announced, setting the food before them.

"Mmm, looks delicious," Richard declared.

"Yes, thank you, dear," said Lily.

"You're welcome. Let me know if you need anything else." They began to eat, Lily quietly and Richard noisily. It wasn't his fault, Lily reasoned, there was something unusually resonant about his large mouth. It made for beautiful singing, but having lunch with him was not particularly enjoyable. He took huge bites and seemed to struggle to breathe through his nose.

"You know Richard, if you're feeling as philanthropic as you say, then you should donate to Halcomb's scholarship fund. We've been hit hard by this recession and may have to cut next year's disbursements by half."

"Oh dear, but you know I don't have *real* money. And a good thing too, I don't think I could handle the responsibility, frankly."

"As I suspected."

"Well that's not servicing *me,* is it?" he laughed, a piece of lettuce taking the opportunity to flee from his open mouth. "And I never said I was feeling philanthropic, that I recall."

"My mistake. I suppose a more accurate word would be entitled?"

"Now Lily, that's not what I meant either. I think you're deliberately misunderstanding me to make me feel guilty."

"Is it working?"

"You know I'll do anything for you. But I'm not Warren Buffet you know. My portfolio has seen better days too. I suppose I can write you a check with a few zeros on it."

"Thank you, Richard. And thank you for lunch. You were right, this salad is delicious."

"Ivan has a way with knives," Richard said, winking.

"You see? Drama and wit. I won't let you give it up. If you ever want to have lunch with me again, you absolutely *must* finish your play."

"Now you're scaring me," he chuckled.

"I'm perfectly serious," she assured him, managing to keep her expression quite stern though she was chewing. "I will not accept your next invitation unless it is accompanied by a copy of the play."

"Lily, you're being too hard on an old scribbler," Richard chuckled. Lily did not crack a smile. It was exactly what he needed, and she was sure it would work. After all, it was Halcomb's suggestion.

15

"LILY!" called Michelle. She was returning from the store and saw her friend out in the side garden of Demerest House. It was a wonderfully warm day; the expected high was sixty-two. Lily had not heard her; she was bent over, her grey hair moving stiffly in the breeze. She was clearing away some old leaves from a clump of daffodils whose yellow tips had peeped up; it would be a few more weeks before they would open. There was a wheelbarrow standing near her, already piled high with refuse. Michelle walked over to her.

"Lily, how are you? Are you in the gardening business now?"

"Oh, hello dear, I didn't think you were home."

"Just got back. I was picking up some things for dinner."

"Look, the crocuses are up," Lily said, pointing to a few dozen of the squat little flowers. There were white, yellow, and purple ones that had opened to the warm air.

"Oh, wonderful. So spring will soon be here, I guess."

"It won't be long. But winter's not done with us yet, I'm afraid."

From her vantage point Michelle could see around the corner to the back of the house, where a wide terrace faced the formal garden. There were many windows there, and two sets of French doors, one from the dining room, one leading to the back parlor, which Lily had always referred to as the family room, as opposed to the front parlor, which she had insisted on calling the drawing room though it was the smaller of the two. Above, there was a balcony for the second floor where there were more French doors providing a romantic view of the garden. By the corners of the house were ancient lilac bushes, reaching up to the second story, already budded in preparation for their spring display.

Michelle had been in the house many times, and knew that room on the second floor had originally been designed as a ballroom. It was the room where all the famous Christmas parties had been held. She missed having seen it last year. She had often thought it would make a perfect studio, facing the north light as it did. From her present angle all that glass revealed nothing more than reflected sky and treetops.

"Does Mr. Westin know you're here?" she asked, thinking, he's probably looking at us right now.

"I have no idea. I don't believe I need my tenant's permission to tend my flowers."

"No. Well you can't pass over a warm day like this, can you?"

"No, I cannot. And I can't bear to let anyone else mess with Halcomb's roses. Here," she said, plucking a few crocuses out of the bed with her gloved hands, "take these home and paint them, dear, they'll be gone in a couple of days anyway."

"Oh! Thank you Lily."

"I expect to see them at the spring show, now," she warned.

"We'll see. I haven't been painting much lately."

"Well now you have to! Mustn't let our skills dissipate as the years go by. Bad habit."

"Right." Michelle looked down at the little flowers in her hand, so transitory. Did Lily think her skills *were* dissipating?

"Perhaps you and Kyle can paint them together, inspire each other."

"I don't think so Lily," she chuckled, "I don't think Mr. Westin paints flowers."

"Oh?"

"Come in for some tea?" she offered, glancing again at the tall glaring windows. "Perhaps Mr. Westin would like to join us."

"Oh, no. I'm expecting my ride any moment. I've got to get back for 'game day'. Catherine Spivak will never let me hear the end of it if I'm not there and she has to partner with her husband for bridge."

"Okay. Well if you need anything, you know where I am."

"Thank you, dear."

Michelle walked back and took the groceries from her car into the house. She put the crocuses in a little vase with some water and a straw, draped plastic wrap around them and set them in the fridge next to the carton of orange juice she had just purchased. She didn't feel like painting at the moment. The flowers would keep for a few days in the refrigerator.

She took her painting seriously and usually enjoyed it, but she hadn't painted at all that winter, she *had* been uninspired. Lily's little jab hurt, though, if she were honest, the implication that she was dissipating in any way. Why had she said it, was it an offhand remark reflecting her own state of mind, in reference to herself, the waning of *her* skills, or her life in general? Not likely, not with Lily; she rarely said what she didn't intend to, yet neither was she apt to say, or even suggest something cruel about anyone else. Perhaps she had simply meant to spur me on, Michelle thought, I have been a little lackluster this winter. However it was meant, Michelle knew she would have to do something with the crocuses before they disappeared for another year, and she was a little peeved with Lily for pressing them on her.

* * *

That weekend there was a nor'easter, which closed all the airports on the Atlantic seaboard. Stephen was stuck in Washington, where he had been giving a lecture. Mid afternoon on Saturday Michelle was standing in *vrksana*, tree pose, one leg bent with the heel tucked up in the groin, gazing absentmindedly out the window of her office at the wet snow piling on the maples, following the instructions of the man on the DVD by breathing. She hardly needed to look at the screen; she was so familiar with this particular program.

Something moved, across the way at Demerest House. The blinds rose up, leaving a clear view (as much as the storm would allow) into the second floor. Michelle lost her balance and fell out of the pose, dropping her foot to the floor. She went to the bookcase and retrieved the binoculars from behind *The Power of Intention* and its adjacent eloquent titles. Training them on the uncovered window and turning the focusing dial she saw a woman pass in front of the window, dressed (jeans and a sweater), thick hair tied back, round face. Moving the glasses slowly, peering past the fuzzy white blobs falling through her field of view, Michelle found the blinds of the other window had also been raised, and she determined that the room had indeed been converted to an art studio. There were easels, tables, photographic umbrellas and lights.

She had taken her own paints out early that morning, attempting to capture Lily's crocuses. She was never able to sleep well when Stephen was away; painting was something she often began before the sun was up, usually on the kitchen counter with a pot of coffee brewing. There were other rooms she could have painted in, but she preferred the warmth of the kitchen, with its dark cherry cabinets and copper range hood. She had turned off the little TV (whose inhabitants had been confirming what she could see out the window, that it was snowing like crazy), put on a CD of quiet music, sat on a stool in her emerald silk pajamas and arranged her palette, paper, brushes, water, magnifier, sponges, and the flowers. She had wanted to do something different with this one, she had wanted to paint *loose*, to paint not only what was there, but what was *implied* by what was there, to show the aura, the soul of the subject — that was art, that would be something.

She started sketching lightly, then erased it. It was pedestrian. Michelle loved flowers of all kinds, but the crocuses were small and squat; their personality seemed equally unimpressive. She had wanted to give them some style, some purpose. They had needed company, a bit more greenery or a hyacinth, something for them to commune with, or cling to with their fat little petals, but there were already eight inches of snow covering the ground outside. With a sigh she had looked about the kitchen for something to add to the vase, a bit of baby's breath or a strip of ribbon, but she had found no such accessory; what she had found was some whisky that she added to her coffee cup. She had turned the flowers this way and that, shifted them in the vase, stared at the falling snow, refilled her cup, and at last found a pleasing composition. It had gone well, she thought, she had tried something rather new for her, a background — subdued, so as not to overpower the flowers, but… expressive, perhaps, with quiet pools of color and motion. Then she had taken a nap on the daybed in her office.

Now, eyes glued to the binoculars, scanning beyond the branches and falling snow, she saw the woman cross before the window again, more slowly, her long hair down now. She couldn't quite see

133

her face, yet she looked familiar. Then she saw Kyle come into the room, talking, smiling, gesturing. Shortly thereafter the blinds went back down, and Michelle was blocked out again.

Looks like he's found his model, she said to herself, slipping the binoculars back behind *Intention* and *Heal Your Life*. After rewinding the yoga program to approximately where she had left off, Michelle returned to *vrksana*, then *tadasana,* or mountain pose, with her hands in prayer posture.

"Heart opening," the yoga master commanded, spreading his arms wide and pushing his chest forward. Michelle followed suit, feeling her arms, shoulders, her pectoral muscles, even her sternum crack and screech under protest, like a creaky old door.

Some Cornell student in need of funds, Michelle thought, probably has no idea what she's getting into.

"Return to center, and breathe. Again, heart opening. Don't worry about how it looks, just feel how it feels," the man suggested.

"Ugh," Michelle groaned, wondering when she had grown so old.

"Now forward fold, and back to downward facing dog." Michelle pushed her heels and palms into the floor.

Clothing optional, my ass, she thought. Not one painting on his website with clothing, unless you count underwear.

"And cobra pose. Don't forget to breathe."

"What a scumbag," she said aloud. Should I tell Stephen? That must be one of his students; I know I've seen her before.

"Now back to down dog. If you need to, bend your knees a little. Lift from the hips."

Can't tell Stephen, Michelle realized, without him asking why I was looking in the neighbor's window. It's none of my business anyway. He can paint whomever he likes. She's an adult, right? Obviously needs the money. There's no reason to suspect anything else is going on anyway. It's not like he's the first man to see her naked, or she wouldn't have answered the ad.

"And heart opening," the master commanded. Michelle spread her arms wide and took a deep breath.

* * *

Forrest Carlson was sitting at the marina in Lauderdale-By-The-Sea, under an umbrella on which was printed *AJ's Café*. He was watching the boats maneuvering through the inlet, having a Cuban sandwich and an orange soda, wondering what manner of swine divinity had blessed the world with the secret of the flavors he was enjoying, and thinking how different life could have been, then *could be*, he reminded himself. He felt quite altered already, after only three weeks of living in the sun and heat. He felt calmer, almost *blithe,* he thought, yet he also felt keener, primed, anticipative of something unspecified. Above all he felt foolish for having waited so long, for having stayed there in the frozen north where his body and his life had inevitably been stiff, slow, and subdued, where they were even now enduring another heavy storm. It amazed him how much the new environs affected not only his mood, but his entire mindset; his underlying understanding of how the world worked and how his life fit in with it, the *feasibility* of the new.

After paying a damn fortune to have a few rooms of furniture shipped down to his new condo, Forrest had gotten rid of most of it. In Ithaca he had seen nothing wrong with the pieces, they were sturdy and durable, and he certainly didn't consider himself one of those people who were wealthy or fickle or careless enough to replace their belongings every time they changed houses, like buying a new shirt when a button was missing. But after arranging the old things in the new place, he realized they were unsuitable, they were keeping him down, they were too heavy, too dark, too much full of *old time* as if they had absorbed and transported to Florida decades of exhaled grief. He just couldn't walk past the hibiscus and frangi pani and birds of paradise into his sunny retreat and face the 'old nuns' as he had inexplicably begun to think of the dresser, the desk, and the dining table; so out it all went.

He drove over to Sunrise and spent a day at IKEA choosing a slim, efficient, light wood life, then spent a week assembling it. He bought coral colored organza curtains to go with the Saltillo tile. He bought a Buddha head fountain, put it in the corner of his living room and hung the calendar Lily had given him next to it, where he could reflect on the quotes to the sound of falling water.

> *Submit to a daily practice. Keep knocking and the joy*
> *inside will eventually open a window.*

He liked that one, and since he had every intention of joining the Buddha each day in contemplation, he bought a huge colorful pillow to sit on. Next he purchased a fish tank, half a dozen Red Serpae Tetras and a little treasure chest to rest on the bottom and promise doubloons. He donated bags of musty, muddy colored clothes and bought Hawaiian shirts and Bermuda shorts and a bucket hat. He bought orchids and bromeliads and succulents and bright pots to keep them in. He even bought a new broom because the old one was blue and it just didn't go. All the while he was performing this presto chango magic act, he heard Lily's voice saying, *You never know what's around the corner*, and thought about how maybe there could be something good around the corner, perhaps *someone* new walking in the door to see his fish or the bright print of a Poinciana tree he had purchased and hung over the sofa. Suddenly there were things he liked in his life, and he wanted to share them.

Now, as Forrest was sitting at AJ's in the cool shade of the umbrella, his hat stretched out on the table beside the half empty glass of sunny orange pop, the delectable sandwich in his hands, the sea breeze tickling his head, thinking *you never know, there are good things in your future*; he saw her. His mouth paused it's mastication while he took in the feasibility of this woman, not terribly young, probably 35 or 40, but gorgeous, fit yet still supple, *really* healthy, not like the pale, dry, creased bark eaters one saw in Ithaca running along the trails trying to stave off death, succeeding only in keeping life at bay. This woman was not like that. There was vitality about her; she's got *chi*, Forrest thought, and felt proud he could recognize this mysterious force he didn't believe inhabited him. She's happy, he realized, taking another bite of the Cuban. Maybe it was as simple as that. She looks a bit like Ellen did when the kids were little, when she still loved me.

She came riding up the sidewalk on her bicycle with her sun kissed red hair flowing behind her, her face rounded by a smile, wearing skimpy orange shorts and a tight T-shirt, which read GATORS across the chest in orange letters. He had seen her before, a few times, he had smiled at her once as she rode by. This time she didn't ride by, she stopped about twenty feet away, at the edge of AJ's seating area, and dismounted, her tanned legs unfolding gracefully. She pushed her bike into a rack there, and fiddled with the lock, incidentally turning her backside toward Forrest. When she finished and turned around his eyes were slow in rebounding, he raised them to find her looking at him, smiling — it seemed to him a sweet, sly smile of acknowledgement and acceptance, of conspiracy, as if to say, I know what you were looking at, I know what you want and it's okay. Did she want it too? He felt a sudden tightening in his lower abdomen, as if her gaze had reached out and touched him there, inside his gut. It was an odd feeling, something he had felt before, but couldn't say how long ago, like a terrible yearning. The GATOR woman made a small gesture like a wave and began walking toward him, still smiling, in fact her smile became broader with every step, this happy woman growing happier as she approached *him*. The tightening inside continued, twisting and turning and grabbing hold of his being, low in the belly, almost the place where a womb would be he thought, if he were a woman, and it truly felt like that, like a new creation, a new beginning, a chance. Was it Hope taking hold? It clamped on and pulled him, he felt flushed with excitement, he was about to break into a sweat; she walked right up to his table... and passed it.

"Hi!" the woman said. Forrest turned slightly and saw her embracing a young man at a table directly behind him. A much younger man than he, a muscular, tall man with chiseled features and a tan perfect enough to match hers, and that same look of *chi*. And Forrest saw himself, pale, grey, paunchy, his rumpled hat on the table, stuffing his fleshy face with pork fat, eating pig like a pig, and he began to laugh. His stomach relaxed, and he laughed at himself until the tears came.

16

LILY knocked. There was no answer. The corridor smelled foul.

"Travis?" she called. She thought she heard something inside, knocked again, then turned the knob and pushed the door open. The room was dark, a single line of dull daylight glowed along the edge of the blinds. The reflected bluish glow of a laptop lit the gaunt face of a young man who sat in one of the two beds, his back against the wall, the covers up over his propped up knees. He closed his laptop as she entered.

"Travis isn't here," he brusquely informed her. He had a slight Germanic accent, and a mature look.

"Oh. Well that's too bad. You must be Andreas. I'm Travis's grandmother. You can call me Lily." She held out her hand briefly, and then realized he was not about to get up out of the bed. She immediately felt a wave of compassion for him, poor boy, all alone in the world. He clearly didn't want her there, but she was not going to leave, not yet. She walked over to the blinds and opened them.

"This is Travis's bed, then?" she presumed, sitting on the other. "When do you think he might be back?"

"I don't know. Four, four-thirty maybe."

"Well that's okay," Lily said with a smile. "I have something for him, but I would just as soon he not know that I brought it. If that's okay with you." She held a small paper bag in her hand, folded closed with a careful crease.

"Sure," Andreas shrugged.

"I appreciate it. Sometimes young men don't want their grand-mothers meddling."

"No."

Lily had received a prayer vision the night before. She had seen Travis holding a baby. He looked frightened. She had become frightened for him, for what she had gotten him into.

"Do you know a girl named Leah?" she asked. Andreas nodded.

"Does she come here very often?"

"No. Only three or four times." Lily relaxed a bit. That seemed reasonable, somehow. She set the paper bag carefully on Travis's pillow. Inside it were three boxes of condoms she had just purchased at the drugstore. She knew in her head that he already had some, that Bryan had already discussed these things with him, that Leah was a cautious and responsible girl, but it made her feel better to leave an additional hint. Things did not come in prayer for no reason. It suddenly dawned on her that the reason for this particular informa-tion might have less to do with Travis, and more to do with Andreas. She had quite forgotten about him. Now that she had seen him for herself, she was hesitant to leave him. He was too thin.

"And how are your studies going?" she inquired. He grimaced and gave her that shrug again.

"What have you had to eat today?"

"I get plenty to eat, Travis's grandmother," he said with a reas-suring smile, "And I pass all my courses, and take all my vitamins and get plenty of sleep, and you need not worry for me. I just say no to drugs. Travis just says no to drugs. Okay?" he chuckled.

"Okay. But I'm going to give you my phone number," she said, rising, pulling a card from her purse. "And if there's ever anything you need, or if you just want to talk, I want you to call me," she insisted. He took the card. Lily put her hand on his blanketed knee, and did her best to convey her sincerity with her wrinkled, withered visage.

"Thank you, Lily," he said. This nicety was just the assurance she needed that he was all right; he knew it, and she knew he knew it. Travis had been right when he told his father that Andreas 'put up a good front'. She smiled at him and walked out into the corridor, leaving the door open, wondering whether she should call Bryan to discuss it, or speak with Travis directly.

* * *

"No, it needs to be wider," Michelle heard someone saying authoritatively as she pushed the door to the shop open, ringing the little bells that hung over the entrance. The cold whooshed in behind her; snow was beginning to swirl in the parking lot.

"Be with you in a minute, Mrs. Wolcott," Mike said. She loved going to the frame shop and seeing the colorful array of samples on the wall. A good-sized canvas and a dozen frame corners occupied the design counter. The customer Mike was waiting on glanced up from studying the different molding samples and saw her. It was her neighbor, Mr. Westin, looking as she remembered, sort of unkempt — not in a sloppy way, more... feral. His hair was tousled, his clothes paint-stained, those boots looked as if he had just emerged from some mountain cabin. He seemed warm and substantial.

141

"Hello," he said, with an inviting smile. Michelle could think only of the young woman she had seen in his studio and how inappropriate it was.

"Oh, Mr. Westin, how are you?" she responded, a little coldly. She felt foolish and small standing there with the little portfolio in her gloved hand, as if her piddling piece of paper could share any space with his bold art.

"Kyle. I'm good. Picking out a frame. I suppose that's what you're here for?"

"Yes." I shouldn't be curt, she reminded herself; I don't want him to know I know. None of my business anyway, who's modeling for him. "I uh... did a little watercolor," she admitted. "It's for the spring show. They always have a floral show downtown. In the spring. Way before anything starts blooming actually, so you have to paint from memory or buy some flowers to paint or paint in the summer for the next year's show," she explained, laughing lightly at the silliness of it.

"I see. So what did you do?"

"It's... I... just a couple of crocuses, not really..." she stammered, opening her portfolio to show the painting.

"No, I mean, which did you do," Kyle clarified, looking at the painting carefully, "did you do it from memory or buy them, or paint them last year?"

"Oh, I did it yesterday. Some of the crocuses are up; they're the first to bloom. They're from your flowerbed actually. Lily's idea."

"Oh? That's right, she came by last week on that warm day. I told her I could take care of it, but she really wants to look after the flowers herself."

"Yes, she loves to garden. It reminds her of Halcomb. Her late husband. He was a great gardener."

"Oh. Well this is very nice, Michelle," Kyle said about her watercolor. A strong frisson pulsed down her arm as he said her name, causing her to drop the portfolio. She felt a slight twinge in her chest. What the hell was that, she thought, bending to pick up the folder.

"I particularly like the background," Kyle continued, placing the painting on the counter beside his own, the canvas which Michelle now saw was dominated by the figure of a nude woman, standing with her backside to the viewer. "Very fluid. Don't you think so, Mike?" he asked the framer, who twisted his head to view it at the proper angle.

"Yeah, it's great. Lot of motion," he said, "have you thought about how you want to frame it?"

"Yes, probably like we did the last one, it was an off white mat with a purple underneath I think."

"I can look it up, if you want to match it exactly, I just need to finish with Mr. Westin's order."

"No, that's not necessary. I'll leave it with you. You can choose the under mat, something that works with the petals. And I think we used a cherry frame last time." She wanted to leave as soon as possible; she was uncomfortable with her neighbor. She didn't know what to make of him, and she liked him too much.

"And what are you framing Mr. Westin?" she asked with proper civility, looking more closely at the oil painting he had brought in.

The woman portrayed was leaning her weight on her right foot while her left was off the floor for balance. Waves of long blond hair undulated down her back and led the eye (if it needed leading) to her perfectly shaped buttocks. Her hands clutched an abstraction of drapery or curtain around which she seemed to be peeking, so that the cloth would be hiding all but the top of her head from the view of whoever might be on the other side of the curtain. All that was visible of that 'other side', however, depicted along the right edge of the canvas, was flame and shadow, as if the curtain were a partition between the woman's boudoir and a large dark room with a vast fireplace.

"Was it this one?" Mike asked, pulling a sample off the wall.

On the left side of the scene, standing behind the woman, was another figure, semitransparent, somewhat smaller, androgynous, with a suggestion of white wings on its back and a slight smile on its face which Michelle could not read — was it meant to be sweet, or more of a leer? This apparition had one hand on the back of the woman, its arm bent. Again, it was unclear what action was intended; was the arm ready to thrust the 'real' woman into the room, beyond the curtain, or was the apparition attempting to hold her back? The figure was rendered well, in lifelike tones and shading, the cloth, and flames were very realistic. The long blond hair reminded Michelle of that girl Stephen's student had brought to the Christmas party. What was her name, Erin? Was that who she saw in his studio?

"Mrs. Wolcott?" Mike asked again. She looked up and met Kyle's eyes; he had been looking at her. She blushed, forced her eyes away and checked the sample Mike was holding up.

"No, not that dark, that one, there." Mike grabbed another and laid it on the table. Kyle was still looking at her; she could feel it, not really trying to communicate with her, but evaluating her, her color and line, as if *she* were the work of art.

"Yes, that's it."

"Okay, if you can wait a minute I'll get it priced out. What's the title of your painting, Mr. Westin, so I can enter it in the computer."

"Uh… I'm thinking of calling it *Nikki's Daemon*. With an 'a'. What do you think, Michelle?"

"So it's a demon, with angel wings?" wondered Mike aloud.

"The wings are not necessarily angelic. I mean daemon in the original Greek sense, they believed every place and person had its particular associated spirit. May or may not be an angel I suppose. Or a demon without the 'a'. That confusion is exactly why I'm hesitating about the title. Maybe it should be *Nikki's Kami*, isn't that what Chieko called it?" he asked, addressing Michelle again. So he remembers her name, she thought, is that what he was doing with those business cards? Will Cheiko be posing next?

"I didn't think *kami* was used that way, for a personal spirit guide, I thought it was more of a nature spirit."

"How 'bout *Nikki's Guardian*," Mike proposed, still focusing on the wings.

"No, it's not necessarily her *guardian*. That's not the way I conceive of it, anyway, it's not that certain."

"Well, guide, guardian, what's the difference?" Mike chuckled. Michelle felt for him, he was simply trying to conclude the sale so he could get back to work.

"A lot actually. A guardian guards, doesn't it. Its aim is to keep you alive, warn you about falling rocks maybe, or a patch of black ice. A guide's aim is to guide you, convince you to do the right thing or get you to heaven, teach you maybe. A daemon has its own agenda. It's not there to serve you; it thinks you are there to serve it. Your daemon's aim is to live through you. You might say it's your alter ego, only it thinks you are *its* alter ego."

Michelle looked at the artist as he spoke. Random images flashed in her mind: Erin combing her long hair in the Demerest House ballroom; gobs of slippery wet paint sliding over a canvas; Kyle, nude, feverishly working the brush. Then she saw Cheiko's bucktoothed smile, and heard her soft accent echoing: *trick you, or guide you.*

"I stand corrected," said the framer, taking a step back with a submissive gesture.

"How about *Nikki's Genius*?" Michelle suggested. He turned to her, and again his appraising gaze slipped away from her eyes and seemed to focus on her hair or her cheeks. She felt her feet sweating, and warmth rising up her legs.

"Yeah, but the modern usage implies a kind of guaranteed intelligence," Kyle chuckled. "I mean, just because you're a spirit doesn't mean you're smart, does it."

"I guess not. So is this spirit about to push Eri... I mean Nikki through the curtain, or is it trying to hold her back?" Michelle inquired.

"I leave that to the viewer," answered Kyle with a disarming smile.

"In that case, I think *Nikki's Daemon*, with or without the 'a', is probably the perfect title."

"Okay Mike, let's go with it. And this frame," he added, handing the sample over. He had chosen a wide frame with wavy compo embossing and a dark coppery finish that reiterated the flames in the painting.

"Great, that's going to be fantastic," the framer promised. Michelle felt dizzy. Her brow was beginning to sweat.

"You'll call me, Mike?" she asked, taking a step to the door.

"Yeah. You sure you don't want your invoice?"

"I trust you. I've got to go."

"Listen, Michelle, I wanted to ask you..." said Kyle, stepping after her, but interrupted himself when she turned away from the door to face him and he saw how pallid she looked all of a sudden. "Are you okay?" he asked.

"I'm sorry, I'd better get home, I feel a migraine coming on."

"I trust you. I've got to go."

"Listen, Michelle, I wanted to ask you…" said Kyle, stepping after her, but interrupted himself when she turned away from the door to face him and he saw how pallid she looked all of a sudden. "Are you okay?" he asked.

"I'm sorry, I'd better get home, I feel a migraine coming on."

"Can I help you?"

"I'll be fine," she called over her shoulder as she stepped out into the snowfall. The wind felt good on her face, but by the time she got into her car she was shivering. She pulled away from the shop and managed to drive around the building before the nausea made her park again, in the back by the mountain of previously plowed snow. The double vision made her close her eyes, but the images would not recede, so she opened them again and thought for a moment that she was on the trail. Rival realities competed for her focus as she struggled to keep the pain at bay. There was the windshield and the snow mound, and a man on the trail. He had a pistol. The baby was crying. It was foggy. Someone was in the water, face down, red pants. There was a man's head, unshaven, gaunt, floating, as if decapitated. And the fox jumped over the railing. Again she heard Cheiko's high voice: *on their hind legs, so one does not know it is a Kitsune at all*. The trail was green, the parking lot was white with snow, and the mourners were in black.

17

"DO YOU think they're trying to tell me something?"

"Who?" asked Sam. Michelle had driven directly to Sam's when her vision cleared. She was glad to find her at home and available. They were in the Healing Room.

"I don't know, angels. My spirit guides."

Michelle had related the severity of the migraine, and the unusual visions accompanying it. Sam had massaged her neck and listened. She told about the Christmas party and the fox in the front yard and *Kitsune* and the dream she had had weeks later where she was an Indian chasing the fox on the trail and the fox, who looked a little like her new neighbor because of the beard, jumped into the gorge.

"Maybe. Maybe you're trying to tell yourself something. You need to make peace with yourself. Something is trying to surface and you are resisting. You need to deal with it. You know it will come back if you don't address the root cause."

"Oh God, I know," Michelle moaned, "I don't want anymore migraines. I just don't know what it's about. I haven't had any in years, why have they come back now?"

"Would you like me to do a reading for you?"

"I didn't know you gave readings, since when is that?"

149

"Well, it's not the sort of thing I like to advertise. People expect too much and take it the wrong way. But in this situation it might be helpful."

"That would be wonderful. I would love a reading. I promise you, I expect nothing. Do you use tarot?" Michelle asked, beginning to sit up.

"You just relax. Put your head back down. Let me get a blanket for you. I don't use cards. I will ask in meditation. Sometimes I see things, sometimes I don't. You don't need to do anything."

Sam seated herself on the zafu and began ringing a bowl. Presently the bowl's singing dissipated. Michelle silently waited, studying the chakra poster. It depicted a figure sitting cross-legged, with brightly colored circles going up the center, a red one in the groin, then an orange, yellow, a green one on the chest, blue at the throat, purple on the forehead, and white and gold on top of the head. She closed her eyes and tried to envision energy moving up her spine and through each chakra. It was hard to see it. She probably wasn't doing it right. Thoughts kept interrupting the colors. She realized she *did* expect something, the way she had expected something when she walked to the bridge that morning. She couldn't say exactly what. Something to do with hope, and the fox, and the shudder she felt when Kyle spoke her name. But that was ridiculous; what was Sam going to do, say 'I see a man in your future, and he's covered with paint'? And what if she did? It's not as though it could happen. She started with the colors again, red, orange, yellow… she dozed.

Sam made a slight moaning sound, inhaled sharply, and stirred. Michelle opened her eyes and turned on her side expectantly. Sam hesitated.

"Well?"

"Maybe this wasn't such a good idea."

"What? You didn't see anything?"

"I did, but you have to remember to take these things with a grain of salt. I can't say exactly where it comes from."

"Well what did you see?" Michelle sat up, swinging her feet off the table, pulling the sheet around her.

"I asked if your guides had any messages for you. I was taken to a library where there was aisle after aisle of books."

"Wow. That's incredible. What do they look like?" She was tingling.

"They looked very old, and were very large, like atlases or old legal ledgers."

"No, my guides. Who are they?" She had often felt her grandfather around her, she thought.

"I didn't see faces. Just beings of light."

"Oh. What did they say?"

"They placed a book in my hands," Sam continued, "and opened it to a particular page. I was given to understand that it was your book, your soul's book. It included every detail of your existence over many lives. The page they showed me was like a contract, they said, a list of things your soul agreed to before coming into this life."

"What did it say?"

"Just one word. Babies."

* * *

"Do you have any more tape?" Richard asked.

"Somewhere. Check under those papers on the coffee table."

"Yep. Got it." He took the opportunity to sink into the couch.

They were helping Sarah Strickland pack. She had accepted the position at Penn State, and was moving the following morning. Lily and Sarah were packing the books and the jumbled occupants of the front closet, while Michelle was tackling the kitchen.

"I believe for the time being, I can best be of service by offering benevolent supervision and moral support," Richard declared with a sigh. "Is there coffee left?"

"Sorry, coffee pot's been packed," Michelle replied, and began to tape up one more box. The truth was, there wasn't much in Sarah's little apartment, but Lily would never let a friend face leaving a place alone. Moral support was what they were all there for, really. It wouldn't take long for them to fill up the trailer Sarah had rented.

"What's to become of us, Lily? First Forrest, now Sarah, next we'll be packing up Michelle and Stephen."

"That seems highly unlikely, Richard," Lily replied. "Such a flair for the dramatic. I hope you're putting it to good use."

"A play will not be born of coercion, not even that of an angel," he grumbled.

Michelle looked out the kitchen window and admired the view; rolling fields bordered with woods. Sarah's apartment, including the stand of birches in the backyard, reminded her of the place she had had when she first came to Ithaca, that unit on Game Farm Road. That was where she had met Marcia; they had rented adjacent apartments and moved in on the same day. Marcia was a grad student; Michelle was already working on campus. Neither dated much that first year so they had spent quite a bit of time together and became fast friends, like sisters Michelle had thought. They carpooled the short distance to campus several times a week, cooked and ate dinner together when their schedules aligned, knocked on the thin conjoining wall to communicate, and went out drinking more times than either would now admit to. They went bowling, played tennis, swam at Buttermilk Falls, shopped for groceries together to make it more fun, rode their bikes around Cayuga Lake, even went to New York together to see *Les Miserables* on Broadway. Marcia was always so cheerful, so full of humor and mischief. She had a humungous orange cat by the name of Riffles. People would say 'Ruffles? Raffles?' 'No, Riffles.' 'Well why did you call her that?' they would ask, 'Because that's her name,' Marcia would invariably answer, and Riffles would meow her agreement.

Somehow in the fall of their second year in those little apartments, they had each bumped into their future husbands on campus, independently, without introductions, only weeks apart. Neither told their 'sister' they had met someone, both saying later because they didn't want to jinx it, didn't want to say *I've met the love of my life* only to have it be a flash in the pan. Michelle found out about Grant, and Marcia about Stephen at the Demerest Christmas party, to which they had each gone with their new men, who were both colleagues of Halcomb. They laughed about it for years with Lily who would always say their shock at seeing the other there, and with a *date* no less, had made it the best party ever. Each was surprised that the other had chosen an older man — well, Grant was not so much older, but he seemed it, prematurely grey and hobbling on bad knees. There had been a little unspoken competition then, which would get engaged first, who would make it down the aisle, which would live in the biggest house. Marcia seemed to win every time, if only by a few months.

In the beginning they had spent several evenings together, the four of them, but Stephen and Grant didn't quite mesh; they both were alpha-males. Their educational philosophies, their politics, their taste in wine always seemed to be at odds. Soon Stephen became far too busy for such dinner parties, the kind where there was no one to meet, nothing to gain but pleasure. Marcia and Michelle continued to get together, but less often. They talked of how they missed the freedom of the old days, and how their husbands worked too much, and about children and how Stephen didn't want any, period. Marcia's eldest son Derek was born after they had moved away. They had three now. Michelle had not met any of them, which was just as well. She would have been terribly jealous.

"You're going to miss this place," Michelle remarked, as Sarah took a soda from the fridge.

"Not likely," the younger woman assured her, "the place I rented down there is bigger, newer, and cheaper. Plus there's a pool."

"What about the view?"

Sarah made a dismissive gesture. "I'll be working too much to care." Michelle nodded. She didn't have the heart to tell her it would be her youth she would miss. Then again, she decided, Sarah might not miss hers.

* * *

Demerest House is a fine old structure; it was designed and erected with care and craft at a time when one's home was the indisputable measure of a man, by the finest architect and workmen Gregory Demerest (Halcomb's grandfather) could buy. The granite portico columns and marble mantelpieces were brought on the train from Vermont, the leaded glass windows had come from Boston, the brass lion head knocker on the front door had been cast in England. From the entrance hall a mahogany banister unfurls its way up two flights of broad steps, accompanied by its elegantly turned balusters and a jade runner. If one happens to posses the magical powers of a daydreaming child, and contrives to slide *up* the banister, one is eventually, at the third floor landing, deposited onto a parquet sunburst in front of the oriel window seat from which Margaret (*Magpie*), Gregory's favorite daughter, once gazed across fields and pastures to the shining waters of Cayuga Lake. One can still see a bit of gray blue shimmer through the tall pines that stand along Highgate Rd.

The artist had covered the highly polished ballroom floor with drop cloths and installed long plywood bins for storing canvases, a couple of large folding tables, three easels, a melamine paint cabinet, various photographic and lighting equipment, a huge widescreen LCD monitor, an old overstuffed chair, and a rollaway bed. The wet bar he stocked with turpentine, varnish, medium, gesso, root beer, and cognac.

There were no curtains or window coverings over the French doors that opened onto the small balcony, so that if one were positioned properly in the few acres of wooded expanse on the hill opposite, one could easily see into the studio. The west wall had two tall windows, facing the neighboring house, Professor Wolcott's home.

Each easel held a painting in a different stage of completion. The first seemed to be dominated by what one assumed would become a breast; there was no suggestion of a nipple, but the shape seemed, to Leah, unmistakable. Another canvas was quite large, at least three feet by four feet, but so far only a sketch marred the white, of a staircase, probably the one she had just climbed. Blocked in on the third was a nascent face, feminine, alluring, an entity seeking animation, impatient to emerge from the canvas and command attention. It was with this face Kyle was intently occupied.

The girl had never before seen a real artist at work; therefore she was quite mesmerized by the process, the speed with which he mixed the colors versus the careful precision with which he applied the brush to the painting. She watched him caress and coax the face into being, as absorbed in it as he was.

This played to my purpose perfectly. It was a matter of timing. Industrious as she was, and anxious to prepare for her date with Travis, she had completed her duties too speedily. I took the precaution to dampen the vibration of her voice, but it was hardly necessary; he kept the music so incredibly loud, and she was by nature too polite to shout. In this manner the required minutes passed, until the music came to its conclusion and she was able to make her presence known, and inform him she had finished.

The occasion was a little gathering at the Stuart's house; the kids had driven up from the city for Easter. Lily hadn't seen them in so long, and the Stuart's daughter-in-law had recently had a little boy.

"Oh, isn't he a big fellow," Lily observed, cradling the baby in the crook of her arm.

"Congratulations!" exclaimed Michelle, "I can't believe you delivered only a month ago."

"Thanks," Jannelle replied, "I've been trying to get some workouts in, but it's hard." She was positively beaming with pride. Her husband, Mathew Stuart was watching Lily like a hawk, to be certain she was still strong enough to hold his precious child. Stephen was already engaged in a heated conversation with Mathew's father about the deer problem.

"But you look fantastic. And he's so sweet! You must be on cloud nine," Michelle said, tearing up. The living room was full of baby paraphernalia and Easter decorations. A giant stuffed bunny sat on the floor beside a combination car seat baby carrier, which, with it's handle sticking up in the air and a bright green blanket rumpled in it, looked oddly similar to the Easter basket on the coffee table, as if it had been delivered by the flop eared toy and the boy had just popped out of a plastic egg. On each end table by the sofa was a large vase crammed with happy daffodils.

"Yeah, it's wonderful. You know everyone says it changes your life, and you're never the same, but you really have no idea until it happens, and then they're there in your arms, and you realize you're everything to them, and..."

"Oh, I'm so happy for you."

"Thank you, Michelle. We're just so glad that he's healthy and has all his fingers and toes, and... there's just so much to be grateful for."

"Here," Lily said, handing little Lucas to her, "You hold him for a while, he's just an angel." But nervous Mathew intercepted his son during the handoff.

"Why don't you have a seat," he suggested diplomatically. Michelle sat and Mathew placed the bundled baby in her arms. His nearly bald head was heavy against her arm; she could feel him wriggling his feet inside the blanket. His little mouth was moist, a tiny bubble formed there and he blinked at her.

"Aw..." she said, "He's so beaut..." she tried to say, but her throat had pinched off the words. The session with Sam was still fresh in her mind. She was overwhelmed with such longing, she wanted so much to take him home, to watch him and feed him and love him. She was beaming while tears of joy began rolling down her face, and when she sniffled, Mathew, hovering, said, "Maybe I'd better put him back in his carrier for now." He didn't want her dripping any fluids on the boy. Reluctantly, Michelle agreed.

She rose and went to the bathroom to recover her composure. Stephen had always insisted that her desire for children was simple genetic programming and had suggested more than once that since her problem arose (as he was certain it did) from physiological changes, she had merely to wait it out; another few years and hormone levels would decline, she would see how she had escaped by the skin of her teeth and she would thank him. Stephen always appeared rational; that was what he was good at. Michelle believed she had finally conquered what he referred to as her 'baby fever'. Now Sam, or her guides or *someone* was trying to stir it up again. She hadn't felt this sad about not being a mother in years. She was supposed to have gone back to Sam earlier that week, but had cancelled, leaving a message on the machine. The crick in her neck was returning. She was starting to sweat. She took three Advil and went back to the living room, joining Lily at the window. Together they looked out at the rain and the melting snow.

"How have you been, Michelle?"

"Oh, fine, fine. I'm sorry; I don't know what came over me. Just such a beautiful baby." She hadn't seen Lily since the reading, and desperately wanted to tell her about it, but knew she probably never would. Lily might inadvertently tell Stephen, and Stephen, who had never approved of Sam, would certainly not approve of getting a reading, particularly one that mentioned babies. He never failed to remind her that she had been well aware of his feelings before they married.

"No need to apologize, dear. I want to smuggle him home too. Of course I'd bring him back after an hour or so," she laughed.

"I guess that would be easier, wouldn't it?" She could ask Lily not to mention it, but Lily's mind was not as reliable as it once was, or so it seemed to Michelle. Of course she had not told Stephen that the migraines had returned.

"Oh, I don't know Lily, I really haven't been myself lately," she submitted, trying to get her courage up to say something about it all.

"Well we all go through a change or two during our lives dear. Just remember, this too shall pass."

A change, Michelle thought, what is she implying? Is she suggesting I'm going through *the* change? I can't be. I'm not. It has nothing to do with that. How old does she think I am? Am I old enough for that? Oh God. I might be. But I'm not, not yet.

"What are you two whispering about?" Richard asked, coming to stand with them and look out the window. He was only able to resist following Lily across the room for a few minutes. "Babies?"

"We were discussing what a big baby *you* are, Richard," Lily advised him.

"Were you indeed," he laughed.

"Did you bring a copy of your play?" she asked.

"Now Lily, you cannot use blackmail on someone my age, it's not humane."

"Such skill with hyperbole, Richard, that will come in handy."

"I didn't know you were done with your play," Michelle noted.

"I'm not. It's a figment of Lily's imagination."

"Oh, I wanted to let you know I won't be able to make it for lunch on Tuesday, something's come up," Lily advised him. He chuckled, opened his mouth to protest, frowned and fell silent.

"You must miss the place terribly," remarked Michelle, nodding across the road and down to Lily's old home. It looked dark and melancholy in the rain. Michelle wanted to go there anyway.

"Not as much as I thought," Lily responded cheerfully.

"It's been nearly a year now, hasn't it?" inquired Richard.

"Ten months. I don't regret it. Certainly don't regret the heating bills."

159

"No, I guess not," Richard agreed.

As they watched, a green truck drove by and turned into the drive at Demerest House. It said *Kampnich's Kitchens and Baths* on it. They heard a honk, and watched as the grand front door opened and Leah emerged. She strode down the walk and got into the passenger side. Mr. Westin waved as the truck, driven by Leah's father, turned around, drove back out to Highland Road and disappeared.

"Oh my God!" Michelle exclaimed quietly, "I can't believe her father is allowing her to do that."

"To clean houses? Why shouldn't he, it's good honest work, the girl needs the money for college," maintained Richard.

"Clean? Do you really think she's *cleaning* for Kyle?"

"What else would she be doing?" Lily challenged, but before Michelle could utter her suspicions, Richard said,

"Of course she's cleaning. I'm the one who recommended her to him; she's a very hard worker. What are you suggesting?"

"Oh, nothing. She was very good at the Christmas party. I didn't mean to imply... I just wondered if that's what Kyle..."

"Okay you three, dinner is served," Stephen said, having been sent to gather them to the table. Michelle wondered how long Stephen had been standing behind them. He aimed his inscrutable expression at her briefly, as if he knew more than she did of her own mind.

"Oh, my, I can hardly wait," rumbled Richard, and he strode off to the dining room.

"Smells delicious, doesn't it?" Stephen agreed, walking with him.

"What is it you suspect Kyle of?" Lily quietly asked as they followed. Michelle felt embarrassed for having said too much, for having thought too much.

"I'm sorry, I have no reason to suspect him of anything. I didn't realize Leah was looking for cleaning jobs. Perhaps I'll use her sometime."

"I'm sure she would appreciate that."

Michelle said little through dinner. Stephen would not look at her at all. Was he angry with her, or did he feel guilty? She thought Lily looked at her funny a few times, with that sympathetic benefactor expression of hers, which somehow only reminded you that you were to be pitied, that your life was obviously not what it should be. Even little Lucas, from his carrier on the floor in the corner seemed to be offering condolences, as if to say, too late, old girl, that ship has sailed.

18

"WHAT?"

"You know, just a kiss, and a hug. He's lonely."

"How is that my problem?"

"Come on, we're all part of the One, right? That's what it's all about; we need to love one another. I mean, what good is it if you just say stuff like that without acting on it. You have to put it into practice. You have to reach out."

"Then you kiss him."

"He's not gay, for God's sake, just depressed. We need to include him."

"Well let's take him to the movies, then."

"I've asked him to the movies, he won't come."

"Then maybe he doesn't want to be included."

"Yes he does, he just... I promised Grandma I would cheer him up."

"And she suggested I make out with him."

"No," Travis laughed, "That was my idea. But I never said make out with him, just one kiss and a good squeeze, you know?"

"Then Lily knows about this plan of yours?"

"No, no. I just think it's... he doesn't ever talk to any girls, he's just way too shy. I think he's a virgin."

"So you want me to fuck him?" Leah asked. This seemed like a fucked up conversation to be having in bed right after sex.

"No, Jesus! I'm just saying, let him know that you care about him, you know? Let him know that there are things to look forward to, give him some hope. Give him a compliment maybe, tell him he's handsome."

"He is handsome. Are *you* gay? Is he going to walk in here now and join us? What the fuck!" She turned away from him, and wound up facing Andreas' side of the room.

"No, God, calm down. Just, next time you see him, let him know you wouldn't mind if he hangs out with us sometimes. I know he likes you."

"Oh, yeah? Did he ask you for permission to have at me?"

"Leah, come on. Don't take it so seriously. I'm just saying, speaking from a male perspective, you know, everyone needs a little attention once in a while, and he's just too scared to ask for it. You could really help boost his confidence, and then I... we, could help him get a date maybe."

Over Andreas' bed there was a poster of a woman's torso, the bottom of which was exposed circuitry, as if she were a robot or something. Long German words framed the image; she wondered vaguely what it said. The woman looked cold and cruel.

"Just one kiss?"

"Yeah, just one. And a hug."

"Whatever."

* * *

There was a rumbling of the windowpane. Several weeks had passed. Michelle was in her office, on the computer. She thought it unusual for a plane to be so close overhead. She had been watching a video her friend Tatiana had posted on Facebook of her daughter Karina eating Cheerios, one at a time, picking them up off the tray of her high chair with her moist, sticky, chubby little forefinger and popping them into her mouth, and at length falling asleep with one still stuck to her finger. The video was nearly five minutes long. Michelle had watched it three times, laughing, then grinning, then yearning.

There it was again, the sound of low, intermittent tones rattling the glass. She stopped the video, opened the window, and listened as it changed pitch — music — a slow bass line. It was a sunny, cool spring day; the peonies had begun to open and were bobbing in the breeze. The bass line continued, but with the window open she could also hear quiet blues guitar, slow saxophone, and a doleful voice calling out lyrics. She liked it, it was bluesy, the sort of music she seldom heard, evocative of something neglected or forsaken. Stephen only allowed classical music to be played in his presence, everything else made him tense, he said. He particularly preferred chamber music. She wondered if he could hear this sexy blues in the study; she rose and closed the door. Michelle had a number of re-laxation CD's; meditative piano, Carlos Nakai, Enya, Yanni, but she only played them in her office or when Stephen was away. Recently she had developed a fondness for Indian ragas.

Looking across to Demerest House she saw that the windows of the studio were open. Bit chilly for that, she thought, especially if he's got someone up there posing. It was definitely where the music was coming from. While retrieving her binoculars from their hiding place in the bookcase, she noticed that the month was almost over and she had forgotten to change the calendar, so she took a moment to do so. The new image was sweet, a man sitting with a baby asleep on his chest. The quote read:

We can't help being thirsty, move toward the voice of water.

Binoculars in hand, Michelle sat next to the window. Little bubbles of words were delivered to her in spurts by the gusts of wind. She heard something that sounded like *Bible*. The back of the easel was visible; the canvas seemed to be shuddering. Something *your Gita*? Interesting song, she thought. Occasionally there was an arm moving, nothing really to see. Now the mumbling voice stopped and soulful harmonica wafted through budding branches to her ear. It struck her as sad, but seemed to provide its own relief from that sadness. The song ended. She shivered, closed the window; went back to her book. After reading a page she realized the glass was rumbling again, and she thought she recognized the same bass line.

"Huh," she said, shaking her head. "Guess he likes that song." She took her book to the opposite side of the house, and curled up in the stuffed chair in the front parlor. To her mind this was the only comfortable chair they owned; she hated Stephen's beloved Arts and Crafts pieces, their slats felt like iron bars in her back.

An hour later, the professor emerged from his study for lunch. She made them roast beef sandwiches and macaroni salad. She drank half a glass of wine, while Stephen had tea. He talked about the new engineering building going up on campus.

"I was thinking of hiking the trail this afternoon," she said, "Would you like to join me?"

"Oh, I don't think I can sweetheart, I have a meeting at three."

"On a Saturday?"

"I'm sorry, I'm just an advisor for this group and they can't meet any other time. But you go, looks like a gorgeous day out there, you should get out and enjoy it. Tell you what, why don't we meet at the Heights for dinner, say 7:30?"

"Sure," she said, "That'll be wonderful."

"That way you don't have to spend any time cooped up here cooking. You should go down to the lake," he suggested, rising. "Take Lily! She'd love that."

"Yes. Maybe I'll do that," Michelle agreed. She hadn't really expected him to come with her; he was always busy. When they first met, his job had not been quite so demanding, and of course she had been working then, so their leisure time was more on a par. Since she had stopped working it had been difficult. Sometimes she missed the activity, but she was not a type A personality as Stephen was. She was glad to be able to live her life at a more meditative pace, but it was inevitable that she should want him home more; she loved him. They were comfortable with each other, when they had time together.

The garage opened, his SUV revved, pulled out, and the steel door clanged shut on the quiet house. She finished the dishes, slipped on her pale pink windbreaker, and went outside. She had decided against calling Lily; she couldn't face her reproachful buoyancy. Intending to take a long walk, she first wandered about the backyard, admiring the peonies and the last of the tulips, checking to see if the gladiolas were up and how the irises were faring. She didn't get down and dirty the way Lily loved to (that's what gardeners were for, Stephen said), but she did enjoy just walking around the beds watching buds appear; spring was her favorite time of year.

As she turned toward the eastern edge of the yard, she heard music again, that rumbling bass line. It drew her further into the wooded area beyond the garden, where the blue spruce was king, where the smell and size of the trees took her away, back to woods of Clarkdale, back to hide and seek and the feeling of disappearing from the world of adults and their confusing cares, out of sight of manmade things, existing in secret like the bunnies and birds, becoming one with the branches and grass and the crisp scented air. She reached out her hand to touch the soft fingers of the spruce.

The music's deep resonance pulled again; she circled round closer to Demerest House, as close as she could get without being in his garden. It was the same song, she realized. How many times was he going to play it? She stood looking up through the trees at the back of the house, at the second floor balcony off the ballroom cum studio, allowing the music to embrace her. He might be able to see her from the window, if he was looking, but no, she thought, he was absorbed in painting, in the zone.

And your stairway, it went, she could hear the words clearly now. Was he singing too?

Reaches up to the moon, yes, one voice was recorded, the other must be Kyle's.

And it comes right back… O my God, she thought, smiling, he's terrible, how embarrassing, I should move out of earshot. But she crept closer. The bountiful pink lilac bushes below his window filled her head with their intoxicating scent.

It comes right back to you. And the harmonica again, which Kyle accompanied with *doo, doo, doo.*

"Hah!" Michelle ejaculated, then covered her mouth and jumped back behind an oak, laughing at the absurdity of the syllables, and at the sheer volume with which he sang. As she went back toward the front of her house, she heard the whole tune begin again. Had his music been this loud last summer? He never heard the doorbell when she had gone over with the brownies, but she had not noticed the music. Why did it catch her ear now?

The next day, Sunday, Kyle's *Gita* song, as she thought of it, again encroached on her windows, rumbling them every time the bass line began. It made her laugh all over again, she could still hear him singing, if one could call it that. He played it for hours. My God, what an idiot, she thought, yet it occupied her all day. She sat next to the open window and listened to it a dozen times, trying to make out the words, until her ear hurt from the chill, until the music had wormed its way into the recesses of her mind. She googled the snippets of lyrics she had discerned. The song was by Van Morrison. She downloaded and played it, synchronized her laptop to the humming glass, and began to understand why he was so hooked on it. There was a reverence about it, woven with an unabashed admission of need, which struck accord with her heart.

Eventually she rebelled against this concordance, this irresistible flow that forced her to visit and revisit and acknowledge the lacunae in the marrow of her being. To escape it, she went to the mall for the remainder of the afternoon and wandered through the stores, distracting herself with colors, patterns, textures, sizes, but the lyrics would not leave her. *I wanna reach you… and your stairway… reaches up to the moon.* She found herself browsing a maternity rack by mistake, then sauntered over to the children's section and bought two adorable bunny suits, one for Connie Ward's granddaughter and one for Jannelle Stuart's new baby boy. *You know what I'm missin'* played in her head as she signed the receipt.

19

THAT night Michelle lay awake, waiting for Stephen to come to bed, looking up through their bedroom window at the moon rising. She had opened the blinds all the way and had turned off the lights just so she would be able to look at it. Both of these actions would annoy Stephen, he preferred the blinds down, and the bathroom light left on until he came to bed, so he could see where he was going without having to disturb her by turning on the overhead. Irritating him was the exact opposite of what she wished, but she had so wanted to watch the moon rising; there was something about Kyle's song which convolved with an image in her mind arising from a book she had read about out of body experiences, and a passage describing the silver cord which connects the soul to the body, and how no matter how far you travel or how high you rise, even if you went all the way to the moon, that cord would stretch and keep you tethered to your body. *And it comes right back to you.*

She rose and flipped the bathroom light on again, opened a drawer, found her diaphragm and carefully inserted it. After removing her nightshirt she got back in bed and looked again at the moon, feeling sad and realizing that their bed was no longer a place where she found peace. It had become a place of confrontation, not necessarily with Stephen, but with herself. It was a place she came to every night seeking comfort and found only her own dissatisfaction.

Stephen was forty when they married, and a part of her realized at the time that she was the younger woman of his midlife crisis, that he was struggling to hold onto his youth, that she might be considered a trophy wife, but she loved him, respected him, and was happy to be what he needed. She knew what everyone said: there's no sex after marriage; but she didn't believe in clichés — create your own reality. Besides, she told herself, she didn't much care about that, it was the sensuality she wanted more than the sex itself, the cuddles, the skin on skin feeling of huddling against the vagaries of life, the companionship. Only after they were married for a while did she learn that affection seemed to be the part of sex Stephen was least comfortable with. When had he become so closed to her? She could not pinpoint a date; it had taken years for him to build his armor, layer by layer. Now it seemed she couldn't reach him, and he appeared to have no desire to reach out to her.

Once, years ago, Michelle had mustered the courage to ask Stephen why he didn't come to bed nude anymore, even in the summer, why he never wanted to cuddle. It was the only way she could possibly confront him about her needs. He accused her, laughingly, of becoming hedonistic and promptly removed his nightclothes, but she didn't want this, she wanted an answer. Of course he had never actually refused to have sex, and he assumed this was her way of asking for it, but when finished he would just put the pajamas back on and turn his back to her. She wanted an explanation, she asked again, why?

"Concessions," he had replied after much thought, his face quite serious, "to the... *baser* passions can only lead to weakness of character, munchkin. Do you imagine I don't enjoy it as much as you? I would get nothing accomplished if I... *abandoned* myself to indulgences. The result would be lost focus, poor quality work, desertion of important goals. Surely you don't want that for me? For yourself?" And in so many words he had managed to make her feel not only that she was hopelessly dissolute, but also that it was to be expected because obviously her upbringing had been woefully inadequate. He had managed to do something her parents had failed to do — make her ashamed of her body — not of her sexuality, but in a broader sense of any physical desire or emotional need, as if she had let him down rather than the other way around, as if she didn't realize the seriousness of life's work, and this new shame made her reticent on the entire subject. They simply never discussed sex.

Following this Stephen apologized for his inattention in his clinical, tactful way, making her feel like another problem solved. She didn't see the pajamas the rest of that summer, but when cool weather returned, they both started wearing their shirts again. Coming to bed nude then became more of a signal between them, to be used if one or the other were very much in the mood. After a year or two it seemed to Michelle she was the only one ever using the signal, and she became even more reluctant to admit she still had 'baser passions'. It made her seem weak somehow. After all, he was the man, he was the one who was supposed to be ruled by his libido, if he could rise above it, why couldn't she? What was most maddening was that she knew full well he was mistaken, that it wasn't healthy to go without sex, that it couldn't possibly be good for their marriage to go through their days with so little affection, but still Stephen managed to make her feel in the wrong. He was so very serious, so committed to his committees, his community, his charities, and his country. Was he not asking her to become a better person, to focus on the needs of those around her more than on her own?

So many nights found her like this one, waiting, hoping, perhaps praying that her husband still had enough interest in her to come to bed naked, just the man, not the professor, not the consultant, not the mentor. Who was she praying to, she wondered, Bacchus? Eros? And what was she praying for? A severe, balding man, beyond middle-age; losing his muscle tone along with his hair, who seemed to have successfully killed off his desire and believed it to have been a good deed. She could see his logic, but there was no part of her that could agree with it. She wanted him to want her in a way he simply no longer did. Why did she love him? *Did* she love him still? Yes, she decided she did, because for all his glib arrogance, she believed him to be a genuinely and profoundly good person. She saw Stephen as one of those rare people who, by insisting on diligence, excellence, and probity, succeeded in elevating those around him to new levels of attainment and understanding. It often made him difficult to live with, but she tried to think of *his* needs, and not belabor the notion that she was dissatisfied. She would try not to bring it up anymore, though it was a disappointment which never went away, no matter how many times it surfaced and seemed to have been dealt with, like a boil which comes to a painful head, disgorges its toxins and recedes, only to return a month later.

Michelle lay quietly, patiently, hoping for 'concessions to the baser passions', noting the progress of the moon in the night sky. *And it comes right back to you...* Kyle's voice sang in her head. Perhaps it was the moon she prayed to, the moon was sympathetic to Michelle, always. She thought she heard Stephen on the stairs. She rose again, closed the blinds, removed her diaphragm, and returned to bed, still without her nightshirt.

The following day in her office Michelle wrote:

I am so happy and grateful that it is spring. I love the dandelions and the tulips. I am so fortunate to have this beautiful home and so many good friends. I am happy that Lily is well cared for and looked after at Crestview. I am so thankful that I am married to such an amazing man, I love Stephen so much, I am so grateful for the many things he has done for me, for all the love he has given me, for all that he has taught me. I am so glad Stephen has helped me to be a better person. I am so thankful we made love last night. I am so happy to be with him. I am so thankful his work is less demanding. I am glad we are making new friends. I am thankful for the time to meditate. I am so happy that Stephen is reconsidering children.

She returned the gratitude book, lit a match to start a stick of incense, then took the book out again and added: *I am excited to meet Lindsay and Paul.* When the volume was back on the shelf and she had settled herself cross-legged on the daybed, she closed her eyes and took a deep breath. She felt irritated; frustrated with herself for not being satisfied with the attention she had gotten from Stephen. Listen to the silence, she told herself, and breathe. When she had finished three deep inhalations, and was just beginning to feel relaxed, the window began to rumble. The bass was there again. She tried to let it go, to ignore it, but it had twined itself within a spiral of images such as the silver thread, the girl on the satyr carousel, *Nikki's Daemon,* Sam's Shiva/Shakti sculpture, and her own idea of what Kyle looked like painting in the nude. She was sick to death of it, but there it was in her head, the crying harmonica playing along with the rumble, the doleful voice still calling for *your Gita, your pillow*, and it was no longer amusing, it was disruptive and made

175

it impossible to meditate. She allowed anger to cover the sadness it brought to the front of her mind, the sorrow she did not want to concede.

"Shit," she said. She would have to go over there and complain, do something to make him stop, before Stephen noticed. He would call the police no doubt, but she didn't want to war with their new neighbor. How would Lily handle it, she wondered. Lily was the most diplomatic person she knew. First of all, she would never go to his or anyone else's door without bringing something, a gift. A bribe. A *replacement*. Perfect, she thought after searching through her music, let him blast this out his window. After carefully gift-wrapping a very graciously used CD of bansuri flute music, she marched over to Demerest House.

There was no answer; she rang the bell again, feeling terribly conspicuous standing there surrounded by the granite columns. Naturally, he was high in the house in the studio with the *Gita* song going full bore; he couldn't possibly hear her. What would Lily do, what would Lily do. She would not be put off, that was certain. Michelle grabbed the old lion head knocker and began rapping it as loudly as she could. Eventually, after a quiet moment in the song, after her fingers hurt from gripping the brass, the music stopped. She kept knocking; still no answer. She kept knocking, for what must have been another full minute. Finally, the door creaked open.

"Good afternoon," she said. Kyle looked at her blankly, as though in a daze. He was dressed in old torn jeans and a spattered, sleeveless t-shirt. Tufts of his hair were standing up at odd angles, smears of various hues of paint marked his hands and arms, his beard, even his forehead. It would have been difficult for Michelle to keep a straight face, had it not been for the intensity of his dark eyes, and the firm grip he had kept on the doorknob, as if he might slam it closed in her face. "I brought you something," she continued, handing him the package.

"What is it?" he asked, releasing the door to take the gift, getting orange paint on the silver paper. There was a note of confusion in his voice.

"Well you can open it," she said, "I thought perhaps you might like something a little… quieter." He tore back the paper, looked at its contents for a moment, maybe reading the title, maybe not, then returned his gaze to her, still in a fog, his eyes focused beyond her somehow.

"See, I'm afraid what you've been playing for the last several days… it… well, it's kind of rattling the windows at our house."

"Oh," he said, looking as if he hadn't heard a word, just staring, not *at* her so much as through her, then uttered what she thought was, "Luminescence."

"I'm sorry?" This seemed to catch him, snap him out of his reverie; he looked at her now, in the eyes. There was an *alignment* of something, Michelle heard a click (perhaps the door latch popping out after having been released), she felt her body react, galvanized by an ineluctability, her head shook slightly from left to right, the shudder ran down her spine to her feet, instantaneously recalling similar moments — when they met and their hands touched, at the frame shop when he said her name — she blinked, glanced away, then back at him. *Namaste*, she thought. She wanted to touch him.

"Are you alright?" she asked, putting a hand on his arm.

"Yes. I just… I… I'll turn it down some then."

"Okay. Or you could play this one instead. I just thought you might enjoy it. The flute. It's very peaceful. Not so much bass."

"I'm sure it's very nice," Kyle consented, his eyes still dark, almost glowering, "but I can't change just now. I mean I'm not fin-

177

ished yet." Now Michelle was perplexed. "If I change the music, it will change the painting. I'd have to start all over."

"You mean you play the same song the entire time you're working on a painting?"

"Well not always only one song, sometimes one album, or one composer, but in this case, yes. It has to be the one song. But I can turn it down. I'm sorry it disturbed you," he concluded, and began to close the door. "But thank you for this."

"It's not that I don't like the song," Michelle said, halting him. She didn't want him to go. She wanted to hear him talk, there was something so soothing about it, something entrenched in the timbre of his voice, some veiled sorrow or joy which she shared with him. Near him she felt less alone. He looked down at her hand, which made her suddenly conscious that it was still on his wrist. She withdrew it. "I mean I wouldn't want you to think I... I only like boring music or anything."

"No. I don't. I understand, I realize it's not a normal listening behavior. It helps me stay with my subject if I identify it with a particular aural experience."

"That's an interesting technique," she noted. "What exactly are you painting?"

"It's an oil," he carelessly said, as if that could possibly satisfy. He seemed to be looking at the ground, or... her hand hanging by her side, the one she had had on his wrist.

"Can I see it?"

"No," he said.

"Oh." She slipped her hands in the pockets of her windbreaker. He returned his dark gaze to her face.

"It's not finished. I only show works that are finished."

"Of course, sorry I asked."

"No problem. Listen, Michelle..."

"Yes?" She shivered again.

"I've been meaning to ask you... I'd like you to pose for me."

"Oh," she said, taken by surprise, unable to keep from smiling. She felt her cheeks flush.

"For a painting," he added, at which she chuckled. "Is that a yes?"

"Will you play this CD when you paint it?"

"I'll have to."

"Then... I suppose so, why not." Now Kyle smiled. She loved his smile. It was not ambiguous like her husband's.

"Great," he said quietly. "You're perfect," and he began to close the door again.

"So..." she inquired, "when do you want me to come?"

"Oh, uh... have to finish this one first. Take a couple days. How about Friday?"

"Okay."

"Ten o'clock?"

"I will knock on your door."

"Well if I don't answer, you know you can just come right in. Don't tell anyone, but I don't keep the doors locked."

"Okay, I won't," she assured him.

The rest of that afternoon and evening, Michelle was excited, agitated. She knew why and a part of her was terribly ashamed, and working very hard to suppress the other part, the galvanized part, the part which was thrilled at the prospect of getting nude in her neighbor's studio, the part which was giddy with the knowledge that someone wanted to see her naked, someone *wanted* her. She felt incredibly flattered by Kyle's invitation to pose, but at the same time she was terrified, not of him but of… herself? It seemed wrong somehow, but it wasn't really. Just because she agreed to pose didn't mean she had agreed to anything else. And she wouldn't, couldn't; didn't really want to, did she? No, she loved Stephen and had no intention of being unfaithful; it was unthinkable. And if being asked to pose made her feel this much better about herself, it was certainly a good thing, right? After all, a little extra self-confidence could only make her more attractive to her husband. Having an accomplished artist paint her could only be good for her marriage. Perhaps Stephen would buy it afterward, and hang it in his study. Maybe they would all become good friends, and Kyle would drop by for dinner as often as Lily had when she lived next door.

Michelle stayed up late that night, later than Stephen. She told him she wanted to finish a book; she tried reading but couldn't concentrate. She tried to call Lily, but Lily didn't pick up the phone. She declined to leave a message. She thought of Sam, but knew she was an early riser and probably already asleep. She emailed Marcia, whom she had not communicated with in close to a year.

She was incredibly aroused, but she didn't want Stephen to know because he had not been the one to arouse her, and she had an irrational fear that he would sense this, and she would confess her appointment to pose, and Stephen would learn the type of paintings Kyle painted and forbid her to go. This was a risk she could not take, so she sat in her office holding a book rather than going to bed and lay next to her husband whom she now desperately wanted because another man had suggested she was attractive enough to be the subject of a work of art. She was beside herself, split, of two minds or more, but she wanted primarily to be kind to her husband, whom she loved with all her heart, and through some contorted logic it seemed to her the best way to be loyal and good to her husband was to stay there in her secure office, laying on her daybed pretending to read *The Power of Intention* until she knew he was asleep. Gradually she became calmer and was again able to cope with her nerves, to slow her heart rate. She got out her gratitude book and wrote:

> *I am so happy and grateful for Stephen. I am glad he still wants me and feels such affection for me. I am happy to be there for him. I am fortunate that our marriage is strong and important to him. I am thankful for the peace we feel together. I am so glad that Kyle is becoming our friend. I am so grateful that little Paul and Lindsay are coming. I am happy to be relaxed and comfortable with my life.*

She put the journal back in its place. After reading a few pages of the book she said she had wanted to finish but in fact had read through twice before, she decided she would be able to sleep and she went up to bed.

For the next few nights, whenever her uncomfortable body urged her to shift, and her mind rose toward the surface, it turned immediately to Kyle, to the sound of his voice, to the dark greenish eyes and that one smile, a smile *she* had put there. It had made her feel important. It made *her* smile, there in the dim light with the blinds closed against the moon, then it would make her feel like crying, and the tears would well up and she would lay there entranced, not dreaming, nor alert, wondering, what's happening to me, what have I done, what am I intending, how many am I, that I don't know myself?

20

[A flash of light, stage right]
Wendell
(whispering)

Did you see that?

Rose

See what?

[more flickering lights]
Wendell
(putting an arm on her shoulder, pointing)

Shh! That, there!

Rose
(whispering)

Where?

Wendell

Just there, in the garden, behind the azaleas.

Rose

No. Why are we whispering?

Wendell
(moving his pointing finger)

Shh! It's just...
(no longer whispering)
oh, now it's gone

Rose

What's gone?

Wendell

The ghost!

Richard was sitting at his roll top desk in front of his computer, typing away. Mitzi was stretched across his lap. The oak desk, its front edge and drawer handles darkened by a century of use, soiled and oiled by generations of hands, was in the second bedroom of his two bedroom apartment, which he had never referred to as a bedroom but as the study, even though he never had nor ever would study in it. He read his papers at the dining room table and books in the recliner. The desk had at one time been useful for grading papers, but lately had only seen use in paying bills and filing invoices from various health care organizations, insurance companies, medical associates, and in rare cases, actual physicians. The top no longer rolled, it had been stuck open for a decade.

Oak bookcases with glass doors covered one wall of the room and held the most favored books of his long life, from his treasured childhood copy of *The Wizard of Oz* to a dog-eared unglued pile of pages that had once been *The Prophet*. He had a vast collection of plays including versions of *The Cherry Orchard* in a dozen different languages, four of which he could read. Richard's prize possession however, was a signed first edition in fine condition with dust jacket of *O Alquimista* in the original Portuguese, which he could *not* read, but treasured all the more because he might learn some day and looked forward with certainty to the esoteric mysteries the nuances of the original language would reveal.

Mitzi was a beige cockapoo with a taste for schnapps and Stilton. Richard secretly wanted to take Mitzi with him everywhere, to the mall, to the doctor's office, to friends houses, but he simply couldn't bear to appear as the sort of person who treats their animals like children and takes them all around town in their cars and in their arms and tries to get away with putting them in the grocery cart at the store. This was ever a source of frustration to Mitzi, who longed to be taken about the town in a soft vinyl carrier with a red crocheted blankie and have total strangers remark on how cute she was and how much she had grown. Richard, thinking, shifted his weight in the chair. Mitzi opened her eyes and groaned irritably. After three months, Lily's lunch date strike had finally had its intended effect. He resumed typing.

Rose

Do you expect me to believe you just saw a ghost in my garden?

185

Wendell

May God strike me dead if I did not!

[Leopold appears behind them, stage left]

Leopold

I saw it too.

[Both Rose and Wendell jump in surprise and turn to look at him]

Rose

Well what did it look like?

Leopold

Like a man, I mean it was all whitish and grayish sort of and a little like fog, but it was definitely a man, with arm and legs and all. A little chubby and wearing spectacles.

Rose

I don't believe you, either of you. I didn't see anything at all.

Wendell

Well it was right there, in the corner of the garden, behind
the azaleas.

Rose

That's where the strawberry patch used to be.

Wendell

Okay, well that's where it was, and it had something in its
hand.

Rose

What?

Leopold

Looked like a bottle to me. It had a foggy, ghostly bottle
in its foggy ghostly hand. It was pouring something out of
it into a dish.

Wendell

More of a... a pie pan I thought.

Leopold

Could have been. Could have been a pie pan I suppose.
But it was definitely pouring something.

Rose

187

Oh my God, Horace used to fuss over those strawberries!
He used to put beer out to keep the slugs off of them. Oh
my God, you don't think…

Leopold

I can only tell you what I saw. Did Horace have a goatee?

Rose

No, he was clean-shaven.

Wendell

So was the specter! I think your poor deceased husband
is still fussing over his strawberries, Rose.

Rose
(faints, collapsing into Wendell's arms)

Ohhh!

[Curtain falls, end of Act II]

"Hah! Fabulous!" Richard boomed. Mitzi lurched to her feet, prepared to jump to the floor if the mountain rose. He put a heavy hand on her fluffy back and she lay down again. "Now all we've got to do is get Rose to see that Horace wants her to move on with her life and marry again! Piece of cake, right Mitz? Of course we've got to make sure she falls for Wendell and not Leopold. That would *not* do, would it girl?"

Mitzi groaned and closed her eyes again.

* * *

Friday morning, after Stephen left for his 9:00 class, Michelle took a long leisurely shower, blew her hair dry, curled it, carefully but sparingly made up her face, and went to her closet to dress. What to wear? She stood looking abjectly at her middle-aged body in the mirror, thinking, no wonder Stephen doesn't want me anymore. She had not gained much weight in the past fifteen years, but she was not an athletic person. She looked unappetizing, doughy, and ineffectual.

"Oh, God!" she sighed, and whimpered anxiously to herself, "What am I doing, what am I doing, what am I doing?" She chose a seafoam green blouse, put it on and stood before the mirror. The color went well with her skin tone, and the sheen of her wavy hair. Thank God for my hair, she thought, still have nice hair. Slowly, seductively, she unbuttoned the blouse, trying to see as he might see, spreading her arms out from center, the reflected motion invoking the yoga master's call *heart opening*, the green fabric plopping on the floor clumsily. He has no idea what he's asking for, she thought. Her boobs, neither large nor small, had never really faced front, as it were, and now they looked particularly splayed out. Played out, she said to herself, she could see the caption in the arts section of the Journal: New Painting by Kyle Westin entitled *Woman with the Walleyed Chest*. Maybe he's *not* asking for it, it occurred to her, remembering that he never specified naked, but the women he's painted with clothes on can be counted on one hand. Maybe I'll refuse. I'll just refuse to disrobe, and that will be that. But I'll get to see the studio anyway. She took her light pink bra from the drawer

189

and put it on, then the seafoam blouse, simple beige trousers, tan flats. She shook her head slightly, watched to see that the tresses rebounded properly. A spritz of perfume and emerald studs for her ears made her feel put together.

The brass lion head stared menacingly as she grasped the doorknob; she had not rapped the bit into its mouth even once, nor had she pressed the bell button. Michelle was trying to be as discrete as possible; she didn't want to stand there in the portico long enough for any of her neighbors to notice her. The door was unlocked as he said it would be. She entered and closed it quickly.

And your stairway, Kyle and Van Morrison were singing. *WhatamIdoing WhatamIdoing WhatamIdoing* went the chant in Michelle's head, her neck knotted, and she felt a tingling warmth entering her left side. Unsteadily she walked across the entrance hall, her chest tight and heavy. It was the first time she had been in Demerest House since Lily had moved out. There was an eerie quality about it; the hall, the front parlor, the dining room, were virtually empty: a single Windsor chair, a love seat, an end table, a lamp. The enormous old hall tree was still there, but not a single piece of clothing hung from its antlers, and its tall, cloudy mirror seemed to reflect nothing but the mists of time. Some of Kyle's paintings haunted the walls, but they were not placed well, not lit, and their lustrous subjects hung like apparitions in the empty rooms.

Reaches up to the moon, they sang as Michelle began her ascent to the studio, feeling dizzy and somehow outside of herself, watching her hand sliding up the magnificent mahogany banister, marveling that her feet were moving in slow motion, as if pushed or drawn up the jade steps without volition by the vibration of the bass and the mournful call of their voices.

And it comes right back... what if Stephen finds out, she suddenly worried; she had no idea what he might be capable of when angered. Would he be angry? Would he care at all?

It comes right back to you

In the hall just outside the studio hung *Nikki's Daemon*, well lit and newly framed in the coppery molding which looked for all the world like tongues of flame flickering up the wall. Its close proximity to the doorjamb gave the impression that the curtain Nikki was peeking around concealed the artist's workroom itself.

"Hello?" Michelle called, stepping over the threshold. The space was foreign to her, transformed; its party room character had been erased. The jumble of legs from easels, tripods, lights and umbrellas, the spattered look of the tarps and drop cloths covering the floor, gave the place a muddled but fecund air, as if any creative seed planted there could not fail to germinate. The colors spilling over everywhere she looked, the brushes and bottles, tubes and tools primed her artistic juices. It was enough to make her want to finger paint, just fill her hands with orange and green and smear them over a clean white field.

On one of the easels sat a square painting of a beautiful baby suckling, its fingers twisting in the long black hair of its mother, its eyelids barely open. He had captured the moment of falling asleep.

"This is beautiful," she noted.

"Oh hi," said Kyle. He was standing with his back to the north windows; an easel supporting a large canvas was before him; a small brush was in his hand. When he heard her, he leaned to the side so she could see him.

"That's my nephew."

"Really! Well he's certainly adorable. And lucky to have such a talented uncle." Kyle said nothing to this. She suddenly felt silly for saying it. Honesty was what he wanted from her, not flattery. Flattery did not make him smile.

"What's his name?"

"Marcus. Marcus Howard Shelton. I call him Hank," Kyle chuckled, "Drives his mother nuts."

"So cute. Looks a lot like you." He didn't respond to this at all.

"Come," he said, making a vague gesture. Michelle crossed the room and stood beside him. He was dressed in the same jeans and T-shirt he had answered the door in earlier that week, and she doubted if he had washed this work attire during the interim; he smelled of strong deodorant, sweat, and turpentine. Oddly, she did not find the combination offensive, but it contributed to her light-headed feeling.

Looking at the painting, she was struck with a powerful sensation of déjà vu; it was of a woman ascending a staircase, the Demerest House staircase without a doubt, she recognized the swirl of the banister, the jade runner, the elaborate balusters; but in the painting the stairway did not end after two flights, it rose to infinity. It disappeared at the vanishing point, after sweeping up and away towards a full moon that occupied the right corner of the canvas. Swirling blue clouds and stars filled the background with motion, almost dragging the stairs along in their wake. On the left was a nude female figure, her legs large in the foreground, her body narrowing with the dramatic perspective of the mounting stairs. Her right hand was on the banister; in her left she clutched a black book. Her left foot was on the bottom step, her right on the fourth, as if leaping up. Her dark hair was swept back; her body and face, in three-quarter profile, seemed youthful, slim, and straight, in contrast to the strong curves of the stairway and the perfectly round moon. In seeing that the woman was such a girl, Michelle stepped out of the picture, she ceased to identify her own climb up the stairway with the painting, and the tightness in her chest eased a bit. A breeze came through the open window; the scent of lilacs dispelled some of the muskiness in the room.

"What do you think?" asked Kyle. "Not really your cup of tea, is it?"

"Well no, but it… it certainly reaches up to the moon," she observed. "I love the staircase. This line is very dramatic." She could not dispel the perception that the girl in the painting was Leah. Had she posed, or had he merely observed her — the farm girl face, the athletic young body — while she mopped his kitchen floor or scrubbed his toilet; was he that good an artist that he could capture her without her consent?

"But do you think it's finished?"

"Well how can *I* say? It's very… effective. Oh. I just saw the face." A large portion of the canvas, the swirling background of dark clouds, made up a male, bearded face, if one saw the negative space, and read the lightest areas as eyes, nostrils, whiskers, and the darker areas as nose, lips, cheekbones.

"Too subtle? Should I accentuate that more?"

"No. No, I think if anything it's not quite subtle enough," Michelle said, stepping back from it. "It's definitely there. It's almost too strong from a distance." Kyle stepped back also, and looked again at what he'd been staring at all week. He grunted.

"Is it Krishna, or you?" she asked.

"Well she's the only one who knows for sure."

"Right. Who was your model?"

"Oh, I didn't really have one. Usually my figures tend to be a compilation. Okay, so let me get set up for you. Can I get you anything to drink? Coffee? Orange juice?"

"No. No thanks. I'm good."

193

"Glass of wine?"

"I don't know... it's awfully early for that."

"Glass of wine it is," he said, reaching under the wet bar to the little refrigerator there. He poured it and handed it to her. She smiled nervously and sipped it while he bustled about moving the armchair, the photographic reflectors, and the tripod. He uncovered a CD player and finally silenced Van, slipping in the disc she had brought to him earlier in the week.

"Thank you so much for doing this Michelle, you're just perfect for this painting I've had in my head for a long time." She blushed again, the familiar flute music filling her head.

"Well. Glad to help," she mumbled, gulping at the glass, trying to nerve herself up to disrobing. So if Erin had posed for *Nikki's Daemon,* she wondered, and Leah for the stairway, was there a painting of Cheiko somewhere, or Sarah Strickland? Am I the last in a long line to ascend this staircase? Surely not the last, merely the latest. Do I care?

Kyle turned on two big bulbs, flooding the armchair with light.

"Okay, so if you could just sit there..." he said, moving behind the camera. She swallowed the rest of the wine and set the glass down on the worktable.

"Did you want..." she began quietly, raising her hands to her blouse.

"Just there, in the big chair. It will only take a few minutes, I promise."

"Oh, okay." She sat. "Do you want me to... should I cross my legs... or..."

"Whatever you're comfortable with. Just relax. I'll just start shooting. If you could turn a little more to the right. Great."

Whatever I'm comfortable with, she thought, hearing the camera click, what does that mean? Does he want me naked or not? She put one hand up and undid her top button.

"There, that's perfect. No, hold your hand there, at your neck, a little higher, with your fingers... no," he came around and took her hand, placing it himself very gently in the position he wanted it — just touching her neck – then unfolded the index finger a bit more, tucked the ring finger and the pinky closer to her palm. His hand was broader and thicker than Stephen's, and very warm. It felt good. She watched his fingers as they manipulated hers. She could sense heat coming from his head, though he did not seem hot or sweaty. His face, this close, was more appealing than from across the room, why was that? There was something so familiar about him, so easy. She wanted to touch him, feel his beard under her fingers. Raising her eyes, she found he was looking at hers, not at her hand at all. Her free hand reached up and slid along his jaw, behind his neck, coaxing his face nearer. She kissed him, softly pressing her lips to his, suspending time, holding her breath. Suddenly she realized that she had moved without intending to, that someone else had intended it, that she was *out of control*, and that recognition jolted her back into time, and filled her with fear. She released his head, pulled away.

"Sorry," she whispered. He held her gaze a moment longer, and then looked back at her hand.

"Never apologize when giving a gift," he said, squeezing her hand, posing it again. "I'm just not sure it's a good idea, since we're neighbors and everything."

"No, of course not. I don't know why I..."

"There, just like that. That would be great if you could hold still for a minute." He stepped back; the camera clicked and whirred quietly beneath the voice of the bansuri flute. 'And everything', she thought, like I'm *married*. God, what's wrong with me?

Kyle lurched up and snapped off one of the lights, now she was lit from only one side. "Perfect," he said, "this is perfect." He took a few more shots, adjusting camera settings, then he reversed the lights, turning the left one on and the right one off and took some more. All the while she sat still, holding her hand to her throat, wondering how he could act as if nothing happened. Probably happens to him all the time, she conjectured, every model kisses him. Can't tell me he didn't kiss Erin back.

"Okay, that's it. We're done."

"Oh," she exclaimed in surprise.

"Thank you *so* much, this will really help," he said, turning off the light. He moved the tripod and took the camera off of it. She arose slowly, somewhat stunned that the session was over. She felt relieved but let down.

"Great. Well..." They stood looking at one another for a moment.

"So... whenever I hear the flute, I'll know you're working on me, in paint?"

"Right, but I hope I haven't misled you, it's not a portrait. You'll only appear in a part of the painting. And you know I don't always get a good likeness," he warned. Then he held out his hand. "I really do appreciate you doing this."

"Anytime," she said, taking it, feeling the strength of it, the shape of it in hers, not wanting to let it go. "I can't wait to see it. I'd love to watch you work."

"No. I never show works until they're done, or nearly done. Besides... I uh... I don't think I could concentrate if you were watching me," he admitted. She released his hand, and turned to go.

"I'll let you know when it's finished Michelle."

"Oh, if you don't mind, maybe I'll just come by... when the music stops. I didn't tell Stephen about it," she explained, blushing, "I'm not sure how he'll react to the idea."

"Sure. Sorry, I didn't mean to cause any problems, I..."

"No, it's fine, just... I'll talk to him." She left the room, descended the stairway, and returned home.

21

MICHELLE felt wretched, rejected, and completely alone, although Stephen was a few yards away in his study. There was no one she could talk with about it; she would be too ashamed to admit what she had done, too ashamed to admit what she had wanted to do. She could not even admit it to herself, could not ascribe it to *Michelle*. Why did you kiss him, she asked, quietly in her head. Why didn't you take your blouse off, was the retort she heard there.

"Now I'm talking to myself." To one of my selves, she thought, pouring another glass of wine. Which one was speaking to which? Was there a good one and a bad one, a right and a wrong? It didn't feel that way, more like a resigned one and a thwarted one, a sad one and an excited one. And for one moment, the other self had been in charge, the one that wanted to live. It was the oddest thing to recall, because she could *not* recall it — the moment when she decided to kiss him — she never made that decision, someone else made it. That moment, so sweet, so electric, did not belong to her, she had only observed it, and now it seemed it had never happened, as if the shock of it had blocked it from her memory, like posttraumatic stress syndrome.

Should she call Lily? No, she couldn't talk about this with Lily, Lily would not understand. Lily would try, she would listen, she would seem sympathetic, but she could never understand, she was one of the disciplined people, one of the strong people. Her life had gone as she had intended, so she was able to care more for others than for herself. Or is that a skill one acquires with motherhood, Michelle wondered, and the painting of the baby nursing came back to her. Marcus is so sweet, she thought, looks just like Kyle. I wonder what it feels like, with a baby.

* * *

She ran downstairs but the rooms had become lost, the doors misplaced, it was all wrong, tortuous, byzantine. It felt like home, like her doll house, the one in the attic in the old place in Clarkdale, like the attic where the dolls sometimes sat without their clothes, and she climbed down the ladder and ran downstairs again, her hands sliding along the broad, smooth, round, red wood, her feet following the jade runner, running from Stephen along long corridors with no exits, only pictures on the walls of degradations and yearnings, scurrying across the hall with *notStephen* after her, calling in her ear: Michelle! Scrambling, now slithering after her on the curving coiling wood, she almost reaching the door but he whipping off the end of the banister, flipping through the air, landing before her to block her way with his green eyes, slipping his fingers beneath the elastic of her panties, lifting her by the haunches, kissing her while she pushed away saying I am married, it's not what I want, and he, yes it is, and she, I'm not one of your... *models*, now pointing at the paintings and the watchers, demanding, do you *fuck* them all, did you fuck her and her and her... and he smiling and answering telepathically, infusing her being with ineffable gnosis, imposing on her psyche the understanding, complete, immediate and irrefutable, that she will never be closer to God than when he, the artist, is in her, and she accusing him of base obsessions, saying: you're sick, and he: I'm dead, stay with me, proposing a red-eyed bargain, life for life, and she: I don't know you! And he thrusting, averring through assured evocative timbres whose soft vibrations ran down her quivering spine: Yes you do, Michelle.

Waking with a start, her arms clamped over her chest, half remembering a lover's clench and something about her dollhouse, her heart aching with an overwhelming sense of guilt, Michelle turned, sat up part way, leaned on her elbow, and looked at Stephen sleeping. He looked suddenly older then, asleep in the grayish light seeping through the blinds, his face seemed ghostly and frail. Of course she was looking older too, she knew that; the little bags under her eyes, the plumpness under her chin, the floppiness of her arms, the various misplaced bulges time had bestowed. She had long known that he was not attracted to her anymore, but now, faced with what had happened to her that week, the things she had felt, the renewed presence of a part of herself she had forgotten, she had to acknowledge that perhaps *she* was no longer attracted to *him*. Did it then follow that if she no longer received what she needed from him, he must not be receiving what he needed from her? Am I giving what he needs, she wondered, what *does* he need, anything? The answer came to her with a great wave of compassion — love, loyalty, respect — these were all he needed, and she did feel such love for him, he had worked so hard for everyone for so long. She began to weep, silently at first like a few tears over a touching movie, and she thought she could control it, but it was not a movie, it was her life, it was his life, she had not been loyal in her heart, and the wave crested, she inhaled noisily and he woke.

201

"Michelle? What is it, munchkin?" he asked, turning and pushing himself into a sitting position. She could not answer because the floodgates were open, she could hardly catch her breath between sobs. "Bad dream?" he presumed, putting his arm around her. Not since childhood had Michelle bawled so uncontrollably, painfully, loudly. Stephen became concerned.

"Calm down sweetheart, it was just a dream," he assured her. She shook her head, wailed louder. "Michelle, what *is* it? What's wrong?" She had never cried this way in front of him. He held her, as her stomach clenched violently, expelling all, emptying her lungs far beyond normal, leaving her with barely enough strength to gasp in, only to wail again in ejection of her pain. He clutched her to him, rocked her, and then pushed her away. "Stop it, now, you're going to hurt yourself!" he commanded. She ceased momentarily, and started up again. Now he spoke calmly, taking her hand, "Michelle, you're becoming hysterical. Whatever it is, you know you can tell me. Please try and get hold of yourself. Take deep breaths. If you can stop crying we can talk about it, reasonably, rationally, like adults. Okay? Can you do that for me munchkin? Take a deep breath." She did so, sobbed once, took another deep breath, and eventually quieted herself.

"There now," he soothed, "You're okay." He reached over to the nightstand, grabbed some tissues and handed them to her. She blew her nose, wiped her eyes. "Can you tell me what's wrong?" he asked. She opened her mouth to speak; another sob came out. She breathed again, feeling ashamed for the crying on top of her other shame, feeling unworthy to be alive. "What *is* it, Michelle, it can't be that bad."

"There's... huhh... something I should've told you," she managed to get out.

"Whatever it is, it's okay," he assured her, "You know I love you. What is it you want to tell me?" She sobbed a few more times before she could answer.

"I didn't use the diaphragm last time," she confessed, and burst into tears again. "I'm sorry, I don't know what came over me, I... I..." Stephen looked surprised for a moment, and then managed a smile.

"Is that what this is all about?" he asked rhetorically, wrapping his arms around her again. She nodded her head against his chest, clinging to him, still breathing unevenly, still tearing. "Well," he said softly, "I'm glad you told me. It's okay, I doubt if one time is going to... cause a stir at our age. I forgive you. We won't talk about it again. Now maybe we can get back to sleep, what do you say?"

"Yes," Michelle sighed, pulling away from him, laying back down, closing her eyes, wondering why she had not told him about posing for Kyle, knowing why she had not told him about posing for Kyle. Stephen gave her one last pat, and rolled over with his back to her. Her head hurt, she felt dizzy, she needed to sleep; she felt relieved, deceitful, foolish, exhausted, anxious, angry and sad. She exhaled again, hoping to let them all go.

* * *

Michelle woke with a stiff neck and took some ibuprofen. Stephen said nothing of the diaphragm, or her crying fit. He seemed preoccupied with work, that is to say, he behaved normally. She fixed him a nice brunch of eggs and home fries and sat with him at the table, but she ate nothing; she was still feeling undone. He read the Journal and mumbled about the editorial page and didn't seem to notice her lack of appetite. Perhaps he did, she thought, but chose to ignore it. Maybe he honestly felt the most considerate thing to do was to disregard her emotions, to forget her 'hysteria', as he put it. And if he had seen her tears as some kind of impropriety, but showed that he was willing to forgive that offense, how could she think him unkind? After all, that's what she wanted, wasn't it, for him to forget the whole thing?

"I've got to be in Prague the last week of July," he divulged, carefully refolding the paper, "Would you like to join me?"

"Of course," replied Michelle enthusiastically, "That would be wonderful."

"Great. I'll set it up." He rose; she stood up too and reached her hands toward his waist. He took them in his and gave them a little squeeze.

"I've got to run or I'll be late for my meeting."

"Oh. What time will you be home?"

"Impossible to say. Not before five I'm sure."

"Okay. See you tonight then."

She was relieved when he was gone, and that he did seem to have forgotten her distress in the night. She was also relieved that the episode with Kyle was over, and that she had not stripped in front of him, that she had retained at least that much of her dignity. Stephen already knew the worst parts of her, and was content with her, what more could she ask for? She began to feel in control again, her old self; she knew who she was, she was Mrs. Wolcott. She had security and stability and a certain standing in the community. And she was going to Prague in July. It would be charming.

The day promised to be quite warm. Michelle opened several windows to the sweet summer air and began a yoga workout to try and loosen her neck. Breathe, the yoga master commanded. She deeply inhaled the aroma of fresh cut grass. As she finished her second *vinyasa*, the drone of the lawnmower ceased, and a different, familiar sound entered the house. It was bansuri flute music; the CD she had given Kyle. He was painting.

She couldn't do it, she couldn't remain in the house listening to that, not now that she had seen his studio and shared that space with him if only for a few moments. The sound instantaneously transported her; her mind was filled with the colors, the smells, the feel of his hands and his lips, but more than that, worse than those sensations of mere desire was the tantalizing jumble of possibilities, the revitalizing, agonizing realization that everyone did not exist as Stephen did; immured in nested boxes of duty, decorum and dogma. Even though she had left Demerest House feeling rejected, she had somehow been given a key.

Michelle could not go back to the studio, nor could she bear to hear him playing that music, her music, her gift. She couldn't keep the vision of him out of her head — plying the color-rich tip of his brush to her half-fleshed face — and she could not sit in the warm house with the windows closed. She set off for the gorge trail, leaving the haunting music hanging in the air.

It was cooler there, sheltered but muggy. The path was still wet with the recent rain. She moved slowly, letting the rustic post and rail wooden fence guide her tactfully away from the edge of the abyss, and back to a simpler time. She listened to the knocks of the woodpeckers, the chatter of chipmunks and jays, the creek running home to the lake, and the breeze speaking with the trees. A hundred hues of green and gold streamed through the leaves as the sun winked in and out of her eyes. It was peaceful. Her neck began to release. A sense of privilege gradually overcame her anxiety. They lived in a place of such unique beauty, such tranquility; she could not help but be grateful for it. She only wished Stephen would take more time to enjoy it, and share it with her.

Formed in the bed of Fall Creek, near the pedestrian suspension bridge, there is a natural wading pool. It is not normally deep in summer, but if one happens to be less than mindful under certain conditions, the stream might carry them down toward the falls where it can be quite difficult to escape the currents. It is easy enough to reach this pool; on the southern side of the gorge there are steps leading down from the trail, not far from where there is access from University Ave, so students often swim there, although it is illegal. The university does everything it can to discourage it, and includes in its literature the fact that several people have perished there due to the unsafe conditions.

As Michelle reached the suspension bridge and began to cross it from the north, she heard voices — laughter — burbling up along with the sound of the water. She paused and looked down through the rods of the guardrail. There were people in the water, not surprising given the heat, but she thought the water must be freezing. Happy squeals echoed along the shale walls. One lanky boy, wearing Cornell running shorts, seemed to have had enough and was crossing the rocks toward the steps. A girl, in a cherry red bikini, was trying to gain her feet on the slimy surface, but another guy still in the water was pulling on her hand, laughing and teasing her, seemingly trying to pull her back in. Michelle thought she heard, amid the shrieks and giggles, the word 'wimp', and possibly a response of 'freak'. It made her smile to see their joy, their youthful abandon. Play, she thought, how do you play?

"Wait!" the guy shouted, but still grinning.

"No!" giggled his friend, wrenching her hand free. Not to be denied, he lunged upward, reaching again for her, his fingers catching on the strap of her bikini top, pulling it down, snapping it off, leaving her breasts bouncing free. She squealed, put her hands over her chest. He fell back, his head submerged in the shallow water.

"Hey!" she shouted. "Give it back!" The boy did not come up immediately. The red cups floated on the surface. Obeying an impulse, Michelle raced across the bridge and headed for the steps down to the water, her hand searching in her purse for her phone, thinking, he hit his head on a rock. She didn't see the boy emerge, laughing, still holding the top, observing his handiwork gleefully.

"Travis!" the girl bellowed.

"Travis!" Travis mocked. *Travis Demerest?* thought Michelle, having heard the name distinctly, twice.

"Fine! Keep it. Jerk off in it for all I care, you pervert," she declared, and picking up a towel, made her way out of the water. Michelle — still scrambling down the steps, her eyes focused on maintaining her footing, now beginning to realize she should stop because Travis was obviously fine, and she would just be embarrassing him — nearly bumped into the lanky boy. Water dripped from his clingy red shorts into his squelching flip-flops. His thin abdomen was stippled with goose pimples.

"Oh, sorry," she said, lifting her head. He nodded, stepped aside and continued on. She knew him. Where had she seen him before? His face had a gaunt appearance; he was unshaven, with light brown hair.

"Andreas, don't you want a towel?" asked the girl from several steps below, holding one up toward him. He didn't even turn around. Travis's roommate, Michelle thought, watching him climb away, his shoulders slumped and his head down. But I haven't met him, why is his face so familiar?

Meanwhile Travis's half naked friend had come storming up the steps, a towel draped over her shoulders, her breasts still slightly exposed. Michelle could not help but see them, they were right *there*, not small, yet standing high on her young chest, the nipples erect with the chill. The girl, perhaps seeing that Michelle was uncomfortable about it, made more of an effort to cover them with her towel. Travis came up behind them, grinning, clutching his red trophy, saying, "Dudes, wait up!" Then he saw and recognized Michelle, who had her mouth open again, as if words were on the way.

"Mrs. Wolcott! Hi!"

"Travis," she managed, now realizing that the girl whose bikini top Travis clutched was Leah Kampnich. "Say hello to your father for me," she muttered, then turned and scrambled back up the steps, while they continued to laugh, as if she were the one being ridiculous.

"Do you think she meant my father, or yours?" she heard Travis joke.

"Oh, give me my frickin' top, you pig," Leah giggled.

Michelle raced up the steps to University Ave in a sudden fury. "How *could* he?" she demanded aloud, grasping her neck, and again thought it, how could he! How could he choose that child, that *slut*, to... to... She's so damn *young*. But why would he want to paint *me* naked when he can paint *her*? Why did I have to run into them like that? She began to cry, cursing them all: Kyle, Leah, Travis; she was so jealous of them for having *fun* without her. Why did Lily have to move out of Demerest House in the first place? Why did the trail have to lead to the bridge? Why did Stephen have to work so hard? This spasm of imprecation was followed by tremendous guilt for blaming all these blameless people, for blaming Stephen for her misery.

There are no accidents, she reminded herself, walking quickly on, but what purpose could it serve, what could it do but bring pain? As the knot in her neck worsened the episode replayed in her mind; the giggles, the bikini top, the sudden fear for a stranger, her humiliating credulity, the awkward recognition, and her childish departure. And in the middle was the roommate, Andreas, walking away with deliberate, methodical movements. With *intention*, she realized, a dogged intention to separate himself from them. She felt a sudden kinship with him in his sorrow, from which arose an appalling empathetic insight: she knew there was no real reason for him to have left, that he was simply unable — no, *unwilling,* due to some misapplied rationale, some inculcated prejudgment — to connect to them. Had she done the same thing? Had she *chosen* to separate from people, from Marcia, from Linda, from Connie, from her ex-officemates... from *Stephen*?

The nausea and vertigo forced her to stop. She found herself at the top of Libe Slope, shaky and sweating, squinting at the glimmering blue lake, sensing the clock tower looming behind her, her head pounding. She sat on the grass, fighting it, breathing deeply. They came anyway, the other places, condensing into coherence, each striving to gain her attention, as if the act of perceiving them ratified their substance, as if choosing one would negate the others, congealing a single tangible world from the vestiges of all. There was the figure falling into the water, the man with the gun in the fog, the rain and the mourners in black, the baby crying out under the oak, the familiar floating face; each coalesced briefly as her focus flitted from them in turn, searching for the sunny slope and the lake which she knew, then doubted, then knew again was there beneath her feet.

22

OUT OF concern for his wife's wellbeing, Stephen invaded Michelle's privacy. It was not something he was proud of, infiltrating her email account, but ever since her previous difficulties with migraines, paranoia, and depression, it had seemed a necessary precaution. The doctor had agreed with him on this score at the time, though perhaps not in so many words. He had made some suggestion about becoming more 'involved' in his wife's day-to-day activities. She never knew of his oversight, of course, he was able to scrutinize her communications directly through the webmail server from his own, or any computer; it was an incredibly facile process, which required no specialized knowledge or hacking ability of any kind, yet she was unaware that such a thing was possible. That was one of the things he loved about Michelle, her innocence. She had absolutely no idea of the dangers; she could not fathom the complexities of systemic manipulation, and would never ascribe malicious forethought to the duplicitous convenience of the digital world.

Fortunately it had taken only a few minutes to determine her password, and she had neglected to change it over the years. It was sweet, really, and he drew an odd compunctious satisfaction from it each time he typed it in: *Auberge*, from the Auberge Saint Antoine where they had stayed in Quebec so many years ago. It reminded him how fortunate he was to have her, as well as how much care she required. He hadn't looked into her account in some time; until recently her mental state seemed to have stabilized. However, her behavior over the past few days had prompted him to perform this cursory investigation, in the off chance that something would reveal itself. Lily had said nothing on the matter, but what could she have noticed from Crestview?

There was little enough activity, which in itself was not a good sign, just a few inane comic forwards from her father, a number of newsletters and ads from her favorite online shops, and a lot of spam. Stephen opened the sent file. There, dated the evening before she had burst into tears in the middle of the night, was an email addressed to marshmellow99@uplink.net:

Marcia,
How're the kids? Stephen and I are great. Spring has finally arrived. Will you be coming to town this summer? We'd love to see you. Check out this guy's paintings, he's the one who rented Lily's place. Pretty outrageous. http://kylewestin.com. I'm going to pose for him. Miss you
Love, Michelle

* * *

"It was just so embarrassing," sighed Michelle, "I had to call Stephen. He came and took me home. He wanted to take me to urgent care but I convinced him it was heat related. I mean I told him it was a migraine, but that's all."

"You didn't mention the... places you were, the body in the water, the person falling, the baby?"

"Oh no, he would think I was nuts for sure."

212

Sam did not immediately respond, she simply continued to hold the pressure points with her fingertips; one hand beneath the thick hair, at the base of the skull, the other near the right shoulder blade. She wanted Michelle to let it go. Listening was important, reply enough to show concern, but not enough to encourage her to begin the cycle again, the doubts, the clutching. She had begun the session with Michelle on her stomach, knowing it was difficult for her to speak into the face pillow, hoping it would help her to quiet her mind.

"Maybe you're not giving him a chance."

"He would drag me to Dr. Wilson for a higher dose."

"Well. I'm not so sure that would serve you," agreed Sam. She reached over with one hand and tapped one of her favorite singing bowls with the mallet. Its resonance joined them; she felt it rising from the floor, up her spine, down her arms, hands, and into Michelle's back. She felt herself rising, riding the hum up out of her head, but Michelle was holding back. She could feel the pain, the fear at the coming transformation, resistance leading to pain, cycling into more fear, more resistance, more pain; contraction, diminution, a spiral of lowering vibration.

Sam could sense there others there, the helpers — Michelle's, in addition to her own. They were patient.

She shifted her right hand to the other shoulder blade, inhaling deeply, exhaling audibly, drawing the tension away, completing the circuit of energy, becoming an alternate conduit for the flow which Michelle's muscles had blocked, the tissues where she had stored her worries, her sorrow, her anger — her unused, unaccepted love.

"Michelle," she said softly, "I want you to relax now."

Michelle sighed, and let out a little sob. "I can't," she said. "I can't relax anymore. I'm just so out of whack. It feels like I'm not really here, or not *only* here. I feel like I'm losing it, like my mind has changed somehow. Like it's been yanked open or something."

Sam released the pressure points. Perhaps it was too harsh a tactic for the present. "Michelle, you're not crazy," she assured her, "Everyone goes through periods of crises."

"Sometimes I think that there is more than one *me* trying to use this body, you know? I just... sometimes it feels like someone else is in control."

Sam oiled her hands and began working the deltoids. "Have you ever heard the term *collective*?" she asked.

"No," Michelle replied. Sam continued the massage and gathered her thoughts.

"We make reference to something other than our bodies and call it spirit or soul because deep down we recognize that our beings don't end at the skin," Sam suggested, slipping her hands along Michelle's skin, working the right bicep, forearm, hand, fingers. "We *are* part of something bigger, whether you call it God or supreme intelligence, or..."

"You mean the collective unconscious? Well I've heard of that."

"Right. Exactly. But the universe is reciprocal, as above so below. Every truth is a paradox; its mirror image is also true. If you are part of something larger, something smaller must be part of you."

Sam inhaled deeply and began pushing on Michelle's gently rounded upper back, exhaling slowly, allowing the pressure to gradually increase, sliding down the ribs and spine, feeling the energy coursing into her, full and bright.

"Your soul is a collective, just as it in turn is part of an oversoul or archangel or whatever designation you favor, just as a family is a collective of the members of that family, but also a member of the clan. So it doesn't surprise me that sometimes you feel out of control. You are a component of greater beings, greater awarenesses, and as such you influence their activity, the course of their existence. Conversely, there are components of your consciousness influencing you, various spirits or energies, each with its mission or goal or desire, hoping to accomplish it through your body in this lifetime."

"Wait…"

"So a balance must be sought, as with a family, as with the chakras. Where there is not balance, when the goals of these entities don't coincide, there is anxiety, there is illness. One spirit may predominate for years, decades even, but eventually it must step aside to allow another to achieve its task. When properly balanced, the body behaves like a dynamo, a conductor, not a resistor."

Here I gave Sam pause. I thought it was ill considered, revealing so much of the nature of things: multiple components, migrating awareness, and the hierarchy of consciousness. Michelle's heart, if not her mind, I did not think prepared to assimilate it. Sam was certain that initiation was imminent; she wanted to go further, though I objected.

She wanted to explain that it is consciousness itself which keeps a body coherent, and breadth of awareness which determines the comprehensiveness of the body, that every named thing is a nexus in the sea of energy called the universe, that her body is a convergence which neither begins nor ends in itself, nor is discontinuous from any proximate nexus or wave or line of force, that each end of the individuation spectrum is identical because the flat line the mind pictures is in fact a multidimensional continuum with a center point simultaneously infinite and singular, which is God which is you.

215

I reminded her of the futility of words. Whether she was aware of my presence, I cannot say, you would have to ask her, however I will point out that she forthwith altered her approach, returning to the sage intention of quieting the mind.

"Okay, you can turn over now," Sam directed, holding the sheet up.

"But which one am I?" asked Michelle, meaning which spirit of the collective. There was a sound of desperation in her voice. Sam sounded the bowl again.

"All of them."

"Then why don't I feel in control?"

"Scoot down a little. Because you're blocking the flow of energy. You're resisting change. You're afraid of something."

"God, I think I'm afraid of everything."

"No," Sam chuckled. "I don't think so." She pulled Michelle's arms back behind her head, stretching the knitted muscles. Michelle exhaled, but there was still anxiety. She was still holding back.

"Can you tell me how long you have had this feeling, that someone else is in control?"

"It's not like it's all the time. I don't know, a few months. I guess since the Christmas party."

"Did anything unusual happen at the Christmas party?" There was something she wasn't telling her.

"Well we saw the fox," Michelle reminded her.

"Oh yes. Tell me again about the fox."

"It was just crossing the yard, we all saw it, but it stopped and looked right at me. Us. I don't know, maybe it was looking at a squirrel, or the lights on the tree, but I felt like it was looking right at me, trying to say something. I guess that sounds insane."

"Not at all," said Sam reassuringly.

"And what do you think the fox was trying to say?"

"I don't know," responded Michelle after a moment. She didn't want to talk anymore; she just wanted to lie there, being touched. "It seemed like an omen. But I felt I could trust him," she professed, "He was so beautiful."

I took a certain satisfaction in that, I admit, but did not hesitate to make full use of the opportunity, now that her defenses were down, thanks to Sam; I again entered from the left, while Sam was busy on the right. Michelle registered a strong sensation of warmth, but attributed it to the massage. I was brief, remaining only long enough to open certain channels, by inhibiting protective patterns, and exciting particular neurons to fire. The technique is simple but effective, and allows the subject to continue to presume autonomy.

"Well remember that beauty," Sam suggested, striking the bowl again. "Hold that feeling. Think of things that bring you joy. And let everything else go."

Samantha rang the bowl again, placed her hands on the top of Michelle's head and let it come — the healing power of acceptance. She surrendered to it, submitted to it, allowed it to gather and be drawn through her. While Michelle floated in somnolence, Sam allowed herself to know that deep well of longing which her friend would not speak of, the wishes she dared not hope for, and the sorrows she fed in the darkness. Sam felt them, and washed away their edges. She sounded a second bowl, allowed her chi to conform to its higher pitch, felt life coursing through her, filling her, overflowing into Michelle.

Sam's vibration rose, and came into the frequency of the radiance, the Light, the waves of love connecting all things, the glorious space, the ironically named dark matter which informs the integrity of the one organism, the living breathing universe.

Ripples of lambent electricity suffused her hands; golden light played in Michelle's luxuriant hair and flickered down her body. She accepted more, spread her awareness further, and saw them, hers and Michelle's; the thin, brilliant, fluxing forms of spirit, the helpers, or guides, or members of the collective.

"There is a child," Sam said, her voice quiet and hollow, "a boy, dark hair, here, now, lying on your belly. Waiting. You have known him before."

* * *

"Mr. Westin," Stephen said when the door finally opened, "Stephen Wolcott, your neighbor, next door?"

"Oh, yes, hi," Kyle said.

"I was wondering if I could have a few words, might I come in?"

"Uh…"

"Thank you," Stephen said, smiling that eyeless smile and stepping over the threshold. "How are you enjoying Demerest House?" Kyle closed the door and faced his guest, who was a few inches taller. He was dressed in an expensive grey suit, possibly silk, likely Italian, yet it looked on Wolcott like it was made of titanium or platinum, as if the cloth itself were afraid to wrinkle or even bend. Kyle was in his paint clothes, barefoot.

"I'm enjoying it very much," Kyle answered.

"Lot of memories here, it's a fine old home," Stephen said, stepping across the entrance hall, casually eyeing the two paintings of Kyle's which hung there. "Designed by Albert Whitly, you know. Went on to work for the Vanderbilts I believe, or was it J.P. Morgan?"

"Well I try to keep it as I found it, I know Lily cherished every inch of it, I have no intention of ruffling any feathers."

"Good. Good. These are… interesting. Your work I take it?"

"Yes."

"Tell me something Kyle, can I call you Kyle? Are all your paintings this… explicit?"

"What can I do for you, Mr. Wolcott?" Kyle asked, his expression turning dark.

"Please, call me Stephen. I understand you're painting a picture of my wife," he said.

"Well, yes and no, it's not a portrait, I'm just using Michelle's hair for a figure, one of several in the painting. It's not just a picture of her."

"Yes, well…" Stephen said, waving Kyle's comment off with a flick of his hand, setting his other hand firmly on the artist's shoulder, "In any case, I'd like to buy the painting."

"Oh? But you don't even know what it is, what it's about."

"What is it about, Kyle?"

"I'm afraid I don't normally discuss works in progress, Mr. Wolcott."

"And why is that?"

"Because it interferes with the creative process. Even discussing the painting this much may affect the finished product."

"Oh, I should hope so," Stephen said, strolling casually across the floor to the foot of the magnificent staircase. "Kyle, do you think I could see the painting?"

"I'm afraid I don't show works in progress."

"Because it interferes... yes. What if I pay for it in advance, Kyle?" the professor said, pulling a check from his inside jacket pocket. "Could I see it then?"

"No."

Stephen smiled, made another dismissive gesture.

"No matter. I'm going to give you this check Kyle, for $15,000. I happen to know you've never sold a painting for more than $20,000, and since there's no commission involved here, I think a twenty-five percent discount is more than fair. Don't you agree?"

The 'B' of bastard formed on Kyle's lips; he was used to saying what was on his mind, and he was angry, for a moment. He almost yanked on that slick silk tie, almost launched into a tirade of the many reasons he did not deserve Michelle, almost threw the arrogant prick out on his boney ass. But he realized that was exactly what the jackass wanted, confirmation of his moral superiority. The moment passed. He could think of no way to refuse without somehow hurting Michelle. And what did he really know about their relationship? Perhaps *he* had reason to be angry. Perhaps he meant no offense at all; perhaps his patronizing manner was so inherent he could not help it. Was it not a compliment to both him and Michelle that the man was willing to pay $15,000 for a painting not yet complete? Then again, maybe Michelle had asked him to buy it.

"It won't be done for at least two weeks," Kyle said.

"No hurry," Stephen said, setting the check on the banister, "And that will include the copyright of course."

"It will still be included in any catalogues of my work," the artist advised.

"Of course. Thank you for your time. I'll be in touch."

23

HER experience with Sam had left Michelle more anxious than before. What was she to make of this *certainty,* 'there is a child, you have known him before'? At first it had felt like an incredible gift, it had brought immediacy to her most heart felt desire. This is what the fox had promised, she thought, this is what she had been resisting, and her resistance, her determination to stand by the premarital agreement with Stephen *not* to have children is what had brought about the migraines. But the joy of this epiphany had faded and turned to frustration. She still had no idea how to change Stephen's mind. If Stephen thought for a moment that Sam had anything to do with it, he would flip out. He would lose all respect for her, accuse her of superstition, and take her back to Dr. Wilson.

Naturally her mind sought alternatives. She had spent much of her time daydreaming about Kyle, and how things might have been different for her if she had married a different man. She had been too embarrassed to tell Sam about posing for him and the attempted kiss, or that she was jealous of Leah and Erin; she had even failed to acknowledge to Sam or herself that Kyle's arrival at the Christmas party had meant more to her than the appearance of the fox. She had been ashamed, but that shame had faded, as if her interest in Kyle had been sanctioned or offset by the reflection of her yearning in the child spirit Sam had seen. Sam had said it was something she had agreed to do in this life. It was as much a contract as her gentleman's agreement with Stephen. She had to find a way to convince him.

Stephen had left early that morning to take part in the commencement ceremonies. Michelle wandered the garden and yard, listening for the sounds of bansuri, tambura, and tabla. For the first time in weeks she heard nothing, which meant Kyle was either not home, or he was done with the painting. In any event, she was determined to see it.

She ducked behind the plum trees and walked nonchalantly along the front of Demerest House, looking to see if anyone were coming down the road. Having verified she was unseen, she quickly crossed the portico, glared right back at the brass lion knocker as she slipped inside, and made her way noiselessly up the stairs.

Only as she entered the studio did Michelle quietly call "Kyle? Hello?" She heard no answer. The room was dim, the lights were off, the west window blinds were down, and a huge canvas propped on two easels effectively blocked the French doors to the balcony. As she approached it, Michelle realized she wouldn't have been able to reach the top without a step stool, and it must have been ten feet in length. She couldn't imagine trying to paint such a large image. Stepping all the way back to the glass doors in order to try and take it in, she turned and regarded the work. It was not at all what she had expected.

It was a twilight scene, rendered in subdued tones. A band of pale blue crossed the horizon, gradually darkening to star-speckled indigo at the top of the painting. The bottom half of the canvas was shadowy foliage and rocky earth; a grey brown pathway wound its way here and there. In the background, small and far away, were several dozen nude figures, men and women, each bearing a torch, walking in single file right to left along the path. This procession progressed up a hill on the left of the painting. On top of this hill was a sort of pool or fountainhead encircled with a natural looking rock wall, from which an eerie luminous vapor arose. All of the people walking up the hill looked young, fit, healthy, and happy; they carried lit torches whose light formed little circles against the dusky landscape. Those walking down the hill (and these were more in the foreground, so larger and more clearly painted) either had no torch, or were dragging them along the ground. They looked ashen, wrinkled, sorrowful, or diseased.

At the crest of the hill a woman was in the act of dipping her torch into the water, dousing its flame. The man standing behind her had a look of panic on his face, as if he had just realized what was happening. It was clear that the entire procession would file past the pool and one by one put out their torches, as if doomed or coerced to do so. In the very center of the canvas was a man who seemed to be bounding away from the pool, and toward the viewer. He was dimly painted, a dogged expression showed on his unshaven face, in his hand was an extinguished torch that he held extended, as if reaching.

The right side of the painting was dominated by a woman, much closer to the viewer than the pool and its hilltop, so close that her feet did not show, she was larger than life-size, the absolute focal point of the piece. Her long, full hair glowed with a shimmering gold aura, as bright or brighter than any of the torches the other figures bore; she was her own source of light. Her hand rested lightly against her throat, as if she were lost in thought, but her eyes looked directly out at the viewer. It was apparent that the dogged man with his darkened torch outstretched was running toward this dazzling woman.

Clearly the woman was Michelle, and she winced to see herself that large, that exposed. It was astonishing; she was thrown by seeing her face reversed from the normal mirror image she was used

225

to, as if the woman were her opposite, her 'other', existing in polar mental states. It was her and not her, was this how people saw her?

In truth, Michelle noted very little about the painting except that the woman, she, looked *fat*. It was all horrifyingly there, her inelegant breasts, her protruding stomach, her lumpy hips and knobby knees, her unsightly bulges captured for all time. She had never been so mortified.

"What do think?" Kyle asked. Michelle gasped, twitched with surprise, and stood quivering in emotional turmoil and adrenaline. Now she saw the artist, off in the left corner of the room, laying on a sheet-less rollaway bed, wearing nothing but spattered orange boxer shorts.

"It's called *Re-ignition*."

His eyes were puffy and his hair was sticking up stiffly as if he had been sleeping. His shoulders, arms and chest looked large to her; Stephen was not as muscular. All this bare skin, including the soles of his feet, bore specks and smears of paint. She was exasperatingly attracted to his unguarded, laid-back demeanor, his comfortable sensuality. She wanted to let herself love him, but he had rejected her, and the way he had portrayed her made it clear why.

"I'm not that fat," she said coldly, "And if you had only asked, you could have seen for yourself." Then she stormed out of the room, tears welling up in her angry eyes.

"Michelle, wait!" he called, clambering after her. "It's not a portrait!" She scampered down the stairs; he slid down the elegant mahogany banister in his paint smeared boxers, raced in front of her, stood before the front door. "I'm sorry, but I'm sure I said before, I never intended it to be a portrait." For just a moment she let herself look at him, into his deep green eyes, she let herself feel the alignment, the gentle kindness there, and the gnosis of her dream resurfaced, the lure of lust fulfilled; but she would not lose control, she would not be rejected again. The desire she was so afraid of turned her on her heel. Being familiar with the house she headed towards the side door by the garage, too proud and scared now to be swayed by the truth of what he said, of what she felt.

"Don't go," he said, chasing her through the kitchen, "It's not really meant to be you, I just needed your hair. I wasn't even going to use your face…" he continued, but Michelle had evaded him, and the door closed on the end of his sentence: "until he paid for it." He let her go, watching, through the thick beveled glass of the door, the lilt of her hips swinging down the drive.

* * *

"Just fuck me, you son of a bitch!" Michelle shouted, her voice cracking, her hands slapping his chest. Stephen held her wrists, an astounded, helpless look on his face; he had never heard her utter such words, let alone *at* him. She collapsed onto him with a sort of anguished growl, and began to sob.

She had been waiting in bed for him, she had gone to his study with a glass of champagne for him, had gone in her sexy red teddy and sat in his lap and kissed him, beckoning him to bed. 'Give me two secs to finish up here, Munchkin,' he had said; she and the moon had waited a full half hour. He seemed interested then, he had disrobed quickly, smiled, climbed into the bed and put his arm around her. She had clamped her legs about him, she had kissed him passionately, she had opened her heart to him, then he had asked, 'Do you have your diaphragm?'

Now she felt like a monster, as if some creature, some succubus had possessed her body and beat her husband.

227

"Oh God," she wailed, "I'm sorry. I'm so sorry, Stephen. I don't know what's wrong with me, I... I just don't know why you can't understand! Why can't you put yourself in my shoes for five minutes?" she pleaded, searching his eyes for some recognition of her soul's plight, and finding none. For whatever the reason, he could not understand, he had no idea why she was crying, what her pain arose from; she would have to spell it out for him.

"I don't want to die without having a baby!" she sputtered, then sighed, "Oh never mind," and threw herself back down on her pillow, mumbling, "I'm sorry." He stared at her with his gunmetal eyes, *considering*, the way he always did before he spoke, considering what he should *say* that he feels before he allows himself to feel it, she thought.

"No. *I'm* sorry. I didn't realize you would be unable to conqu... I didn't know it would mean so much to you."

"Well neither did I," she confessed. They had had this conversation before, or some milder version of it, in which he forever ascribed her general 'neediness' to the steady ticking of her biological clock. *Baby fever*, he called it, like it was a disease, like it was somehow wrong to create life from love. Michelle had submitted to his judgment, her tactic had been to simply ignore the ticking; now she felt like she was hearing a countdown, and only seconds remained before she would explode.

Stephen gently stroked her brow, but she flinched at his touch.

"Perhaps it would be helpful if you saw Doctor Wilson, he could adjust your dosage."

"Oh fuck you, Stephen, fuck you! I don't need a doctor; I don't want any more fucking drugs. I need love! Is that crazy? I want a baby! Does that make me sick? How hard is it to understand, how can you not want me to have your child?"

He sat there in the bed, his boney knees pointing at her, the calculation showing on his brow, though he did his best to hide it. At least she had succeeded in wiping that glib smile off his face. Before he could respond, she stated with incontrovertible gravity, "If you love me, you'll make me pregnant."

He looked dismayed. She suddenly felt, for the first time ever, that she had the upper hand; that maybe, just maybe, he was going to *give*.

"Well, perhaps we could consider adoption," he finally said, and she recognized it as a great concession. She had begged him to adopt many times before, since his argument had always been the 'cruelty' of bringing another life into the world — get one that was already here. She would take care of it by herself, completely, she had said, he needn't be bothered at all. *Naïve* he had called her — she had no conception of the responsibilities and risks involved, or she would not have broached the subject. Children were not toys one picked up at the mall like a new set of luggage, they were a twenty-four seven commitment, he was not prepared to attach himself to any such encumbrances, his current slate of obligations simply did not allow it, nor would it for the foreseeable future. One did not have a child for fun; had she thought about a dog, he had wanted to know. Of course she had been made to see he was right, Stephen was always right, he could always fit your truth into his, like an artist working with found objects. But each of his chosen words was a wound, planted firmly in her memory like thorns, and when she stepped on them they fed a certain creature which part of her battled with behind her mind and here, now, that creature, that *other* had come to the fore, was running the show, and saw its opponent on the ropes.

"No, I want to be pregnant, damn you, don't you get it? It's what people *do,* it's what I'm *made* for, it's what you're made for;

it's why we're here! I want to have *your* baby Stephen, why won't you do this for me?" she shouted, and reached for him. He looked crestfallen, defeated. Part of her hated to have hurt him this way, to impugn his love, but another part felt triumph within reach. Yes, she wanted a child for herself, but she refused to judge this as a selfish act; did not the self include those who came before and those who would come after? Was she not more than one body; was she not her family, her nation, her species? Did not Paul deserve a chance to be born? She would not back down, she could not; coming to grips with this had been too costly for her to quit now.

"I can't, Michelle. I've had a vasectomy."

"What?" She was stunned. "When?"

"Several years ago," he admitted.

"Without telling me? Without asking me? When was this? Why didn't you tell me?"

"It was a long time ago, sweetheart. But listen, we will look into adoption, all right? First thing tomorrow, I'll..."

"How long ago Stephen, how long have you been making me shove that stupid diaphragm up here for no reason?" she demanded, palming her crotch, rising up and out of the bed. "Why didn't you tell me, you bastard? Why the hell would you do that and not even tell me?"

"Because I love you," he shouted, "because I didn't want to upset you." Michelle grabbed her robe, put it on and headed out of the room.

"Munchkin, please, come back to bed. Let's talk about this," he suggested, rising, taking her arm. She slapped him as hard as she could.

"Stay away from me you fucker!" she screamed, grasping the doorknob, turning back to snarl through clenched teeth, "I'm sleeping downstairs, you just stay the hell away from me!" and she slammed the door, hoping he would not follow. She went down to her office, grabbed her keys, her wallet, her laptop, and a pair of sandals. In the laundry room she pulled a dirty yellow sundress out of the basket and threw it on. She went to the garage and got in the sedan, but decided she didn't want the noise to alert him that she was leaving the house. She didn't want him coming after her; she didn't *know* him anymore. She didn't want to be reasoned with or made up to or otherwise pursued, she just wanted him to leave her alone. So she got out of her car and quietly left on foot, through the side door.

24

JESUS, what am I doing, Michelle wondered, I don't even know where the hell I'm going. How could he have lied to me all this time? How could he have made that decision without me? What's happened to us?

A light summer drizzle was falling. Her eyes blurred with tears and raindrops. The dark wet roads were smeared with white streaks of reflected street lamps. Her mind filed through the years, trying to identify a turning point, some milestone she could grasp and say, this is when he stopped loving me; this is when his heart closed to me. Had he ever loved her, or was their entire relationship based on one moment of their lives, that first weekend in Quebec, that one evening of beatific mutual sentience?

I can't stand to think of him right now, she thought, I won't be able to see him again, to look him in the eye without hating him. How could he have done so much for me, yet not do the one thing I wanted, needed; how could he be so stupid? He never respected me; never saw me as a person. How can I ever forgive him? What the hell am I going to do now, a fat cow like me?

"Son of a bitch goddamn fucking liar," she swore, trying to spit him out of her head. Her mind returned to the other man who'd been consuming her thoughts for weeks, but found little satisfaction.

How did Kyle know that's what my boobs look like, she wondered, how did he know that's where my hips bulge? If he didn't intend it to look like my body, why was it so similar? Am I really that fat? No. I should have shown him. I could have, wearing that dress. I could have flashed him, just pulled it up, to prove I'm *not that fat*. What if I had grabbed him, there on that rollaway, what would have happened, would he have even touched me? At least he likes my hair. Stephen never said anything about my hair, or any part of me, really. He used to say I looked nice, or spectacular, if we dressed up for some function, but not in years. When did he stop wanting me? Did he ever want me?

"Fucking son of a bitch," she sobbed.

* * *

On her knees by the little twin bed in her Crestview apartment, Lily was lost in prayer. She had attended to all the flowers in her garden, sent her love and blessings to all the people who made up the collective family of her heart, praised God and Jesus with glowing, sincere gratitude, and shared a smile with Halcomb. Then, eyes still closed, hands still clasped, she received a very strong gift, a vision almost. She was given a picture of dear, sweet Michelle, out in the rain, alone, frightened, and full of sorrow. And she was made to feel that Michelle was afraid of her husband.

The day before, Michelle had left a message on her machine, suggesting they get together for lunch. Lily had been out of town and had not been able to get back to her yet. She tried to recall if there had been any distress in Michelle's voice. These feelings, this vision, moved her very much, but she knew there was nothing for her to do at the moment. She had learned the hard way that you cannot approach someone; they must approach you. You cannot say, I have received the gift of your pain, I have been made aware in prayer; you cannot help someone who thinks you're loony. You cannot call in the middle of the night, wake someone, and ask, are you all right, Jesus told me to help you, or, I had a bad dream and in it you were crying. She would call first thing in the morning, they would get together, and perhaps then she could help. Surely there was nothing to fear from Stephen.

* * *

Despite the late hour, Michelle rapped loudly on the door. It was quite dark inside. No one came. She had walked without purpose for several blocks, and then realized she was nearing Linn St. It was the perfect solution; Sam would take her in, let her spend the night — probably let her stay as long as she wanted, knowing Sam. She tried again, sure she would be forgiven for waking her, but Sam did not appear. The neighbor's dog barked. Her car was in the drive. It made no sense at all. Why the hell didn't I bring my phone, she cursed. It was in the car with her keys, laptop and wallet. Michelle looked up at the second story, trying to guess which window might be Sam's bedroom, wondering if she could toss a pebble like they did in the movies. She rapped a third time, looked to see if a light went on upstairs. No Sam. She felt something furry brush against her wet bare leg, and heard a pathetic mew.

"What are you doing out here in the rain, Mouchey?" she whispered. The cat put her paw on the door, fully expecting the human to open it and let her in out of the rain. Michelle tried the door, but it was locked.

235

"Where's your mommy, puss?" She bent down to pick Scaramouche up, but the cat ran off. Michelle stood there on the concrete step, water splashing on her as it dripped off the eaves, wondering where on earth Sam could be, and feeling utterly alone.

What she could not understand, what few would ever understand, was that 'Samantha' was with me. Us. She reached out to comfort Michelle, and began to realize the difficulties of trans-dimensional massage. We laughed. Poor Michelle could not perceive the cycle *in toto* as we could. The challenging compression phase was nearing completion, but she had no way of knowing that.

After a time Michelle wandered away from the Healing Room, back the way she had come, to the end of Linn St., then up University Ave. She was tired now. The adrenaline had worn off. Still, she couldn't bear the idea of going back to that house, back to that *liar*. Their entire life had been a lie, what was left for her? What point could there possibly be in continuing, just getting older and older, becoming less desirable, less needed, less, less, less. It was too late, she would never have a child, she didn't deserve one, she had failed some test, had broken some vow by keeping to her agreement with that bastard. Sam was gone and with her the child she had seen. Of course it was impossible; she did not deserve happiness. Her childless marriage to Stephen was a punishment for some unfathomable offense, she didn't know what, but if there had been no transgression there could be no retribution; the pain was real and so her guilt must be severe. She did not deserve happiness.

As she passed the towering Johnson Museum, feeling there was nowhere left to turn, she saw the opening in the trees, and the pole light illuminating the steps which led down to the gorge trail. Some memory of peace remained associated with walking there; she went to it and began her descent. It was dark, but the light of the footbridge was not far off. It drew her on under the dripping branches, along the muddy trail. She was soaked through, her feet were sliding in her sandals, and her hair was clinging flatly to her neck, which began to tighten up from the chill.

Beneath the fuzzy glow of the tower lamps, in the gathering fog, she stood staring down into the gorge. Here and there dull gleams blinked in the black where the movement of the water managed to refract what little light reached the creek. Is there someone there, she wondered, some being down in the dark looking back at me? She placed one foot on the crossbar and lifted herself, leaning her head over the railing. Did she have significance to the *kami;* was there something she could do for this spirit, could a connection be made, would she be welcomed? The dim light, the mounting vertigo, the rain and fog, played with her depth perception. It didn't seem so far to the bottom. It would be okay, she thought, preferable even; she wouldn't be alone. She could feel positive about it, and that was the important thing, right? It seemed, at that moment, that it would be a movement forward in the progression of her spirit, a way to make contact with a larger realm.

As she lifted her other foot off the concrete deck, she thought she heard something. It resonated in her chest first, then came echoing down the hills toward her, borne on the wind; the plaintive sound of a child's voice calling *Mama,* and again, *Mama.* An involuntary cry escaped Michelle's lips in response; her arms trembled. She scanned the dark watercourse for a hint of movement, certain a child was lost and alone. The haunting call came again: *Mama, Mama.* With tears rolling down her cheeks, Michelle crossed the bridge and stumbled along the trail, searching everywhere, her eyes wide and desperate for light, her ears waiting to hear the child's cry again, hearing instead echoes of owls and frogs and scuffling in the bushes.

Dizzily she slipped to the ground, battling nausea, double vision, panic, and crushing pain. Competing images emerged, dissolved and confounded her. She saw the figure falling, men and women running on the trail, Sam rubbing her feet, Kyle's head floating; all juxtaposed with the face of a baby crying — *her* baby. With her head cradled between her hands and her eyes clamped shut, Michelle whimpered, wanting the quiet trail to return, then needing, pleading for just one of the worlds to fully constitute itself, no matter which time or place, so long as there was only one, so long as the terrifying disparateness stopped, please God. Slowly focus was restored, a singular vision: a fall day, dry leaves under the oak, the baby's cry fading away, the buckskin flapping against her legs, the pain in her belly, in her heart, tears dripping down her face as she ran.

Night creatures cringed at the sound of her wailing. We remained nearby until that with which she was familiar condensed again, and she was able to resume control of the body, and regain her feet. In this I assisted. It was not my intent to push her out, but to fortify, clarify, and guide her footsteps. I was never so much *in* her as along side, adjacent, concurrent.

* * *

The street was silent, the house completely dark; a trio of deer blinked their red eyes at Michelle across the shadowy lawn, iridescent with the dew. She tried the door, it was unlocked, the knob turned, but the warm rain had left the old wood swollen and tight. Forcing it would be noisy, yet she couldn't stand outside all night.

238

Gently she leaned in and pushed with her legs, it popped open with a dull thrum, the outer screen door answering with a metallic tink as she lurched forward and it slapped her calves. Slowly, cautiously, she crept in, holding the screen so it wouldn't slam, leaving the wood door out of the jamb instead of shoving it completely shut. Wet through and cold, her head pounding, her stomach shaking with anxiety, anger, and sorrow, she stood listening for movement in the house, and heard none.

What am I doing here, she wondered. She had followed the fox. It had been there when she opened her eyes, when the migraine eased, just standing there, watching her, it's white chest and gleaming eyes showing in the darkness. Then it went away down the trail, and crossed the bridge. She followed, knowing she should, not knowing how or why she knew, but trusting, too tired to doubt. Then it had been obvious — because the door would be unlocked, because it would be safe.

Only after she was inside did Michelle begin to question her actions, but it was so good to be out of the rain. After leaving her shoes by the door, she stole through the kitchen and dining room, dripping on the dusty wooden floor. Silently she crossed the dark entrance hall, glad it was clear of obstacles, and entered the living room, where she thought she might be able to spend the rest of the night, on the loveseat. She peeled off the soaked sundress; it dropped with a squish on the floor. She was about to sit down when the overhead light in the entrance hall went on.

Kyle appeared in the doorway, looking in, wearing only those orange boxers, concern on his face. Can he even see me, she wondered momentarily, for his face was in shadow, and she stood just outside the trapezoid of light, which had revealed the trail of her wet footprints. But of course he could see her, she realized, just as she could now see the two lurid paintings hanging on either side of the door, their vague figures distinct enough to convey the eroticism intended, visible enough to make her ashamed that her real naked body did not conform to this artistic ideal. She crossed her arms over her chest, not knowing what to say, how to excuse herself, her intrusion, her nudity, her need.

"Michelle," came his quiet voice out of the dark, "are you okay?" The sound of her name in his mouth, the kindness with which it was uttered, dissolved the resentment she had felt about the painting.

"I'm not that fat!" she protested, uncrossing her arms and throwing her hands up momentarily as if to prove it, then crossing them tightly over her breasts again.

"No, of course not," he said, stepping through the lit space without haste, reaching out, wrapping his warm, heavy arms around her chilled flesh. She sank into his chest, letting her weight sag into him, fighting back the tears, smelling his smell of paint and sweat. He stroked her hair, rocking her gently back and forth.

"You know, Michelle," he whispered, that sympathetic resonance filling her head, "the woman in the painting is not fat; she's pregnant."

25

DR. STEPHEN J. Wolcott III, professor, advisor, consultant, seated at his beautifully crafted Georgian pedestal desk in his private study, was unable to concentrate. He had not slept well. He had waited, expecting Michelle to come back to bed. He had been fully prepared to offer forgiveness. Her anger was understandable, given the circumstances. He had dozed, waking periodically to find her still absent. It soon became apparent she intended to spend the entire night in another room of the house. This was, as far as he could recall, a first in their marriage, but he had felt certain that crowding her at that juncture would be imprudent. Finally succumbing to deep sleep, Stephen woke late, dressed, and went downstairs. Michelle had not yet risen, which he ascribed to the same lack of sleep he had suffered. After such an emotional outburst, it was only natural. He had decided to let her sleep, had made his own coffee, and came into the study to get a start on the day. In that way he might make more room in his schedule, free up some time to speak with his wife, when she was ready. He might even begin looking into the adoption question, if he had time.

Now it was eleven o'clock. He went to her little office. She wasn't there, and it didn't look like she had slept there. He passed through the kitchen, dining room, and parlor, then went upstairs and opened the guest bedrooms. Those beds had not been disturbed either.

"Michelle?" he called, heading back through to the master bath. She was not there.

"Michelle?" he repeated, returning downstairs, checking the kitchen again. He opened the garage door. Both vehicles were present.

He called her cell, but there was no answer. He accessed her email, but found nothing of significance. He briefly looked for her laptop, in hopes it might offer some indication of where she had gone, but couldn't find it, and stood there in her office, thinking, noticing with irritation that she had left those blinds wide open, when she knew he preferred them closed, and he went to close them, even though it was an incredibly foggy day, and no one could possibly see in. That's when it hit him, where she might have gone. He had not thought her capable of it, and realized, for the first time in his life, that he might be guilty of arrogance.

Stephen returned to his study, where he located a phone number for Kyle Westin with a few clicks of the mouse. He called the number, Kyle did not pick up. He then unlocked and opened the lowest desk drawer to his right, removing from it a pistol and a pair of thin leather gloves. After checking the clip and making sure the safety was on, relocked the drawer, shut down the computer, and stood. The pistol he slipped into the waist of his trousers, then he donned his suit coat, the gloves, and left the house via the back door.

The fog was so thick he could barely see across the yard. Perfect, he thought, for it seemed prudent to enter Demerest House quietly and perform a cursory search. Avoiding the street, he slipped quickly through the wooded area into Lily's garden, approaching from the rear, up the broad terrace steps. After peering through the

French doors and finding the rooms uninhabited, he selected a key (obtained many years previously) from his ring, inserted it, and found upon turning it that the door had not been locked at all. He allowed himself a slight snort of contempt as he carefully wiped his feet on the mat and stepped into the family room, closing the door behind him.

From here Stephen stole along a hallway, quietly checking the unused rooms, and thereby came into the entrance hall, passing by the side of the elaborate staircase. He still hadn't heard a sound from the rest of the house. As Stephen passed the hall tree and neared the front door, he peered into the drawing room. There was a sofa, a lamp, and dull light coming through the curtains. He noticed feminine footprints in the dust, a wet spot on the floor, he felt the cushions; they were damp. He could imagine her there where she must have lain, his wife, his Michelle, her beautiful hair, darkened by the rain, spread out above her head, that sleazy man's dirty hands on her. His jaw tightened.

Quickly now he went up the stairs, scanned the studio, cleared the master bedroom, and then stormed up past the oriel window, its impressive view blocked by the fog. He checked the small rooms there on the third floor, once servants' rooms, now vacant except for haphazardly hung, immodest images designed to inflame and consume. Convinced there was no one in the house, he descended the stairs, walked through the kitchen and opened the door to the garage. One side was occupied by a van which looked about thirty years old and was painted flat grey, the rest of the space was stacked with flat packing crates such as would accommodate large paintings. The concrete was dry. Could that be his only car, Stephen wondered, unable to recall any other vehicle coming or going, and the grey van only rarely. Stephen retreated, exiting the house through the dining room's elegant doors.

* * *

As Stephen crossed into his own backyard, he noticed there were other dark footprints in the pale dew-wet grass, two sets side by side, crossing from Demerest House through his lawn to the street. He also noticed a blue Volvo in his drive, no one inside it. Quietly, he entered the garage and opened the big door.

"Lily," he then called, walking around toward the front of the house as she, having received no answer at the door, was making her way back to the car. Two paces behind her was Richard Cole.

"There you are," she said.

"I was just leaving. Is there something I can do for you? Hello, Richard."

"Good Morning."

"Well I wanted to talk to Michelle, is she still asleep?"

"I have no idea. I was about to call you, actually; we had a bit of a misunderstanding last night. Apparently she was more upset than I thought, and now I have no idea *where* she is. I was hoping you might know. I thought perhaps she went to see you."

"No," Lily said, "I haven't seen her in a couple of weeks." She considered relating the prayer vision; Michelle out in the rain, and that poignant feeling of sorrow, but she couldn't quite trust him just then. It seemed *he* was the trouble his wife was in somehow. Why, she wondered, on such a warm summer morning, did he have a pair of dress gloves in his hand?

"She left me a message yesterday," Lily revealed, "and I couldn't get back to her until this morning. I've tried her cell phone, but no answer."

"Yes, I've been trying too. Perhaps her battery has run down."

"Have you tried her father in Clarkdale?"

"No I haven't, Richard, not yet. She's not close with the old man, and her car is still in the garage."

"Oh, I see," he replied, then mumbled to Lily, "So she really was out in the rain."

"A misunderstanding about what?" Lily was bold enough to ask.

"I'd rather not say," Stephen replied, glancing Richard's way, "but I believe you are aware of some of our... issues."

"Yes," admitted Lily, and felt she could assume they had argued about children again. She had never understood his hesitancy on that score. She wanted to respect his choices, and his privacy, but she also wanted to warn him.

"If you don't bend a little, you're going to lose her," she said quietly. Richard took a step back, studied his shoes and feigned deafness. Stephen's face reddened, his glib smile curled toward a sneer.

"I had every intention of *bending* this morning. But if she doesn't have the decency to keep me informed of her whereabouts, I..."

"And you don't have any idea where she might have gone?" Lily pressed.

"I'm afraid I don't, do you?"

"No," Lily lied, "Perhaps Linda Morse would know. I think I have her number."

"That would be very helpful, Lily. Do call if you hear from her, won't you?" Stephen requested, "I really need to speak to her, I'm afraid I owe her an apology. I've got to go now, something's come up." With that he strode into the garage and got into his SUV. Lily and Richard returned to the Volvo, backed out of the driveway and continued along Fall Creek Drive.

"Go around the block," she instructed him.

"What?"

"Is he behind us? Just circle back around."

"Lily, what's going on?"

"Please Richard, I think I may know where she is."

As instructed, he turned and wound through to approach the street as they had a few minutes before. Lily checked behind to be certain Stephen turned toward campus.

"Turn here," she said, indicating the drive of Demerest House.

"Lily, what on earth?"

"I'll only be a moment, Richard, either way." She hustled up the portico steps and smacked the brass lion in the mouth with his own bit, something she had not done in close to seventy years. She half expected Halcomb's mother to open the door. No one answered. She still possessed the key of course, and as landlord, the legal right to enter, but she never dreamed of it. If Michelle were there, she might well be indisposed. She knocked a second time, listened for activity, heard none, and returned to the car.

"Oh well," she sighed, "It was just a hunch."

"You think Michelle and the artist…"

"It's not as though I have good reason. Just the way she looked at him."

"That's as reliable a reason as any, I'd say. Now what, call Linda Morse I suppose?"

"Yes. But you drive," Lily replied, taking a battered address book from her purse.

"Where to?"

"Linn Street."

26

KYLE'S head seemed removed from his neck, as if floating free on the gentle black ripples. Did she look the same to him? She felt an ethereal connection, as if their bodies made no difference whatsoever, yet she had never felt such strong desire. His chin just touched the mirrored surface; beads of water adorned his beard and dripped from his thick eyebrows. Those dark green eyes held her motionless.

"Happy?" he asked.

"Yes," she replied, grinning, amazed that she was still breathing, that one could survive so much change in so little time, that the world had not collapsed on itself in violent cataclysm, and that the gorge walls above them were in fact still standing. It seemed so easy now, she had simply asked, and love appeared. Why had she been so afraid for so long?

They had spent the night making love on the sofa in the drawing room, kissing, caressing, exploring like virgins, hugging when too spent for anything more, dozing in each other's arms. She had awoken lighthearted, irrepressible, and eager. She wanted to celebrate; she wanted to *play*. Seeing the thick veil of fog outside, she had been immediately inspired. 'Let's go skinny-dipping,' she had said. The gamut of Stephen's responses to such a suggestion could never have included *yes*.

Gerald R. Stanek

Like naughty children they snuck along the trail and crossed the bridge. The fog made everything perfect, there was something sacred about it, to them, tempting the abyss, stepping out into the void without being able to see the other side; a test of faith, a testimony to the strength of this new love. With Kyle she could face the dizzying spell of the mutable worlds. He would be there supporting her, should a migraine surface.

Holding hands, they went down the slick stone steps toward the water, now solemn, now gleeful, pushing through wet ferns and mud puddles, the trees dripping tears of joy on their heads. In the fog she felt free to be absurdly silly or incredibly loving without fear of being seen and derided or scolded. As if sloughing old skin, they disrobed with ritual slowness on the bare rock, and stood touching, looking, laughing. At first the water took her breath away, but the cold revived her, restored her, it was an elixir for her soul, like a baptism. She realized she was being given a chance to begin anew, to be a different person.

Her hands slid down to his waist. She gripped him tightly, as if to verify that he was real and would not dissolve away from her like some of the places she had seen, like the elusive fox, like the baby under the tree. She felt incredibly grateful to him, as though she could never repay him for appearing in her life. Why is he being so good to me, she wondered, why should *he* love *me*? And then she saw it, and her eyes went wide with wonder.

"There's light all around you," she observed, and a frisson of energy coursed through her spine.

We smiled, Samantha and I. It is always heartwarming to share that moment, when the blind begin to see, when the initiate recognizes that en*light*enment is literal.

250

"In this fog?" Kyle chuckled, "What are you talking about?"

"You're an angel," she said earnestly, marveling at the corona she perceived illuminating his head, at the power, and the love he emitted.

"Oh, *that* light," he said, understanding her. He knew of the radiance, and he knew that her seeing it now had nothing to do with him or his spirit, and everything to do with her open heart.

"Well don't let the wings fool you," he quipped, pushing his foot between her legs, "my intentions are not entirely honorable."

Michelle squealed and tried to step away from him on the slippery stone, but he caught her arm and pulled her back to him. She laughed and kissed him, holding his shoulders, straddling his knee. He felt so solid, so secure.

"I love you," she said, still seeing the aura about him. He smiled.

"Kiss me my little naiad."

"Naiad?" she asked, pushing her nose against his, tasting his mouth. Was that to be her new pet name, her new identity?

"Yes, you're my water nymph. It's a shame I didn't bring my camera, I think I'll have to paint a portrait of you here in your natural habitat. Put some flowers in your hair."

"Or make one of those wreaths you see in all those old paintings, what are they, laurel?"

"Yeah, but it would have to be from the water... a seaweed wreath."

"No, lily pads, a lotus blossom tiara with lily pads, we could go down to the farmer's market, they've got lotuses there. Or Houston Pond."

"Oh, you'd do it, too, wouldn't you, you nymphet, you would get naked with the koi."

251

"Yes," she chuckled. She loved the idea. A portrait of her new self. It was completed now, realized, worth commemorating. She was aware of a definite shift, as if the person she had been with Stephen, *Munchkin*, was now on the back burner, and this new person, *Naiad*, had been brought to the fore — or was it that she was simply looking at the stove from the opposite side, that it was the cook who had moved, not the pots or burners at all? There would be papers to fill out, complications perhaps, but the new Michelle felt no fear, saw no obstacles, and marveled that old anxieties should have been so cleanly erased.

"Only you have to promise to make me look thinner this time, and younger."

"How many times have I told you, it's not meant to be a portrait," Kyle chuckled, "and the woman is pregnant."

"I know, sorry. It just looks a lot like me."

"I swear by the ghost of Leonardo, I'll make you immortal this time, a goddess. You can't make the immortal younger, it's impossible."

"So if I'm a water nymph, what does that make you, a sea monster?"

"Absolutely. I'm your Leviathan, your Moby Dick." She laughed, grabbed it and kissed him.

"You know I wasn't even going to use your face until he bought it, I was just after the hair."

"Until who bought what?"

"The painting. *Re-Ignition*. He didn't tell you? He bought it."

"Who?"

"Your husband."

"What?"

"I thought you knew. I thought you asked him to. Gave me a check for fifteen grand."

"I never told him about it," she mumbled. The mere utterance of the word 'husband' made her neck knot up. The Light had disappeared. The old pattern of fear recycled itself. How had Stephen found out, and why hadn't he said anything about it? Fifteen thousand dollars?

"Kyle," she said, her voice now serious, "I don't know what I'm going to do. I don't think I can go back there. I can't walk into that house again."

"Then don't," he said, "Stay with me." She looked in his eyes to see if he meant it, and then started to cry. "I can call a lawyer for you. If you want. We can leave if you want. I have a few friends in Soho that would put us up. I mean if you want to... be with me."

"God, yes," she said, wrapping her arms around his neck, "Anywhere, just let me stay with you."

"Always," he said.

* * *

"I'm going to go around back," Lily informed him. Like an obedient puppy, Richard began to follow. "No, you stay there, in case she comes to the door. And keep knocking." He did so. No one came.

Lily peered through the windows of the Healing Room, of Sam's living room, of her kitchen. No one was there, yet her car was in the drive.

"She must have gone for a walk," surmised Lily as she rejoined Richard at the front door.

"Should we leave a note?" he asked.

"No. Michelle's not here. I've already left Sam a message on her machine."

"Well now what, shall we get some lunch?" Richard suggested, maneuvering his bulk back into the Volvo.

"Honestly, Richard, how can you think of food at a time like this. Go back up the hill, maybe she's home now. Let me try her number again."

"Certainly. I didn't mean to appear insensitive to the situation, I just thought, since we have come to a dead end." He backed out of the drive; his stomach gurgled noisily.

"Well we have, that's exactly why I'm so concerned. It's not like her not to answer her phone, and if she didn't take her car…"

"I'm sure she's fine, just had enough of Wolcott's sterile company. The man is heartless. She's probably at the mall right now having a pizza. We should go see if we can find her."

"Stop!" Richard stopped the car and looked where Lily was looking, in the small parking lot near the public access to the gorge trail.

"What?" he asked.

"Pull in here."

"There's nowhere to park, they're all taken."

"Don't you see, that's *his* car," Lily explained, pointing at a black SUV. She undid her seatbelt and opened her door.

"Whose car? Lily, what are you doing?"

"*Stephen's*. Why didn't I think of it? She loves to walk the trail," she said, getting out.

"Lily, where are you going?"

"Oh for God's sake, Richard, park the car," she instructed, hurrying somewhat unsteadily toward the gorge. Richard, unaccustomed to sudden movements, sat in flummoxed flaccidity, watching her disappear into the wilderness, until it dawned on him she might endanger herself. He pulled off the road, parked illegally, and paddled after her.

* * *

The wall of the gorge is quite steep and unstable; old leaves and pine needles float on the myriad layers of silt, clay, and shifting shale. Trees here may live a hundred years, tenaciously holding together with their own roots the rocky soil that supports them, or they may wash away into the creek after a few short seasons. Living on the edge of the abyss is a tenuous position.

There were people speaking below. Stephen stopped to listen, long enough to satisfy himself that his wife was one of them, although she sounded strange. There was an unusual timbre of elation in her voice. He began to descend the steps that led to the gorge floor, but decided against such an open approach. Still fifty feet above the water, Stephen carefully left the stone steps and moved off to the side, creeping cautiously downstream in the soft footing.

I followed at a respectable distance, not wanting to make my presence known until precisely the right moment.

"God, I'm starving," noted Michelle as she stood up, "I could go for a big steak."

"My ass is going to be sore for a week," Kyle laughed. He had lain on the wet rock; Michelle had been on top of him.

"Well it was your idea," she protested.

"I know, I didn't say I was sorry. I just couldn't leave without... celebrating I guess."

"That's a new way of putting it. Police arrest couple for inde-
cent celebrating in Fall Creek Gorge."

"Oh, it's still too foggy for anyone to have seen," he insisted,
tossing her sundress to her. But that was not entirely true.

Stephen was watching them, leaning on a young beech, which
was in turn leaning out over the gorge. He had not seen them copu-
lating, but he had seen them helping one another to their feet; he had
seen the smiles on their faces. He was watching, and I was watching
him. I saw him slip on a pair of thin black gloves, pull a pistol from
his waistband, brace his left elbow against the tree, and steady the
gun over his forearm. It was unclear to me which one of them he
intended to shoot; it may have been unclear to him. This was of
little consequence. The disparity in the vibrational frequencies of
redemptive violence and restorative justice is substantive; that between retribution for betrayal and retribution for seduction is slight.
I knew that the energy produced by his hostile act would not be
supported regardless of his aim; it would alter the *kami* in the gorge
and rouse the *ara-mitami* — the aggressive soul, and so I chose this
moment to act.

I leapt forward with all the weight of the small body at my disposal. A dry branch snapped as my front paws landed on it, Stephen
whirled around, pointing the gun at the flash of white-tipped tail.
His foot slipped on the wet rock, his skull smacked against the tree
and began to bleed. The gun fell into the water as he grasped the
trunk with both arms, and the beech, its roots newly exposed by the
recent rains, ceased to be a tree. The *kami* released it; the weight of
its July-green head wrenched the remaining tendrils from the rocky
morass as it fell toward the water below, taking Stephen with it. The
roar of the nearby waterfall and swoosh of the branches muffled his
one brief cry.

Through the fog, Kyle saw the tree moving, slowly tipping over and tilting down like a drawbridge opening.

"Holy shit," he said. Michelle turned just in time to see the crown of leaves entering the water, followed by the trunk, and the man clinging to it.

"Stephen!" she cried, lunging toward his falling form. As she saw her husband hurtling through space, their life flashed before her eyes: his diligence, devotion, and protection, his kindnesses, solicitude, and love. She lost her footing. Her head went under the water just as her husband's did. The shock of it all — that sound of the gorge letting go of the tree, seeing him *there* where she had just betrayed him, seeing him drop — arrested her reflex. She floundered, took in water, tried to get to him but he was caught in the current, his limp body drawn over the edge of the falls, and she had to be pulled away, choking and shaking, by Kyle.

27

STRANGE, what happens to time and perception during moments of crises, and what happens to memory with the passage of time. What is observed by one participant may not be what is recalled by another. History teaches us the awful truth: there is no truth, or rather everything is true somewhere, sometime, for someone. Whatever the subject or event, the truth of it is in the middle, and all around, evasive but ever-present. The universe is a torus; the mind hasn't enough eyes to survey the entirety of its ever-curving surface.

Much of what occurred between the falling of the tree and the moment Michelle was released by the paramedics failed to make its imprint on her memory. She had no recollection of crying out, of flailing her arms about, or slapping Kyle when he had pulled her from the water. She was quite unaware that Lily had been there, had been the one to call 911, and had helped her into her clothes while Kyle and Richard raced to the bottom of the falls to do what they could for Stephen. She only remembered the disorienting sensation of being under the water, unable to go where she intended, and Stephen's face, and the revelation.

She was told these holes in her memory were normal, she had been in shock, and it was a natural defensive reaction to trauma. But as she stood there, with Lily holding one hand and her father holding the other, watching her husband's casket sink into the ground, it seemed to her that expunging selective events for her own protection was not what her mind had done. It had not blocked those things out, it had brought other things into focus, because how she got out of the water or into her clothes or even what happened to Stephen after he fell was not the point of the experience, that's not what it was *set up* for. And it *was* set up, she could see that now, the chain of events necessary to bring them all to this place could never be thought of as accidental. She saw that it had played out with a life of its own, as though they were all pawns in some drama arranged by others — these guides or angels or daemons — not in order to change their *lives*, but in order to change their souls. For it was in that moment of turning toward Stephen, as Shakti turns toward Shiva, that Michelle realized it was *her* heart which had been closed, all along. It was *her* judgment of him which had kept them distant, not his, of her. This was why she had been unable to pinpoint when he had stopped loving her — because he had not stopped, she had.

For this, and a thousand suspicions and misgivings she felt terribly guilty. For Stephen's complicity in the destruction of their lives, she felt ashamedly angry. How had he known Kyle had painted her? What was he doing in the gorge, anyway, and why had he been wearing gloves? Was he spying on her? If the tree had not fallen, would he have asked for forgiveness? He had lied to her for so long, why had he not lied at the last? Why had he not simply said, 'Yes, Michelle, let's try now, let's have a baby.' They might have continued like that for years. Things may not have unfolded as they had, he might still be alive, she might not have had to experience this horrible pain, this terrible grace of God, this knowledge of her own selfish iniquities.

Yet even as she wailed, expelling her guilt and grief on the scene, a part of her was separate, watching it all in slow motion, apart, above, from a discrete center, for she knew the whole situation was beyond her control, beyond Stephen's control, beyond Kyle's control. A part of her had known it when she first touched Kyle's hand, when she heard her name in his mouth. This part did not feel culpable, did not regret her actions, could not regret having found him at last, would not deny having asked for him to enter her life. Still crying, she leaned back into Kyle's arms, allowing him to support her, to enfold her, and provide a sensation, a memory for this moment other than the sound of dirt contacting wood, and the black ring of mourners.

28

LEAH Kampnich pulled into the drive at Demerest House, turned off the engine and sat with her hand on the handle of the car door, wondering what she was doing there and if it wouldn't be better if she just backed up and drove away. Yes, she had been invited, but by whom? The invitation had *Kyle & Michelle* printed on it, but had been sent by Mrs. Demerest who had written: *Dear Leah, please come, Travis is excited to see you!* and signed it *Lily*. But was he really? It seemed unlikely, she hadn't heard from him in months. Not that she had expected to. Leah had been attending cooking school for the past year and really enjoyed it. Travis had been pretty supportive about it, he had helped her to fill out the applications, told her it was a great idea, but hadn't bothered to visit her. Andreas had visited her, though. Shortly thereafter Travis stopped calling. She knew he had slept with other girls. Not that it mattered. She didn't love him, probably. She had been on a few dates but hadn't clicked with anyone. She didn't know if she wanted to see him again, yet she was there, in the driveway, her aging Escort parked beside the Lexuses, BMW's, and Volvos.

She got out of the car and went through the side yard, where a bunch of kids were playing soccer, and stepped through the gate. Tons of people were in the back, sitting around the tables on the terrace, wine glasses in their hands. No one greeted her; they didn't really see her arrive. Was it just a formality that she had been in-vited, and she was supposed to have had enough sense to decline, to realize it was time for her to return to her natural station in life? Travis was on the opposite side with a group of guys, holding a beer, his back to her. She walked on into the garden, thinking she might just turn around and leave. It would have been different if they had hired her to help, now more than ever she was most comfortable in the kitchen, and she could have used the money.

Lily, standing on the balcony, beside herself with joy, had failed to see Leah arrive, there were too many things to observe at once, too many circles of love to inhabit. All her dearest friends were there, and many new ones, laughing, eating, enjoying the garden, their children playing ball on the side lawn; it was heaven to her. From her vantage point she could see the Rananda's from Highland Road ad-miring the rhododendrons, the Bermeyers crossing the footbridge to see the little pagoda, two of her new friends from Crestview kicking their legs on the bench swing in the gazebo, and Leonard Parkhurst playing peek-a-boo with his granddaughter around the privet hedge.

Below her on the terrace was most of the old gang, including the Stuarts. Bryan and Gretchen had come, bringing along Sarah and her friend Tina from Pennsylvania. Sarah seemed quite changed, confident and happy. (When she would later leave, everyone re-maining would agree that Sarah had really come into her own, that Tina, although she wore too much makeup, was very good for her, and that they made a lovely couple.) The Williamsons, who had bought the Wolcott's home next door, had dropped by. They seemed like pleasant people, one son was in high school, and the other in elementary. They had three Russian wolfhounds.

Halcomb too, was rejoicing, she could feel it. Not since he had passed had everything seemed so right. It was the start of a brand new tradition: the Fourth of July neighborhood barbeque at Demerest House — Kyle's idea. Kyle fit into the family wonderfully, Lily thought. Bryan and Travis had helped him with the grill, the three of them joking together, burning the meat; she and Michelle and Gretchen manning the kitchen — it had reminded her of when Halcomb's mother had been alive and his sisters had joined them so many times; the delicious food, the sounds of babies and laughter. To have the house so full of joy again gave her more pleasure than she could ever express. Now, the meal over, they were all lounging on the terrace watching the shadows lengthening on the lawn.

"There you are," said Richard Cole, joining Lily on the balcony, wondering vaguely if it would hold his weight, "We've been looking for you everywhere." In his arms was Mitzi, snuggled in a red crocheted blanket, despite the warmth of the day. She snuffled out a quiet woof, as if to concur with her master.

"I just couldn't resist the view. Halcomb and I used to sit up here on summer evenings you know. What do you think, Mitzi?" The dog wagged her little tail at Lily through the crook of Richard's arm.

"Isn't the garden magnificent," he said, gazing out at the display, "Kyle and Michelle have done a wonderful job keeping it up haven't they? Just look at those gladiolas."

"Kyle and Michelle indeed, they'd be lost without me, they don't know a gladiola from a snapdragon."

"I stand corrected. *You've* done a wonderful job, Lily dear."

"Well... I've done my best to keep it the way Halcomb always did. Except I let the strawberry patch go. Do you remember how he used to fuss over his strawberries?"

265

"I do. I was thinking about that not long ago, actually, and how delicious they were. Didn't he used to feed them beer?"

"He fed the beer to the snails and slugs. Otherwise they would devour the berries before we could pick them."

"Of course, the snails. Well I know nothing about gardening, except it requires too much bending over."

"It would do you good, you should join me sometime."

"It's a date. I will trundle your barrow, my lady." Mitzi assented by putting her paw in the air and waving it three times.

"Oh, Richard, I do love having everyone here! I can't tell you what it does for my heart."

"Yes. Quite a party, eh?"

"Couldn't be better."

"You're certain of that, are you?" Lily did not answer but looked askance at her old friend. His voice had betrayed him; there was something up his sleeve. He stepped closer, put his hands on the rail and leaned over, looking down on the partiers.

"Everyone, I have an announcement," Richard boomed.

"Oh?"

"What is it?" Heads turned, everyone looked up at him expectantly. He milked the moment, pausing for maximum effect, spreading his hands wide.

"I have at last finished my play!" he proclaimed.

"Oh, wonderful!" Lily cried, clapping her hands twice.

"What's it about?" Forrest asked. He had abandoned the Florida sun for the summer and was happily mooching off various friends and family in the cool northeast. With him was his bride of five months, Grace. She was slim, but not too slim, warm but not fiery, and reportedly made a mean Cuban sandwich. Lily thought she was delightful. Forrest told them all the story of how they had met at an early bird buffet, and she had said yes, she would go to a movie with him, and that yes was such a shock to him that in a fit of temporary insanity he had run out and bought a ring. Through sheer force of will he had managed to wait three weeks before proposing, and was utterly astounded that she said yes again. They had been married on the beach at sunset by a gay minister whose lover provided accordion music and took the photographs. Now they were inseparable and he had gained fifteen pounds.

"Well, actually… it's about all of *you*," Richard replied, although among those present there were many he had never met. Those whom he referred to, knew who they were. "I changed the names of course, and occupations… ages…"

"Is that *all*?" Sarah asked with a chuckle.

"Oh, some body types may have been altered to protect the innocent, I mean how else could I appear as my true svelte self?"

"Indeed," agreed Lily.

"And in some cases I may have changed one's race, gender, creed. Naturally the locale is completely different…"

"So, it's about us except we're not in it," Michelle laughed.

"Come come, none of those things matter, do they?" Richard remarked, "It's your spirit that inhabits the thing. Or should I say spirits?"

"So it's a ghost story," Bryan surmised.

"You are correct, sir. It *is* a ghost story. It's a mystery-romance, full of supernatural happenings. And *spirits*."

"I love a good mystery," Tina remarked.

"I thought you were supposed to write what you know," Sarah challenged, "I didn't know you were versed in the supernatural."

"I don't teach my students *everything* I know. An old man has to have some secrets."

"Congratulations Richard," Gretchen said, "When do we get to read it?"

"I don't have copies just now, but you'll all get to see it next year. I convinced Mark at the Hangar Theater to put it on."

"We can't wait to see it!" Kyle said in a singsong voice, "Can we?" He spoke both for Richard's benefit and for little Lindsay's, and he bounced her on his knee and raised her hands in the air when he said it. Lindsay laughed that irresistible way babies have when they first learn to laugh and they use any excuse to practice their new trick, such as being bounced on their father's knee.

"Not so hard, you'll make her spit up," Gretchen warned.

"Uh-oh!" Kyle said with mock concern, bouncing her again, setting her laugh off one more time. "Spit up? Uh-oh!" Everyone looked at Lindsay expectantly now, waiting to see if she would.

"You would never do that, would you, Lindsay," Sarah said, "You won't ever spit up 'cause you're a lady."

Richard, still on the balcony, said quietly to Lily, "I never thought I would see Michelle so happy. Isn't it grand."

"Yes," Lily replied.

"When are you going to get a little brother or sister?" asked Gretchen of Lindsay, who was clearly not prepared to answer.

"Oh for God's sake, give them a chance to breathe!" Forrest laughed, "This one hasn't even cured yet!"

"But she expects a brother, don't you?" Gretchen went on, "What do you say, Kyle?"

"Don't look at me, it's all up to my little nymph over there." Michelle rolled her eyes.

"We'll see," was her only comment.

"Well you don't want to wait too long," Grace pointed out.

"Leah!" Lily called from the balcony. Leah had spent as much time as she could wandering through the garden, avoiding. Lily waved vigorously at her. She waved back.

"Welcome!" Richard boomed in turn. Following Lily's lead, many of the seated people turned and greeted her as she approached the terrace steps, whether they knew her or not, whether they remembered her or not.

"Leah, how are you?" Forrest asked enthusiastically.

"Good."

"How's school?"

"Great, actually, I really like it."

"Fantastic," Jacob Stuart observed, "What are you studying?"

"I'm at the CIA," she said. She loved doing that. Several people looked ready to believe her.

"The Culinary Institute of America," Michelle clarified to the group.

"Oh, hah. You had us going there," said Gretchen.

"You've gotta watch out for this one," Travis warned loudly, crossing the concrete to embrace Leah. He kissed her sloppily on the cheek. Shit, she realized, he's drunk.

"Djya miss me?" he asked.

"Maybe," she answered, trying to guide him away from the center of attention. What the hell good would it do to talk to him now?

"I missed you," he confessed into her ear.

"You've got a funny way of showing it," she said quietly, blushing, smiling, embarrassed for him. She pulled him into a chair away from the others, "Can I have that beer?" she asked, trying to keep it from getting worse. Maybe he had been just as nervous about seeing her as she had been about seeing him.

"Sure," he said, handing it to her, "I'll get another."

"No, don't. Sit here with me." She took a swig and put the beer to one side. He looked at her disapprovingly.

"You think I've had too many beers," he observed.

"Yes."

He chuckled. "Had to do it, babe. Had to," he whispered hoarsely. "It's just too weird, being here."

"Oh yeah?"

"I keep thinking I see him walking around, you know, in my periphinal vision, just checkin' it out, just keeping an eye on things, you know?"

"Who? Who's walking around?"

"You know, Dr. Wolcott."

"Oh. But… it's been over a year," she said, "I didn't realize you were that close."

"Yeah. No, we weren't, but I mean, I knew him all my life, you know? And now they're living in Grandma's house."

"Must be awkward for you."

"Kyle's okay, don't get me wrong. And it wasn't their fault, really. I guess I just got creeped out."

"About a six packs worth," she noted. He laughed.

"It's really good to see you," he said, "You're sweet."

"Let's talk later," she whispered, "okay? Maybe tomorrow?"

"Maybe tonight," he suggested.

"Hush," she said. He grinned, put his hand on her knee, and pushed his nose in her ear. "I love your laughing eyes," he slurred. She smiled, put her hand on his and wondered how soon she could decently leave. At least people had stopped looking at them.

"It's good to see you too," she conceded. Or it would have been, she thought, if you weren't wasted. He leaned his head against her shoulder.

"You didn't have to fuck him," he said. Leah turned beet red, pushed him off and got up to leave.

"Well he needed me," she explained, "I thought we were supposed to be there for people." She turned and slipped out the side gate. There was no reason to stay any longer; she had the answer she had come for. He would never be able to let it go.

"So stupid," she muttered to herself as she got back in her car. What did it matter now? Andreas flunked out and was back in Germany, neither would ever see him again. She had given him a few moments of joy in the midst of a difficult part of his life, how did that hurt Travis? She pulled out of the drive and sped away.

Travis heard her car leave. He leaned over and retrieved his half finished beer. His father was holding forth on some pointlessly abstruse topic, obviously trying to impress Tina, the most overtly sexual female present. It didn't seem to matter that she was gay. Maybe he thought he could turn her with the size of his humungous brain. Why does Mom put up with it, he wondered, am I like him?

"Because it's a cooperative relationship, not a compulsory one. Social media creates a social holon; it's a collective consciousness, not an individual one. There is still free will."

"But how do you know that?" Tina fired back, "What makes you so certain? The *perception* of free will by an individual does not constitute free will. I think you're making a lot of assumptions with no basis." She gestured as she spoke, her long red nails flashing accompaniment to her words. "Maybe you only think there's not an individual consciousness in control because it's not *yours*."

271

"Maybe a holon has created the social media, not the other way around," Sarah added.

"Yes, well, if it comes to that," Bryan countered, "it may be *you* are a social holon, and your individuality is merely a misguided perception. But I think we can make the assumption that is not the case, I think therefore I am, etc."

"So what's been happening in good old Ithaca while I've been at the beach?" Forrest tactically interrupted.

"You haven't missed much, I can tell you that," Bryan laughed.

"What do you know about it?" Sarah demanded, "You don't live here."

"Well there was never anything going on when I did," he chuckled.

"Maybe you just weren't very observant," Travis slurred as he crossed the terrace toward the ice chest.

"Actually, there was quite a mystery last summer," Doris Stuart revealed. "They came and did a story for TV about it, and every-thing."

"Oh?"

"A woman disappeared," she said.

"Oh yes, Samantha Reyes," Rick Williamson put in, "did you know her?" Forrest shook his head.

"She was a massage therapist, Michelle used her, didn't you?"

"Yes," she confirmed. "She was an amazing person."

"Was?" Sarah asked, "I didn't hear about this, what happened?"

"She disappeared," repeated Doris.

"What do you mean disappeared?" Grace asked.

"Just that, there one day, gone the next."

"Like, packed up her stuff and left town?" Forrest suggested.

"No, like no one ever heard from her again. Clients showed up for appointments, no one there. Lily tried to see her one day, I think."

"Yes," Rick agreed. "Eventually the police went into the house, no one was there, nothing touched, no break in or anything, suitcases still in the closet, all her money still in the bank, just disappeared off the face of the earth."

"Probably went for a hike and fell in one of the gorges," Bryan suggested coldly.

"Without driving there? Without her cell phone?"

"Well people have been known to walk, dear," Doris's husband Jacob reminded her. He disliked her love of the dramatic.

"No, no. I don't believe it, not with her purse, her keys, her credit cards, her phone, all in the house and the door locked, her car still in the drive? Why would she go for a walk and leave her keys in her house? How did she lock the door?"

"Whoa," sounded Travis slowly, "that's reeaally weird."

"What are you suggesting, she was kidnapped?" Gretchen asked.

"But no one took anything, no sign of a struggle. Just lucky there wasn't a fire because she left all these candles burning."

"Come, come," Jacob Stuart protested, "The police said there was no sign of foul play, how do you know she isn't exactly where she wants to be? For all we know she was in debt up to her eyeballs or something and ran off to escape prosecution."

"But she wasn't in debt. At least they didn't say so. There is still money in her bank account."

"Maybe she was whisked off her feet by a wealthy lover who took her away from all this," Tina suggested playfully. Having never met the woman in question it did not affect her personally, it was simply a curiosity, one of those things you hear about.

"My God," said Sarah, "I'm shocked. I can't believe I didn't know. Why didn't you say something?" she asked of Michelle.

"I... I didn't know you knew her, I..."

"I'm sorry, you had a lot to deal with."

"Well that *is* something," Forrest said, "So she ran off without telling anyone. Maybe *she* was with the CIA." Grace laughed appreciatively at her clever new husband.

"Could be," agreed Doris, "She was always an odd one, by all accounts, really out there."

"Why, because she touched people?" Michelle asked pointedly, "Because she was easy to talk to?" She looked upset. Doris fell silent.

"She didn't mean anything," Jacob assured his hostess.

"I think it's time for someone's feeding," said Michelle, taking Lindsay inside. Immediately, as she passed through the family room, she regained her composure. She loved Demerest House with all her heart, it made her feel so secure, so loved, and gave her such a sense of permanence. She carried her baby up the superbly crafted staircase, so familiar now, yet still so enchanting. It seemed somehow to forecast euphoria each time she ascended.

As Michelle was going up, Richard was rushing down with his little white bundle.

"Ah, the joys of parenthood," he said sympathetically, as if they were in exactly the same situation, "I think Mitzi needs a bit of lawn." Michelle chuckled, Mitzi whined, Lindsay blew a bubble.

Lily, having overheard a bit of the conversation and seeing Michelle upset, had made her way back through the studio and met her friend on the second floor landing. She put an arm around her and smiled consolingly. "I'm sure Sam is at peace, wherever she is," she offered.

"I know, it's just... I never really thanked her, properly. I never could have made it through everything without her."

"I'm sure she knows, dear. I feel certain she's here now, listening. She knows you love her."

"Oh, Lily," Michelle sighed, hugging her back, tears in her eyes, "You're amazing. You have the most incredible faith. I might as well say right now I could never have made it through without you either, you know that. You know how much I love you, I hope."

"Of course, dear, but it's nice to hear it," Lily said. "Now let's go up and enjoy the view."

Together they ascended to the third floor, and settled on the window seat in front of the oriel. Michelle unbuttoned her blouse and began nursing her girl, gently stroking her short, thin hair.

Lily demurely turned her eyes away, and looked through the tall glass, down at the neighborhood kids still playing soccer on the glowing green lawn, their voices shrill with excitement, the glimmering, quivering leaves of the birches and poplars behind them seeming to cheer them on in celebration of play and summer and youth; and in the opposite direction the dark green stand of pines, majestic, constant, the little bit of lake peeping through, navy now in the decline of day, the sunset reflected in streaks of rippling light, and beyond the water the hazy sage of the far shore resting below the yellowish western sky.

"I never tire of this view," Lily admitted.

"It's just incredible. This is our favorite place to nurse, isn't it, dumpling?" Lindsay's only answer was to open her eyes for a moment.

"I can still remember Robert sitting there in the sun," said Lily, pointing at the shiny parquet sunburst, "tracing the design with his tiny fingers. And when they were older they would zigzag their toy cars around like it was a winding mountain road."

Here Michelle felt a pressure in the center of her back, and dismissed the momentary impression that it was other than what it must be: a knotting of her muscles produced by the tug of her child's weight, a movement of tissue produced by the strain.

"It must have been magical to grow up in this house."

It was not, could not be a touch, she thought, some contact from another, because Lily was not near enough, and they were alone at the top of the house. She dismissed any such notion, even though the pressure, the pull of ligament or *unknotting* of muscle felt good, not like a strain at all, even though a shiver washed a wave of sorrow from her body, she dismissed it as a reaction to the pull of her child, or a draft coming through the old window.

"Halcomb thought so. He was offered positions elsewhere, you know, but would never consider leaving this place. I was so grateful. None of my children seem to have been so sentimental about it. I can't tell you how glad I am that you and Kyle decided to stay here," she confided, "so that I can still enjoy it. I know it's been hard."

"Well... it was at first," Michelle admitted, "But not so much anymore. I think it had something to do with the Williamsons moving in over there, the sound of their dogs barking. I don't know, I feel... released now. Finally. It's hard to explain."

"You don't need to. I think I know. There comes a time, eventually, when the pain dissolves."

"Maybe so, maybe it's the time. Or maybe I've just got better things to think about," she cooed, smiling at Lindsay's sleepy face,

oozing maternal affection. Then she turned the smile on Lily, who reflected it, and Michelle let out a little giggle.

"I'm so happy it scares me sometimes," she said, "like one of those perfect May days which are so beautiful it makes you sad somehow."

"I think I know what you mean; you feel a pang because they aren't all like that, and you feel sorry for the days which could have been beautiful but weren't. I sometimes feel that. But this isn't like that, Michelle. You needn't be frightened. This is going to last."

Now Michelle began to weep softly, tears of release. Lily moved nearer and put an arm around her. Lindsay, disturbed, detached her mouth long enough to make a slight mew of protest.

"That's right, Lizzy, tell Mama all about it," Lily urged, "Tell her life is beautiful."

"Oh, no," Michelle chuckled, "We're not using that for a nick-name, no way. If you won't use her proper name, you can refer to her as your highness, or cutie pie, or even baby doll, but you may *not* call her Lizzy."

"No?"

"No, in fact I'm prepared to cause all sorts of confusion and start calling her Lily before I permit that particular appellation. She is definitely not a Lizzy."

"Oh well, suit yourself. But these things have a way of developing organically, and parents' wishes rarely have anything to do with it. My father never called me anything but Eleanor as long as he lived, but it was his own sister who began calling me Lily, or so I was told, and it stuck like glue, and he never forgave her for it, and I was never so grateful to anyone as I was to her," Lily laughed. Lindsay's head tipped back, but her mouth remained in an 'O', and her lips kept working the missing nipple.

"She's out," Michelle pronounced, "I'd better put her down for her nap."

"Such an angel," Lily breathed.

"Yes."

Together they descended to the nursery and settled the angel in her crib.

Paul remained there on the window seat, anticipating. The anxious period was over, he was quite confident now, tranquil in his waiting. Of course he had had to let Lizzy go first, it was the gentlemanly thing to do, but he harbored no doubts, the day would come soon. Kyle and Michelle were just as eager as he.

The sun was below the horizon, the moon not yet risen, but for Paul the yard of Demerest House was aglitter with the diamond radiance of life linked to life, streaming lines of love stretching from leaf to leaf and tree to tree, waves of sparkling joy resounding from heart to heart to heart.

He was unaware of us, Sam and I and those of our collective. We had no reason to disturb him; our presence was no longer required. Michelle had others coming into her field, each to their own time. Prolonged attachments hinder the work. Progression, expansion through the hierarchy, requires embracing all, yet holding none.

About the author:

GERALD Stanek has written numerous children's books, several of which have been illustrated by his wife, intuitive artist, Joyce Huntington. The couple lived for a decade in Ithaca, NY, the setting of Gerald's latest novel, "Skirting the Gorge", titled after and partially inspired by a painting Joyce produced several years earlier. They now reside in Sedona, AZ.

More books by Gerald R Stanek:

The Eighth House
A Novel

Sonoran Ruminations
(novellas and shorts)

For Children:

Emmalina's Dream

Emmalina's Flight

Emmalina in the Woods

Sarah 'n' Dippity

The Day the World Fell Away